THE DECEPTION

Lauren Hudson

Publisher Page
an imprint of Headline Books, Inc.
Terra Alta, WV

The Deception

by Lauren Hudson

copyright ©2018 Lauren Hudson

To order additional copies of this book or for book publishing information, or to contact the author:

Publisher Page
P.O. Box 52, Terra Alta, WV 26764

Tel: 304-789-3001
Email: mybook@headlinebooks.com
www.HeadlineBooks.com

Publisher Page is an imprint of Headline Books

Cover design by Kevin T. Kelly / www.kevintkelly.com

ISBN 13: 9781946664327

Library of Congress Control Number: 2018941402

PRINTED IN THE UNITED STATES OF AMERICA

To my parents.
You made my dream a reality.

I

Triplets Jinx, Felix, and Desdemona sit with Hazel and Kade in the House cafe for breakfast before classes start. Today's menu features over-easy eggs with pancakes in the shape of Headmaster Belton's face. Normally, the food prepared by culinary-gifted Asterian chefs tastes like heaven, but today it's bland and starchy. Normally, Asterians surround them, cramming for tests or doing the homework they should have done the night before. Instead of air filled with chatter and laughter, the cafe falls dead silent. This morning all eyes remain glued to the large projector screen in the middle of the cafeteria.

SURVIVORS FROM JANE ANCHOR'S ARMY FINALLY SPEAK OUT! The headline slashes across the screen. The onscreen reporter, Abigayle Rollens, presents a sympathetic affection as she glances at the timid boy standing before her. She averts her eyes from him, staring directly into the camera as the film begins rolling.

"Nearly nine months ago, Jane Anchor rose once again, hypnotizing hundreds of Asterians with her many powers. Jane's own three children, Desdemona, Felix and Jinx Anchor, came to our rescue. These remarkable triplets entered The House for initial training just a few months before facing Jane. The Anchor kids—armed with their Asterian-family powers to see the past, present, and future—defeated Jane and liberated the Asterian race," the reporter begins.

As the Anchors feel multiple sets of eyes glance towards them, the reporter continues, "Finally, one of the only sane survivors of

Jane Anchor's Asterian Army, Jason Curb, has chosen to speak with us about his experiences under Jane's influence. Jason, how did you first get involved with Jane Anchor?"

After what seems like a long, but necessary pause, the dark-eyed boy answers the reporter. "I made a conscious decision to reach out to Jane. After a recent death in the family, I was desperate for someone to give me hope they could bring my sister back. Jane promised me that. She told me if I followed her, I would see my sister again."

Ms. Rollens nods understandingly, tears appearing to well in the corners of her eyes. "What was it like while you were in her fortress on top of Truchas Peak?"

Jason takes a deep breath. This answer appears harder than his last. "At first, I was excited to see what was going to happen, thrilled about the opportunity to see Julia again... But then, after a few weeks, the feeling faded and I just felt... numb. Lost. Almost like a robot."

"Once escaping Truchas Peak, were you happy to find that the Anchor children succeeded in protecting the Asterian race from Jane once and for all?"

Jason nods. "Yes. Once I got away from Jane and her followers, I came to my senses. I realized she lied to me about bringing Julia back. It was all just a trick to get me to stand with her. I never want anyone to be tricked by her again, and thankfully, no one will."

Ms. Rollens quickly thanks Jason for being on air and speaking of his experiences. She turns back to the camera, beaming. "Now, here's Helen with your Asterian Society update."

Slowly, the noise and bustle of the room resume. Turning away from the screen, Desdemona shares a look of closure with her brother and sister. Despite having won the battle against Jane, it isn't something they talk about. They follow an unspoken rule: no one mentions their mother unless absolutely necessary. Unfortunately, Jane comes up often in their Asterian history books. It is impossible to avoid her entirely.

Hazel searches desperately for something to break the tension between the members at the table. No one hates mentioning Jane more than Hazel. She served as a right-hand man to Jane; she even considered Jane a friend. Even now, when she looks back on her naivety, she cringes.

"Hey, I am eligible to go for my mentor training today!" Hazel exclaims, finding words to end the silence.

"Has it been nine months already?" Felix asks, counting the months on his fingers since they returned to the House. "Yeah, I guess it has." In order to become a mentor at the House, the student must complete all required courses, be older than seventeen, and live at The House for at least nine consecutive months. Hazel, having completed the first two requirements nearly ten years ago, has finally reached the third prerequisite. Finally, she's ready to begin training to become a mentor for new Asterians.

Kade squints his eyes, looking at the date on the bottom of the news feed still chattering in the background. "Oh! You guys start new courses today, right?"

Desdemona nods, picking lightly at her egg breakfast, still a little shaken from the news broadcast. "Yes, we do."

"And these two royal idiots signed us up for Ancient Asterian Runes, the hardest course in The House!" Jinx sticks her tongue out at her siblings, pouting over the time and effort she will have to put in to do well in this course. "Since I'll have to study the night before now, I guess I will be forced to speak to all of you at breakfast instead of rushing through the homework."

Kade laughs. "Oh, what a shame that will be." Kade's laughter causes everyone at the table to snicker, ending the awkwardness from the earlier broadcast.

"What are our other courses?" Desdemona asks, reaching over Felix's shoulder to pull the schedule out of his backpack. "Hmm... Let's see. Well, we start with Ancient Asterian Runes that Jinx is oh, *so* excited about and then we go to Asterian History 202. Next—my personal favorite—Intro to Interpreting Prophecies and we end the day with Power Ethics.

"Why do we need Power Ethics anyway? It's a waste of time," Jinx said.

Kade, stepping into the mentor role he still likes to fill although the Anchors completed their apprenticeship nearly three months ago, speaks up quickly. "Power Ethics is a course crucial to your development as an Asterian. It teaches you when it is and when it isn't appropriate to use your powers, particularly in the presence of humans."

Desdemona laughs at his didactic demeanor, "Okay, Kade, we don't need a lecture today. I'm sure we'll hear enough of that in class."

Asterians rise from breakfast tables and begin to make their way to their first course of the new semester. Felix wants to arrive at class early – as always – to get a seat right up front. Grabbing her breakfast tray, Desdemona follows. When Jinx gets up with a groan, Kade pops up right after her. He moves around the side of the table to grab her tray and take it to the trash can.

As he walks away, Hazel smirks at Jinx. "You know, I can't believe you finally got my brother to stick. He's always been hesitant about dating even though every girl who lays her eyes on him wants him."

"Don't remind me," Jinx scoffs. "I never really liked relationships either, so that makes two of us." When Kade comes back to the table, he shoots Jinx a hesitant smile.

Jinx grabs her backpack and points a finger at him. "Now, don't go getting all soft on me, Kade."

That boy is something special to be dealing with her, Felix hears Desdemona think to him, snickering.

We're all something special to be dealing with her, Felix thinks back, waving at Hazel and Kade as the triplets make their way out of the cafe. The hallways teem with Asterians. The usual laws of traffic don't apply in the House, with Asterians going every which way to get to their classes.

Felix, Desdemona, and Jinx push their way to the stone staircase and climb up three floors to their Ancient Asterian Runes class. They arrive to a full classroom and take the only available table, which happens to be the one in the very front. A large scroll of paper with unintelligible scribbles sits on their group desk.

"Are we supposed to be able to read this?" Jinx asks, running her fingers over the paper. Desdemona rolls her eyes at her sister, not even bothering to provide the obvious answer. If they already knew how to read Asterian Runes, they wouldn't need to take this class! Felix starts to reply anyway, but when their teacher slams the door shut, Felix topples out of his chair.

The teacher struts up to their front table and extends his hand to Felix. "Good morning, Mr. Anchor! I am Dr. Hagin, your Ancient Asterian Runes teacher for this semester." Dr. Hagin helps Felix up from the floor and, once upright, shakes Felix's hand firmly.

Flustered and halfway annoyed at Dr. Hagin for singling him out, Felix pushes into the minds of other students to hear their reactions to the teacher's obnoxious introduction.

Finally, a professor who isn't going to bore me to sleep every class. Felix hears from a boy in the back. A girl in the front of the class swoons about the teacher's swoopy hair and perfect smile. Now that he sits back in his seat and gets a good look at Dr. Hagin, Felix understands. Judging by the way Desdemona flamboyantly pulls her hair into a ponytail to attract Dr. Hagin's attention, she agrees with the other girls in the class.

"I'm sure you've heard from Asterian mentors or Asterian graduates this class is the worst. While I disagree with them, I'm not going to lie to you; this course is far from easy. Learning how to translate Asterian runes is as rewarding, yet as difficult, as learning a foreign language. In fact, it is a foreign language. More like a lost art, really."

Dr. Hagin pulls down a large map at the front of the room and smacks Asia with a yardstick. "Quick history lesson before we dive right into content. Asterian runes are believed to have developed here in South Asia. Some historians claim they have been structured like Egyptian hieroglyphics, but the symbols differ significantly from those of Ancient Egypt."

With a sweep of his hand, Dr. Hagin pulls down yet another board in the front of the room. This one, however, reveals hundreds of different scribbles and symbols, each more confusing than the next. Desdemona glances at Felix with wide, startled eyes.

Are we going to have to know all of these? Desdemona thinks, fearfully. Felix shares a look of apprehension with his sister, shakes his head, and turns back to Dr. Hagin.

"These are the various symbols of Asterian runes. As you may see, we have quite a few of them," Dr. Hagin chuckles. "But, don't worry. While we have over a thousand Asterian symbols, only fifty-seven are commonly used in ancient and current runes."

"I imagine some of you right now are wondering how these differ from Egyptian hieroglyphics. Now, there are many minuscule differences, but the biggest difference is Egyptian hieroglyphics have to be physically written by hand." Dr. Hagin pauses, taking in the confused faces of the student sitting in the classroom. Jinx cocks her head to one side, wondering where this is going.

"Asterian runes, on the other hand, are not written, per se. They appear. In fact, nearly every inch of the Asterian world is covered in runes which many cannot, or will not see," Dr. Hagin lectures. "Many runes simply appear before Asterians when they need them most. However, some Asterians, such as myself, have the power to uncover them at will."

Dr. Hagin takes one step towards the front desk where the Anchor siblings sit, dumbfounded. When he places his hand on the table, symbols appear in the wood as if pulled from inside the oak.

"You're telling me there are things like this everywhere? And we just can't see them?" Jinx questions out of turn.

Dr. Hagin turns his yardstick towards Jinx. "Miss Anchor, please raise your hand if you wish to ask a question."

Jinx takes a deep breath, attempting to suppress an involuntary eye roll. She raises a half hand, repeating her question.

"Yes. Many appear when their messages are crucial to the task or survival of an Asterian. For example, if an Asterian were to be lost somewhere, runes could appear to help them find their way."

"But..." Jinx begins, stopping herself before she can speak out of turn again. She quickly raises her hand and continues when Dr. Hagin nods at her. "Where do these runes come from? They can't just appear on their own everywhere."

"What an excellent question," Dr. Hagin enthuses. "I imagine you will touch on this in your Asterian ethics class, but each member of the Asterian Society receives the power to create these runes. In fact, a big part of being in the Asterian Society is placing these runes in spots where Asterians in need can utilize them to their full potential. Once the Society creates a rune, it sticks in that spot forever."

As he speaks, Dr. Hagin moves around and rubs his hand on each family's desk, making a rune appear, leading to a series of gasps and awestruck faces from the students. "The Society has placed the runes on the desks and all around the room specifically for learning purposes."

Dr. Hagin makes his way back to the front of the class and in passing lays his hand once more on the Anchors' desk. Dr. Hagin suddenly jumps back in shock as another, seemingly unexpected rune rises from the table. Trying to pass it off, Dr. Hagin scans the rune and brushes it away with another swipe of his hand.

Although Kade told Felix he should not use his powers of the present to snoop into a teacher's mind, Felix tries to justify this mind reading. It's only right for Felix to make sure Dr. Hagin is okay, isn't it? Swiftly, Felix enters Dr. Hagin's mind.

Felix finds himself in a brightly lit room cluttered with papers and files, almost like an office.

The room in Dr. Hagin's mind appears nearly empty, yet files have been strewn about as if recently sifted. Felix tiptoes around the room, noticing each file has been labeled by year. Thinking it impolite to snoop through personal files, Felix readies himself to leave Dr. Hagin's mind. He then notices a statement written in bold letters on the chalkboard in the back of the room. In flowy script, the board reads:

Teach them well. They will need it.

The sound of Desdemona chirping in Felix's ear snaps him back into the classroom, "Felix? Felix? Earth to Felix?"

Felix blinks rapidly, noticing each family filing one by one out of the room as Dr. Hagin puts his pull-down maps away. "Sorry, I was daydreaming a little."

Desdemona scoffs. "No, you weren't. Stop lying to me. Jinx and I both know you were using your powers. Class is over. Walk with us and tell us what you saw."

Gathering their things quickly, the Anchors begin to make their way to their Asterian History 202 class. "Spill," Jinx orders Felix.

"Well, I thought it was kind of weird that Dr. Hagin's demeanor changed after the last rune popped up. My curiosity got the better of me," Felix admits.

"Oh, Felix," Desdemona scolds. "You didn't."

Felix nods, pretending to be ashamed. "I did. I went into his mind, but I also found something intriguing."

"Kade is going to hear about this, you know," Desdemona reminds him.

"Mona," Jinx stops her. "Kade isn't our mentor anymore, remember? We don't have a mentor since we're past our first three months. Kade doesn't need to know when we use our powers to snoop."

Desdemona purses her lips at her siblings. "Guys, it's not good to look into other people's lives when we don't need to."

"It's not good to look into other people's lives," Jinx repeats in a mocking coo as she turns back to Felix. "What's the scoop?"

"As I was leaving the room in Dr. Hagin's mind, the board was blank. But then I turned around and noticed the board said 'Teach them well. They will need it.' I think that's what Dr. Hagin was concerned about."

"Do you think it's about us?" Desdemona inquires as the trio walks through the House's bustling class wing hall.

Jinx slaps her sister on the arm. "Who else would it be about? Did anyone else save the Asterian race a few months ago?"

"Hey," Felix stops her. "Don't go getting a big head. Lord knows you don't need more food for your ego."

Jinx rolls her eyes. "No, guys, I'm serious. 'They will need it.' Who else would need Asterian Runes?"

Desdemona shakes her head when she feels a rough push on her left shoulder. As she turns around to identify the culprit, she notices a girl with shiny red hair similar to Margret, their traitorous "friend" from the year before. Mona holds her arm out, causing both Felix and Jinx to slam right into it, stopping them in their tracks.

"Look," Desdemona stage-whispers, pointing at the Margret look-alike. She raises her hand to her forehead, running her finger down the length of the fading scar over her eye left by her mother, Jane, on Truchas Peak. When someone mentions Jane or that trip, Desdemona involuntarily rubs the wound which still mars her face.

"Is that...?" Felix's voice trails off.

"No. She's too young," Jinx notices. As if on cue, the doppelgänger drops her class book and reaches down to pick it up. As she does, the triplets notice a face considerably rounder than Margret's. Her eyes bug out like a scared freshman in high school.

"Could that be her sister?" Desdemona wonders aloud.

Felix shrugs his shoulders, resuming the walk to class. "Asterians do usually come in families. I wonder if she feels out of place because of what her sister did."

"I don't trust her," Jinx adds immediately.

"You don't even know her, J!" Felix scolds, turning to Desdemona. "Mona, tell her."

Desdemona shakes her head. "I have to go with Jinx on this one. Whether it's right or not, my gut tells me to be leery of her."

As they enter their classroom, Felix sighs. "Just because their powers may be alike doesn't mean they are alike. I mean, look at Jane and her siblings. Marcus and Stacy are blessings, while Jane turned out to be as evil as Voldemort."

"This isn't one of your nerdy Harry Potter adventures, Felix. This is real life," Jinx reminds him. Since Felix returned from Truchas Peak, he's been binge reading and watching all the Harry Potter movies. Because they don't keep them in the House library, he ventured into the normal world to get the novels. Jinx's favorite hobby has become teasing him for cherishing those books like a mother cherishes her babies.

Felix turns to give Jinx the stink eye as they sit down at their table in class. "You'll be happy to learn I've moved on to the Lord of the Rings books."

"You've evolved from a wizard to a hobbit. Congratulations! Should we throw you a party to celebrate your accomplishment?" Jinx laughs.

Desdemona hides her giggle, trying to stand up for her brother. "I think it's great Felix got into reading! You need a hobby, Jinx."

Felix pushes into Desdemona's mind. *No, Mona. Jinx has already got a hobby.*

Desdemona raises her eyebrows. *What?*

Yeah, Felix begins. *Her hobby is making out with Kade in the left wing staircase when we're in the rec room!*

At this, Desdemona bursts out laughing. And not the pretty, girly laugh. No, this is a full-out bellow, complete with snorting and table slapping. Jinx looks with dismay at her brother and sister, upset a secret joke has seemingly been made at her expense. Just as she opens her mouth to order Felix and Mona to tell her what's going on, their professor enters the room. A short, stout woman, she grabs a step stool to write on the board at the front of the room. In all capital letters, she writes "THE ASTERIAN SOCIETY."

"Good morning, class," she begins in a tone so bland it practically puts Jinx to sleep with a single sentence. "My name is Mrs. Tall."

Before she can stop herself, Jinx lets out a snort-laugh at the irony of her name. Mrs. Tall responds, cocking her head to the side and waddling over to the Anchors' table. She narrows her eyes at Jinx.

"Is there something funny about my name, Miss Anchor?" she questions, straightening her tweed blazer.

Jinx snaps up and shakes her head wildly. "Oh no, Ma'am. Not at all."

"Don't think just because you defeated Jane Anchor you get special treatment," Mrs. Tall reminds her with a stern expression. "There are many things you don't know about this world, Jinx

Anchor. It would do you good to stay awake in my class and learn a few things about the world you 'saved.'" She finishes with mocking air quotes.

With a swing of her hip, Mrs. Tall makes her way back to the board and Jinx looks at Felix and Desdemona with concern. Despite her sass, Jinx hates getting torn up by professors as much as the next student. Turning her attention to the board, Jinx zones in on the lesson for a change.

"For our first lesson, I thought it would be appropriate to cover a huge part of our world: the Asterian Society. You may not see or hear of them very often, but they're nearly always watching. Very few important things go on in the Asterian World about which the Society is unaware."

Jinx blinks her eyes, already bored despite her efforts to stay engaged. As if taking pity on Jinx, Mrs. Tall halts the lesson, looking around at a class of half-asleep teenagers.

Sighing, Mrs. Tall motions to the book placed on the shelf in the front of the classrooms. "Since you all are so very interested in this subject, I'll allow you to finish reading about the Asterian Society in your textbooks for the entirety of class. The chapter starts on page 56."

"I got them," Desdemona told her siblings, getting up to grab three Asterian history books. Lugging them back to the table, she drops one in front of both Felix and Jinx and turns to page 56. Focusing intently, she reads the Asterian Society contains twelve members at all times and when one dies, various competitions occur to replace them.

Turning the page, her eyes skim until she pauses on a subtitle reading SOCIETY CREATED TO SAVE THE WORLD. Intrigued, she continues to read. In thin letters, the book tells all Desdemona needs to know.

When the first Asterians were placed on this earth, they were created by God to do only good deeds. They were told to help the humans on earth when they were in disastrous or life-threatening situations. However, the Asterians did not always follow the will of their creator. The first Asterian to go rogue was a woman by the name of Cecily Cross. Born in 192 BC, Cecily found her unique power of illusion by hypnosis at the regular age of fifteen. Her mother, also an Asterian, aided in harnessing her powers, working with Cecily to teach her the benevolent ways of Asterians.

One night as Cecily trained, she became upset and used her powers to hypnotize her mother into letting her out of lessons for the day. After this revelation, the misuse of Cecily's powers became frequent. Cecily would often go out into the human world and, instead of using her powers to save the humans, she tricked them into performing her selfish deeds. Power-hungry and greedy, Cecily began ravaging the human and Asterian world.

Desperate to stop Cecily, a group of five Asterians convened to form an army against her. The great Clarence Abbot led them to victory against Cecily in what became known as the Battle for Mankind. After Cecily's defeat, the original group of five Asterians formed a coalition against evil. They decided to continue to meet as a council to preside over events occurring in the Asterian community; this became known as the Asterian Society. Granted powers of knowledge and sight by God, the Asterian Society can watch over chosen Asterians individually. They can also assist these Asterians by placing hidden runes around the world, revealing them only when necessary. To this day, the Asterian Society continues to guide chosen Asterians in their quest to protect the earth for humans.

The sound of a door knock interrupts Desdemona's reading. Mrs. Tall bustles over to open it, revealing a clean shaven Kade with a clipboard tucked under his arm. He whispers something to Mrs. Tall which causes her to scrunch up her face in a scowl.

Giving in with a sigh, Mrs. Tall turns back to address the class. "Jinx Anchor, your presence is requested." Jinx slams her textbook closed quickly, tucking it away in her backpack and turning to her siblings. Balling her hands into celebratory fists, Jinx mouths, "Yes!" She waves innocently, leaving them stuck in the class with snarky Mrs. Tall and their textbooks to keep them company.

Rushing out to meet Kade, Jinx closes the door behind her and raises an eyebrow at her boyfriend. "So, do you have something to say to me or were you just looking to have some quality time?" Jinx smirks, matching his stride as he begins to walk towards the elevator.

"As much as I know you loved being pulled out of class just for the hell of it, I have a genuine request for you today," Kade informs her as he clicks the elevator button to take them down to the lobby floor of the House. "But, I'll appease you for just a second." Glancing around as if to make sure no one watches, Kade takes Jinx's cheek in the palm of his hand and leans in close, touching his lips to hers in a sweet kiss. Much to her dismay, Kade pulls away just as she begins to sink into his touch.

"Oh, c'mon, that's all I get for the hard work I've put into this school day?" Jinx teases.

"J, you were in class for approximately a period and a half," Kade reminds her with a laugh. Jinx responds with an eye roll, remembering even though Kade is no longer her mentor, he still likes to keep their relationship on the DL. Jinx, not one for PDA, doesn't mind this setup. However, when they do get some rare seconds alone, she can't help but want a little affection. Despite her efforts to remain stone-faced, Kade has a way of brushing the dust off her feminine side. With him, she can't help but want to giggle like Desdemona does when she flirts with anything that breathes.

The ding of the high-speed elevator pulls Jinx out of her stream of consciousness and reminds her of the reason for Kade's appearance. "What is it you wanted to ask me?"

Kade exits the elevator and makes his way toward Mr. Belton's office. Knocking briskly, he leans in close to Jinx's ear and whispers, in a deep, musky tone, "You're going to hate it now, but I promise you'll thank me later."

Mr. Belton, with robes much like that of wizard dragging the floor, flies open the door with a sweep of his hand. "Ah, Mr.

Defrates! I'm so glad you succeeded in securing Miss Anchor's agreement to our request."

Before Jinx can open her mouth to protest, Kade places a hand on the small of her back, signaling for her to once (just once) not jump the gun. Jinx snaps her mouth closed and her eyes drift to the mini-Margret who bumped into Mona in the hallway earlier. With shiny red hair and tan skin, the girl is drop-dead gorgeous.

Just like her sister, Jinx thinks to herself, narrowing her eyes at the girl. Why does *Kade want Jinx to interact with the blood relative of the girl who completely betrayed our trust, almost getting all of us killed?*

"Jinx, this is Maxine, Margret's younger sister. I know you and Margret had some... um... disagreements," Mr. Belton begins.

"Disagreements?" Jinx interrupts him, not being able to hold herself back. "She set us up for murder!"

Kade snaps his head back at Jinx, once again touching her back and signaling her to hold off just one more second.

"I know, and I'm sure you and your family are still very upset about that incident. However, Maxine is new to the House. She just turned fifteen yesterday and her mother delivered her to us this morning. I am thrilled you have agreed to become a guide to Maxine as she finds her way around the House," Mr. Belton cheers, thrusting a sheet of parchment paper with Maxine's schedule at Jinx. Feeling the anger build in the pit of her stomach, Jinx is one second away from throwing the paper back at Mr. Belton. Kade, sensing her anger, quickly intervenes.

"Yes, Mr. Belton, while I know Jinx is eager to begin showing Maxine around, I think we should allow her to grab some lunch before giving her the full tour," Kade suggests. His stiff tone makes his request sound more like a demand. If Jinx didn't know any better, she would think Kade, not Mr. Belton, runs the House.

"Of course, of course!" Mr. Belton nods furiously. "Please, Miss Anchor, let Kade accompany you to lunch. No one can give a thorough tour on an empty stomach!"

Jinx, bewildered and furious, dares not open her mouth. If she says one word, she knows she can't control what follows. This is a fight Kade, not Mr. Belton, deserves. Following Kade out the door without another glance at Maxine, Jinx mentally prepares to give Kade the verbal butt-kicking he deserves.

2

"YOU VOLUNTEERED ME TO GUIDE MARGRET'S LITTLE SISTER WITHOUT ASKING ME!" Jinx shrieks as they move out of earshot from Mr. Belton's office. She balls her hands into fists and steps in front of Kade, stopping him in his tracks. She punches him not so lightly in the chest and despite her attempt to make it hurt, Kade doesn't even flinch.

Ignoring the punch, Kade begins, "I knew you would say no if I asked you first."

"Uh, DUH!" Jinx yells. "In case you've forgotten, Margret betrayed us!" Thinking back to just nine months ago, Jinx recalls how Margret served as their guide when they first came to the House on their fifteenth birthdays. Margret showed them all the ropes. She was even nice enough to entertain Felix's far-fledged crush. Then, when Jane "kidnapped" Margret, the Anchor kids and Kade came to rescue her.

Jinx's lip turns into a curl as she remembers the look on Margret's face when Margret stood by Jane atop Truchas Peak. Jane's plan to use Margret and lure them into a trap worked flawlessly. It took everything the triplets had, plus Hazel, Kade and the Asterian Jewel to end Jane's reign of terror once and for all.

"J," Kade begins. If she weren't so mad at him, the use of her nickname in that musky tone of his would have made her blush. "Maxine can be of use to us, don't you understand? She knows Margret better than any of us ever did. Maybe we can decipher things about Jane's rise to power."

Jinx stops for a moment, realizing he has a point, but knowing she cannot give him that kind of satisfaction. "Why didn't you pick Mona or Felix? Either one of them would have been a better guide for this devil child!"

The frustration in Kade's tone becomes clear. "She's not a devil child. She is *not* Margret."

"She sure looks like her!" Jinx points out, throwing her hands in the air.

"Well, you sure look like your mother!" Kade screams back. Jinx feels all the air whoosh out of her system as if someone just punched her in the stomach. Hurt, but not daring to let it show, Jinx gives Kade one last shove before barging away, forgetting all about lunch.

Knowing her brother and sister will be finishing Asterian History, Jinx slumps up against the wall outside of the classroom. She doesn't dare go in for fear of people seeing her current state of rage. As a part of their agreement to discuss Jane only when absolutely necessary, Kade was way out of bounds mentioning Jane and Jinx's uncanny similarities. Nearly the mirror image of her evil mother, Jinx even carries Jane's former nickname: "J." Having nearly forgotten entirely about Maxine, Jinx wonders what Kade had been implying. Kade knows the doubts Jinx has about the good in herself, and yet Kade still thought it was okay to say that. The nerve!

Just as Jinx tries to shake off her worries, the classroom door opens and students begin to flush out. Jumping to her feet, Jinx waits until Felix and Desdemona exit the room before rushing to their side.

"We need to talk," she tells them. The smile they both wore falls from their faces as they notice Jinx's tone. Felix can tell this isn't one of Jinx's usual, petty predicaments. No, this is something bigger than that.

"Let's go to our room," Desdemona suggests, also noting Jinx's unusual behavior. Jinx and Felix both nod before entering the elevator to take them to their room. Rushing up to the door to their suite, Desdemona places her hand on the wood and whispers "Anchor," the only way to enter an Asterian's room at the House. It prevents theft, Desdemona guesses, and it's easier than having to keep up with a key.

Entering the room the triplets sit on the couch in the living area. Desdemona and Felix look at Jinx expectedly while Jinx sifts through her mind. Deciding to leave out the sour ending to her fight with Kade, Jinx explains how she wound up unwillingly designated to serve as Maxine's guide.

"Wait," Felix stops her. "So Kade just signed you up for this job and didn't even tell you?"

Jinx nods. "He said he knew I would say no."

"Of course you would!" Desdemona agrees.

"This was my reaction exactly, guys," Jinx informs them. "But, since there's no way I'm getting out of doing this, I think we should use our powers to get into Maxine's head a little."

"But we're not supposed...." Desdemona starts.

Jinx shoots her sister a glare. "Mona, shut up with the goody-two-shoes stuff! This is an appropriate time to use our powers. If Maxine is all buddy-buddy with evil like her sister, we deserve to know."

Desdemona shrugs her shoulders, realizing this time Jinx is right. They need to know what they are up against. As the room swirls away, Desdemona allows her Asterian power to consume her, entering Maxine's past.

Desdemona finds herself in a dark bedroom. Blurry walls painted baby pink with fancy white trim around the edges surround her. Feeling soft cotton under her fingers and her head, Desdemona realizes she lies in bed somewhere. Blinking her eyes to adjust to the darkness, she glances over and sees another twin bed across the room. A lumpy shape stirs in the bed before sitting straight up, looking directly across at her. It only takes Desdemona a second to realize a disheveled-looking Margret occupies the bed next to her. Only this time, Margret looks noticeably younger than she did when the Anchors first met her in the House.

"Margs, are you okay?" Desdemona feels herself say. Running her hand through her red hair, Desdemona realizes she must be seeing this vision of the past from Maxine's eyes.

Margret breathes heavily from across the room, jumping out of bed and beginning to fumble through the closet near the blank television. "Margret, what are you doing?" Desdemona asks.

Margret doesn't answer at first. Then, jumping up with a crazed look, she runs to the edge of Desdemona's bed. She grips Desdemona's covers and leans in close to her face with wild eyes.

"I have to go. She's telling me to come with her," Margret whispers to Desdemona. As Margret begins to throw clothes hastily into a bag, Desdemona notices Margret's normally perfect hair has become a messy, tangled knot. Margret looks... stressed. She looks nervous. Desdemona would feel sympathy if she hadn't betrayed their trust.

"What do you mean? Who is telling you to do this?" Desdemona asks.

Margret doesn't answer her question. Instead, she slings the bag over her shoulder and rushes over to Maxine. "Tell Mom and Dad I went back to the House."

"Why are you rushing so much if you're going back to the House? You aren't supposed to go back until tomorrow," Desdemona asks Margret in a squeaky voice she guesses must be Maxine's.

"Max," Margret gets down on her knees to look Desdemona in the eyes. Desdemona notices Margret is at least a year or two younger than when they first met at the House. "You have to trust me on this one."

Desdemona cringes at the nearness of Margret, but feels herself reach out and hug her "sister." "I don't think this is a good idea, Margs."

Margret abruptly pulls back from the hug. "I have to go. If I don't, I will be in big trouble."

Margret stands up and throws open their first story window. "Who? Who will get you into trouble?" Desdemona whisper-

yells, jumping out of bed and following Margret to where the night breeze blows through the open window.

Margret takes one last look at Desdemona with a scared, searching expression and jumps out of the window without another word.

Desdemona slowly comes back to the present, blinking her eyes to notice Jinx and Felix talking fervently with one another. When they see her watching, they suddenly stop and look her way.

"What? Have I got something in my teeth?" Desdemona asks, jokingly raising her hand to pick between her teeth.

Felix laughs a little, but Jinx remains stone cold. Since Jinx returned from her meeting with Kade, she has been strange. More strange than something like this would usually make her. Desdemona wonders if something more went on with Kade than just the Maxine thing.

"What did you see?" Jinx asks all business.

Desdemona quickly relays her vision of the past to them before adding, "This means Margret was in with Jane even before we knew about our powers."

"And it means Maxine didn't know anything at all about Jane," Felix notes.

Jinx shakes her head. "She didn't know it then, but she might know now."

"Felix, what did you see about the present?" Desdemona asks, deciding not to respond to Jinx's skeptical comment. Although Desdemona usually disagrees with Jinx's cynicism, this time she might have a point.

"I didn't see much that was helpful about the present," Felix admits, shaking his head. "But I did find out her power is a lot like Margret's: Persuasion. Margret can only persuade boys to do what she wants, but Maxine can get anybody to follow orders."

"What's the catch?" Jinx asks, knowing no power can be that simple.

"They only follow her orders for thirty seconds," Felix finishes. "Although, maybe someday her Embellishments will extend that time."

Jinx groans. Embellishments, heightened Asterian's powers, have felt like both a blessing and a curse. A blessing because all three of them have received wicked Embellishments, but a curse because so did everyone else who has tried to kill them.

Not waiting for anyone to ask, Jinx jumps right into telling what she saw in her vision of the future. "Actually... what I saw was kind of sad. Well, it will be sad if Maxine turns out to be good. I saw Maxine sitting in her one-room suite at the House and she was crying... crying because everyone else has these close family relationships and she can't even find Margret."

"Does she know what Margret did?" Desdemona asks.

"I'm not sure," Jinx answers truthfully. "I assume she does just because it was all over the news, but I can't be sure."

Felix looks between his sisters and raises his nose in the air like a snobby heiress. "So... we're saying I was right and Maxine is trustworthy?"

Jinx gets up from her seat on the couch and sighs. "She's not completely in the clear, but from what we've seen she doesn't seem to have the desire to do anything as drastic as her sister. Let's not get too close though, okay? We can't afford to be tricked again."

"Hey, there's one more thing I think you guys should know," Desdemona adds, thinking back to when she first saw Maxine's face in the hallway. "Her forehead says DIVIDED."

Jinx, remembering Desdemona's power to see the past can include a bizarre Embellishment where she sees a word written on a person's forehead, ponders the message. The word usually describes an important component of their past. "Like their family is divided?"

Desdemona shrugs. "That's what I assume."

"Are you going to agree to be her guide around the House?" Felix asks.

Jinx begins to walk towards the door, deciding she will get something to eat since Kade interrupted her schedule with his uncalled for and unbelievable attitude. "I'll give it a shot."

After grabbing lunch, Jinx makes her way back to Mr. Belton's office, knowing her nut-job principal will want her to show Maxine the way to her room and her afternoon classes. After Jinx knocks forcibly on the door, Mr. Belton swings it open and greets her with a shout. "Miss Anchor! I'm so glad you're back. Did you get enough to eat? I sure hope so. You've got a lot of touring to give Maxine."

Jinx glances over Mr. Belton's shoulder to see Maxine sitting in nearly the same spot as when Jinx first came to the office. Her round face and sweet eyes raise to meet Jinx's. Jinx has to stop herself from visibly flinching away from the eyes of Margret.

Mr. Belton shakes his hand in front of Jinx's face, pulling Jinx away from Margret's blue eyes. "Her room is on floor 111 and it says Loelan on the front. Your hand, as well as hers, have been programmed. You can show her how to get in."

As she watches Maxine rise from her seat, Jinx realizes this is her cue. She slowly leads Maxine out of the room, feeling a mixture of nerves and hatred balling up in her stomach. Whenever she looks at Maxine's face, she can't help but be reminded of Margret's look as she stood side by side with Jane, plotting to kill her and her siblings. Attempting to put the thought out of her mind, Jinx opens the elevator for Maxine and they enter in awkward silence.

"Um..." Maxine begins in a tone as soft as a mouse. She pauses for a second, unsure whether to continue. Finally, she does. "I just want to say I'm sorry for what my sister did to you..."

Jinx glances at her out of the corner of her eye. "It's not your fault."

At least, I don't think it is, Jinx thinks to herself, hoping Maxine will someday prove her to be correct.

After another tension-filled silence, the elevator button dings and Jinx steps out. Maxine follows briskly.

"Oh, the elevators are high speed," Jinx informs her. "In case you didn't realize." Maxine nods in response and Jinx continues, not sure what else to do. "The House is actually much larger than it seems. From the outside, it looks like a regular home. But there are 365 floors total."

When Maxine again doesn't verbally respond, Jinx notices the difference between the two sisters. Unlike Margret, Maxine is quiet and reserved. While Margret was always eager to meet and greet, Maxine seems to be one to keep to herself. Who knows, maybe Jinx can get along with this girl.

Walking down the hallway, Jinx passes her room before stopping at the room directly next to hers.

Oh, you've got to be kidding me! Jinx thinks to herself as she realizes Maxine has been placed in the room directly adjacent to her own. As she begins to show Maxine how to get into the room, students pop their heads out of their rooms, yelling behind them at their siblings to hurry up. Each family rushes out of their suites and down the hall towards the staircases and elevators. Confused about the commotion, Jinx stops Jackie French, a girl she recognizes from class last year, to ask her what's going on.

"Didn't you hear? The Asterian Society has an announcement!" Jackie enthuses. "We're all meeting in the arena!"

Jinx glances between Jackie and Maxine, wondering what to do with the newbie now their tour has been torn apart. As if they can sense her nerves, Desdemona and Felix exit the room right next to them.

"J! Good! Now we can all go down together," Desdemona says excitedly before her eyes trail to Maxine, who looks meek compared to Jinx.

Felix, always the people pleaser, quickly introduces himself and Desdemona to Maxine. "Why don't you come down to the arena with us? We can show you the way."

Maxine nods excitedly, prompting Mona to scream into Felix's mind. *Hey! What did we say about getting too close?*

Mona, we can't just leave the poor girl standing here all alone. Felix scolds her.

The last thing we need is you falling in love with another devilish redhead. Mona raises her eyebrow at him. Felix shakes her off and leads the way down to the arena.

They arrive to find nearly the entire population of the House already seated, talking and laughing with anticipation. The arena looms as tall as it did when the Anchors participated in the Hunt just nine months ago. Remembering the adrenaline rush he felt when Mr. Belton crowned the Anchors winner of the Hunt, Felix licks his lips, imagining the lingering taste of celebratory Asterian Ale—the single best drink he's ever had the pleasure of consuming. Still lamenting the fact that Asterians serve the Ale only during celebrations, Felix leads his sisters and Maxine up to the top row of the arena, the only one still open.

Mr. Belton steps up to the podium near the far end of the arena and raises his hand in the air. The Asterians quiet quickly, causing the dust on the arena floor to settle onto the ground before he continues.

"As many of you may already know, the Asterian Society has a very special announcement for us here today. Now, hosting the Asterian Society is a tremendous honor for the House. The last time the Society visited the House was very nearly a century ago. We need every single one of you to represent the House well. Extend to the Society your fullest attention and respect."

Just as Mr. Belton finishes, eleven Asterians appear out of thin air in the middle of the arena, causing the brown powder to stir once again. The crowd of young Asterians cheers wildly, screaming and yelling at the top of their lungs.

"Show offs," Jinx whispers under her breath. Desdemona elbows her sister in the ribs, clapping along with the crowd.

"Respectful, remember?" Desdemona says.

Jinx, although not responding verbally, mouths "respectful, remember?" with a mocking expression, making sure Desdemona notices her retaliation.

When the roar of the crowd subsides, a tall woman dressed in traditional Asterian Society robes, complete with black stole, begins to speak. "Hello, young Asterians. My name is Mrs. Tary. Usually, my colleagues and I would be wearing golden stoles.

However, we come before you in a time of mourning. We have recently lost a dear friend, a friend who completed our dozen: Jerald Young."

At this news, many young Asterians in the crowd begin to murmur, muttering about how he could have died and how they plan to replace him. The woman raises her hand in the air and the speaking stops instantly.

"Although we are heartbroken by this loss, it is of the utmost importance we fill this empty spot as soon as possible. My colleagues and I believe a young Asterian would bring a new dynamic—a new perspective—to the Society. What better place to pick a successor than the best Asterian training house in the world?" At this, the arena erupts with cheers once more.

"And that is why," the woman pauses for dramatic effect, "members of The House will compete to decide who will fill the empty spot of the Asterian Society. The competition will be held in two weeks in Las Vegas, Nevada!"

Felix nods his head in appreciation and raises his hand for a high five from Desdemona. "We're going to Vegas, baby!"

Desdemona slaps his hand just before Jinx interrupts their celebration. "That would be great, but the last time we went out West, we almost got ourselves killed!"

"This is different, J," Desdemona tells her. "This time we're being supervised by the Asterian Society themselves!"

"And even so, Jane is dead. She can't hurt us from the grave!" Felix raises his fist in the air in celebration and turns his attention back to the woman as she quiets the crowd once more.

"As much as I know every young Asterian wishes to have this opportunity of a lifetime, there are restrictions. To participate, you must be under age twenty-one and you must have studied at least ten months at the House, two of which need to be under the supervision and training of a mentor," the woman informs them.

Jinx mentally checks these items off her list. Jinx and her siblings have been at the House nearly a year now and Kade trained them for two, two and a half months (if you count the time spent together on Truchas Peak). Jinx curls her lip and feels her stomach twist at the thought of Kade. Jinx, too stubborn and angry to go to him first, knows it must be Kade who bridges the gap and apologizes. If they are going to make this whole relationship thing work, he can't exploit her deepest, darkest fear.

He'll apologize, Jinx keeps telling herself. *He has to.*

3

"What's the point of going to class today?" Jinx whines as she follows Felix and Desdemona to their Ancient Runes course. "We leave for Vegas tomorrow!"

"For the last time, J, we can't just ditch class because we're not going to be here tomorrow." Felix scolds. Over the past two weeks, Felix and Desdemona have worked hard to motivate Jinx to continue going to class, but it hasn't been easy. At times she is thrilled about leaving for Las Vegas, but five minutes later she mopes about something petty. The constant mood swings remind Felix of when they first arrived at the House and Jinx practically rejected them as her family.

Upon arriving at class, they take their usual seat at the front of the room just before their beyond handsome professor closes the door behind him.

I have to admit, Felix hears Desdemona tell him in his mind. *I sure am going to miss him in Vegas.*

Felix shakes his head, laughing at his sister's stereotypical girly crush and zones in on Mr. Hagin. "I hope you all did your homework because we're having a pop quiz!"

The entire class groans in unison as they clear their desks, preparing for their unavoidable fate as Mr. Hagin passes out single sheets of paper to each Asterian. When Desdemona receives her paper, she sees six lines of Asterian runes.

"Write the translation of these runes below each question. When you're done, flip your paper over. We will go over it in fifteen minutes," Dr. Hagin announces. "You may begin."

Reluctantly, the Anchor kids grab their pencils and begin scribbling answers. Fifteen minutes pass and Dr. Hagin stops the class to reveal the answers.

"And the last question, number five, says 'Our superintendent, Mr. Belton, works very hard to run the House.'"

Desdemona glances down at the white sheet, looking at the sixth question, which Dr. Hagin overlooked. Raising her hand, Desdemona mentions "Dr. Hagin, I believe you forgot about number six."

Dr. Hagin's face twists with confusion. "Number six? The quiz only has five questions."

Desdemona silently reads her translation once more: "Las Vegas holds exciting, yet dangerous feats. Beware." Desdemona, comparing this last translation to the original five, realizes it differs from the others. The first five are generic statements about life at the House, while the sixth question appears as a warning message. Dr. Hagin rushes over to Desdemona and hovers, looking over her shoulder at the paper. Normally this action would make Desdemona swoon and bat her eyelashes, but not this time. This time she watches as Dr. Hagin's face morphs from confusion to dread and he grabs the paper from her desk.

"Alright," Dr. Hagin starts, his voice shaky and unsure. "Everyone give me your papers. You all receive 100% and you are dismissed. I will see you when you return from Las Vegas."

The Anchor kids quickly gather their things, excited to be getting out of class early. Although Felix often scolds Jinx for wishing to bail on class, even he loves it when teachers cut classes short. Especially when they're going to Vegas in less than twenty-four hours! Various classmates give them high fives on their way out, thanking the Anchors for earning them all 100s on their quizzes.

"Did anyone find out what the competition is yet?" Desdemona asks Felix and Jinx. They both shake their heads. The Asterian Society has been keeping the competition details under heavy lock and key since announcing the location.

"We only know our flight leaves tomorrow at 10:00. We're supposed to meet in the lobby tomorrow at 6:30," Felix reminds them.

"Why so early?" Jinx complains.

Desdemona slaps her sister on the shoulder. "J, we're getting an all-expense paid trip to Vegas. Stop complaining!"

Just as Jinx is about to give Desdemona a taste of her own medicine, Kade appears next to her. "Can I speak to you, Jinx?" he asks rigidly.

Desdemona and Felix both feel palpable tension in the air between the pair. For one, Kade never calls Jinx by her full name. It's always "J." And, despite Jinx's efforts to hide it, both Desdemona and Felix know Jinx and Kade haven't talked much over the past two weeks.

Jinx nods quickly, leaving her brother and sister without so much as a wave goodbye. She follows Kade down the crowded, dimly lit hallways into the elevator. They travel up to the 125th floor and Jinx scrunches her eyebrows, wondering where they are going. Not wanting to be the one to break the silence, Jinx holds her tongue. Finally, the elevator dings and Jinx follows Kade to a wooden door with the name "Defrates" carved into the mahogany.

Jinx's eyes grow wide as she realizes she is about to be in his room. Kade's room. Alone. With Kade. In the middle of their fight. Jinx closes her eyes and prays Hazel is in there to diffuse the tension.

Much to her dismay, the suite is empty. Set up much like their room, with a living area just across the hall from the bedrooms. Kade leads Jinx to the soft, brown couch and motions for her to sit.

"Why are we here, Kade?" Jinx asks, finally breaking the silence.

Kade stuffs his hands into his pockets—a nervous habit Jinx always, or almost always, finds endearing. After taking a deep breath, Kade speaks. "Everyone is in all the rec rooms because they're excited about going to Vegas. I need to speak to you alone."

"Why?" Jinx questions, already knowing the answer.

But the answer Kade gives her is even better than expected. Taking his hands out of his pockets, Kade takes her face in his calloused hands and kisses her forcefully. Before she can succumb to his touch, Jinx pushes him away as a reminder he still hasn't apologized to her yet.

"You can't just kiss me and think everything is peachy, Kade," Jinx tells him, determined to stand her ground.

Kade sighs, knowing she is right. "Look, J, I'm sorry for what I said. I've seen you fight against Jane and I know you're anything but her pawn. Just because you look like her doesn't mean you act like her."

Kade pauses, but Jinx waits for him to continue. "I'm going to Vegas with Hazel and I don't want to be fighting with you while we're out there. This competition could be the best experience for all of us, but if you aren't speaking to me, it will be my worst experience."

Jinx melts at his words like putty. She rises from the couch and throws her arms around him in a tight hug, exhaling when he wraps his muscular hands around her back.

Kade sighs in contentment before exclaiming "Oh! I almost forgot something very important." Kade yanks open the drawer of the table next to the couch and it reveals three objects: a dusty book, a pink hair clip, and a Polaroid photograph. Before Jinx can ask, Kade explains himself. "The Council can't allow young Asterians to walk around Vegas with their weapons. They have enchanted our weapons to appear like everyday objects."

Jinx takes the trio of household items and looks them over. Nothing appears out of the ordinary, but she guesses that's the whole point. "Felix's is the book, Mona's is the hair clip, and yours is the photo. To make the weapons appear, tap the object three times fast. The same goes for closing them."

Excited to take the objects back and explain them to her siblings, Jinx looks at him with a lopsided smile. "We're going to Vegas, baby!"

"Flight 1254 with service to Las Vegas is now boarding zone two. All zone two passengers may board at this time," a sweet voice announces over the intercom at the airport. The sun streams through the glass windows in the early morning, revealing the large passenger jet outside on the tarmac. A group of nearly forty Asterians from the House lug their bags from their chairs in the waiting area to the flight attendant standing in front of the gate.

"What is our cover story again?" Desdemona asks Felix, securing her pink hair clip just above her right temple. Instead of having forty teenagers with hidden magical powers drawing attention to themselves, Mr. Belton—who is accompanying them on this trip—briefed them on a story to tell anyone who asks about the purposes of their travels.

Felix answers in a lowered voice, making sure the humans around them can't hear. "We're here for an academic team competition." He tucks his enchanted book/sword under his arm.

Desdemona nods as she hands her ticket to the gangly, blonde airport attendant. "Have a great flight," the woman says with a coy smile.

"You, too!" Desdemona replies out of habit before she can stop herself. Felix, overhearing the conversation, tries his best to suppress his laughter. Desdemona sticks her tongue out at him.

"Don't act like you've never done it!" Desdemona responds as Hazel hurries up next to the pair.

"I was feeling like a third wheel back there," Hazel said, smiling as Desdemona and Felix look back to see Jinx and Kade laughing with one another as they hand the woman their tickets.

Felix knows Jinx and Kade fought, but all that seems to have passed. As he watches them laugh with one another, Felix can't help but smile at his sister's happiness.

As terrible as Truchas Peak was, everything seems to have worked out, Desdemona tells Felix in his mind with a head tilt towards the happy couple.

Felix agrees and notices Desdemona always seems to be on his wavelength. *Don't speak so soon, Mona,* he reminds her. In all his favorite novels (most recently, *City of Bones*), things always seem to fall apart right after everyone has their best moment.

Finally reaching their seats, the Anchor family settles into row five while Kade and Hazel sit directly behind them.

"Don't you want to switch seats with Hazel, J? That way you can sit next to your boyfriend." Felix teases under his breath, wagging his eyebrows at his sister. Jinx slaps him harshly on his arm in retaliation and shifts to lean away from him, closing her eyes to try to get some sleep. Just as she closes her eyes, she rubs the scratchy seat covering and feels her power to see the future taking over.

Jinx finds herself in a dilapidated, rancid hotel room. Stains of all colors cover the torn, off-white bedspread. Raggedy curtains hang crookedly, blocking only half of the incoming light rather than covering the window. Something small and furry scuttles across Jinx's feet, making her squeal like Desdemona. Knowing she can't be heard or seen, Jinx hops across the ripped carpet and throws open the top drawer of the chipped bedside table, looking for something to tell her where she is. Inside the chest lies a small piece of paper containing the hotel's address: 3570 S Las Vegas Blvd, Las Vegas, NV 89109.

She repeats the address to herself to commit it to memory as a certain red-haired beauty strides in from the bathroom. Just when Margret slings a backpack over her shoulder, Maxine bursts through the door, yelling.

"Give it to me, Margret," Maxine orders, standing tall against her sister. Jinx thinks for a moment, remembering Maxine isn't old enough to be in the Asterian Society Competition. They left her at the House with the other newbies. Why is she in Vegas?

"Go away, Max," Margret retorts. "This is none of your business."

Maxine balls her hands up into fists. "It is my business. Where is the Jewel?" Jinx doesn't even bother to stifle her gasp. After the Asterian Jewel helped save the Anchors' lives and kill Jane on Truchas Peak, Mr. Belton locked it up somewhere deep in the House, but she doubts it's there anymore. That man is a scatterbrained basket case—the last person who should have been trusted to safeguard a magical jewel.

"You're too late," Margret tells her, taking a step towards the door. Maxine side steps to block Margret from exiting the room. Despite being a head shorter than Margret, Maxine's unwavering stare and powerful stance give Margret pause. "Trust me."

"No," Maxine retorts back, but then she pauses as if she's actually considering the request.

"C'mon, you know I'm not going to hurt my baby sister," Margret convinces in a voice practically dripping with honey. And with that, the vision abandons Jinx.

Glancing skittishly at Felix and Desdemona, Jinx ponders whether to tell her siblings about the vision. She decides against it, realizing both are asleep (or at least trying to sleep) and not wanting to disturb them. This can wait until they get to the hotel.

When the plane lands in Nevada, Felix recalls their last incident at an airport when they teamed up with Kade to hijack a car to get them to the bottom most point of Truchas Peak. The memory brings a smile to Felix's face.

I sincerely hope this trip is less eventful than the last one, Felix thinks to Desdemona. Desdemona snickers and nods as they grab their bags from the overhead bin, following Kade and Hazel off the plane. Asterians talk excitedly, stepping into the Las Vegas airport. Immediately, flashing lights fill the air as colors bounce off the gray, plastic looking airport walls. As they continue through the airport, slot machines seem to appear out of thin air. It takes Felix only a few steps to realize the airport has a mini-casino.

"Gambling? Already? We haven't even left the airport!" Felix notes aloud.

Kade, overhearing him, responds. "Welcome to Vegas!"

4

As the Anchors enter Caesar's Hotel in Las Vegas, their jaws drop with amazement. A tall white tower with red lettering, the hotel stands out on the Vegas strip. Sure, from the outside, the hotel looks nice. But the interior of the hotel makes the exterior look like a beaten down apartment building. In the entryway, as if guarding the hotel, stands a larger-than-life statue of the famous Caesar himself. Behind him and off to both sides, casino games stretch as far as the eye can see: blackjack tables, slot machines, poker games, and roulette wheels everywhere!

"I can't believe we're not twenty-one yet!" Desdemona overhears one of the boys from the House lament. Shaking her head, Desdemona runs her fingers over the milky marble walls as the group bypasses the casino towards the lobby. The lobby, even more extravagant than the casino area, sits in a giant rotunda with concierge and check-in desks all around the perimeter. In the middle, the splashing sound of water in an oversized fountain fills the air, forcing Mr. Belton to nearly yell as he turns to address the group.

"I have paired each of the younger families up with an older family or mentor. Mentors, please lead your group to the assigned spot," he tells them, beginning to read off the assignments. Jinx crosses her fingers, praying Mr. Belton pairs them up with Kade.

"The Anchors and the Defrates," Mr. Belton finally announces. Jinx lets out a deep breath she didn't realize she was holding and follows her siblings towards Kade and Hazel.

"How can the House afford to pay for rooms for all these people in a hotel like this?" Desdemona asks, still in awe of the circular designs of all colors on the ceilings.

Kade leans in close to make sure no one outside their group can hear. "We don't have to pay for it."

Before Desdemona can ask what he means, Kade and Hazel flip around and head back towards the casino with their luggage in tow.

"Kade, aren't the rooms that way?" Felix taps him on the shoulder in a futile attempt to stop what now appears to be a rush by Kade to the slot machines.

When Kade ignores Felix's question, Hazel answers, "Can't you guys be patient for just a minute? We know what we're doing."

Felix furrows his brow at his sisters as they blindly follow Hazel and Kade. Instead of stopping in front of the entrance to the casino, Kade barges right into the casino despite none of them being of age. Circumventing the colored lights of the slot machines, Kade swerves around the gambling guests towards a nearly full blackjack table. Kade nods at Hazel, who moves around to the side of the table towards the haughty-looking dealer. She whispers in his ear and he flashes a smile.

"Come with me," the man orders them. Ditching the players of the game, the dealer rushes towards the back of the casino without even a glance back to make sure the Asterian group follows. Lucky for him, they are.

The man stops once they reach a red velvet curtain drawn tightly to conceal a dark room behind. Too busy looking around the casino, Jinx runs flat into Kade's back.

"Sorry," she murmurs.

Kade smirks. "No, you're not."

Trying to suppress a small smile, Jinx leans over Kade's shoulder as the dealer speaks. "It's right through this curtain. Be discreet about it though. Some of the less informed staff don't understand why a large academic team is staying at Caesar's of all places." The man pauses before continuing. "I can take your luggage, please."

Hazel gives her bags to the man, pushes the curtain to the side, and enters with the rest of the group close at her heels. They begin climbing down a black, winding staircase. The lack of light forces Felix to run his hands along the stony walls to feel his way. Felix feels every curve, bump, and ridge in the wall on the pads of his fingers. He hears every step and breath of his group loudly and clearly. Hesitating at first, Felix remembers. When an Asterian loses one sense, the rest heighten to pick up the slack.

"We deserve some answers," Jinx sneers at Kade and Hazel in the darkness.

Kade lets out a deep breath before responding. "We can't answer questions we haven't heard."

Felix jumps at a chance to clear up the confusion of the past half hour. "Who was the man who took our bags?"

"That was Harry. He's an Asterian with a gift for gambling, so naturally, he works at a casino," Hazel answers as they continue to descend the dark staircase.

Beginning to wonder how far these steps go down, Desdemona thinks to pass the time by asking, "What is going on with this hotel? Is the competition held here?"

Kade's deep exhale signals to Jinx this isn't going to be a short answer. "The land on which Caesar's Palace sits has been an important location for Asterians for centuries. As you would have seen for yourself in just a few minutes with a bit more patience, deep below this hotel is miles of space available for Asterian use."

Kade stops momentarily, allowing his footfalls to echo through the never-ending darkness. "The ancestors of Harry, the guy you met earlier, occupied this land when Cecily, the evil Asterian who spurred the creation of the Asterian Society, went on her rampage. It was originally a safe house for Asterians, with thousands of supply rooms, but now the Asterian Society uses it as one of its headquarter locations."

"You're telling me this is an Asterian hotel and the humans don't know a thing about it?" Jinx questions.

"Pretty much," Hazel finishes.

Soon, Felix begins to see a light at the end of the staircase opening through the darkness. As they near the light, noise begins to penetrate the concrete walls to end the fallen silence. When the staircase finally levels, the noise grows louder and the source can be heard. Hundreds of voices, all having different conversations, fill the air.

"Wow," Desdemona murmurs as they enter the lobby of the hotel under the hotel. Unlike the entryway of Caesar's Palace, the floor of the underground hotel has no slot machines or other gaming. Instead, more young Asterians than they can count stand on the white marble floors. The white marble of the floor mixes with grey and black as it scales the wall. Slowly fading towards black, more marble covers the ceiling. The center of the lobby, just as in Caesar's, features statues. But instead of a large statute of Caesar, five different statues adorn the lobby. As she approaches the first, most prominent figure, Desdemona notices the engraving on the base.

"Clarence Abbot," Desdemona reads aloud. "Where do I recognize that name?"

Felix jumps in, answering. "That's the name of the founder of the first Asterian Society. Remember? We read it in history class that first day."

His statement jogs her memory and Desdemona realizes the five statues pay tribute to the group of five Asterians who defeated Cecily and saved the Asterian race.

"What's the name of this place?" Desdemona asks Kade.

"It's called the Ironwell," Kade answers. Desdemona can't help but notice his indifference towards the magnificence and beauty of the underground hotel. Wondering if this isn't his first trip to Vegas, Desdemona makes a mental note to ask him more questions about the Ironwell.

Losing her train of thought, Desdemona notices more Asterians entering through dark staircases much like their own all around the lobby area. With faces just as starstruck as hers, questions pour out of their mouths to their leaders.

"Why are there so many people here?" Jinx asks. "The House only brought forty people."

Hazel attempts to hide a laugh, causing Jinx to jump at her like she often does. "Why are you laughing at me?"

"There's just so much you don't know," Hazel informs them.

"Well, we would know a lot more if Kade didn't keep getting upset whenever we opened our mouths!" Jinx accused.

Trying to stop the anger before it comes to a boil, Felix intervenes. "What I think Jinx is trying to ask is who are all these extra Asterians?"

Kade, shooting an inpatient look at Jinx, responds, "The House isn't the only Asterian training facility. There are other ones in other parts of the world."

Felix nods, wondering why he never thought about another school before. Obviously, Asterians who live in Europe aren't going to move to the United States. It only makes sense to have multiple training areas.

"How many are there?" Felix looks around, noting there must be three hundred people in the lobby and probably more elsewhere in the Ironwell.

Hazel furrows her brow in confusion. "How many other training schools?" Felix nods in response.

"Oh, there are hundreds!" Hazel exclaims as if they should already know this. "Some are smaller than others. The House happens to be one of the larger ones."

Taking in the information, Felix notices everyone in the area seems to be waiting for something. Just as he opens his mouth to ask another question, he receives his answer.

The marble ceiling parts from the top, creating an enormous opening. From this fissure, an oversized stage lowers. The eleven remaining members of the Asterian Society stand proudly on the stage. The woman who spoke to the House, Mrs. Tary, stands at the stage's edge holding a microphone. At the sight of the Society, the immense group of Asterians becomes immediately quiet.

"First and foremost," the woman begins with a smile. "I would like to thank you all for choosing to participate in this once in a lifetime experience. As I am sure you're all aware, ONE of you will complete the Asterian Society as its newest twelfth member."

The families whisper excitedly amongst themselves, each of them sure it will be one of them.

"Since I know you're all curious to find out how the competition works, I will start by saying it isn't going to be easy. A member of the Asterian Society must have patience, perseverance, vigilance, and critical thinking skills. And that is why the first aspect of our competition is..." she pauses, allowing the anticipation to build. "A scavenger hunt!"

Jinx lets out a snort. "A scavenger hunt? What is this? Elementary school?"

As if she heard Jinx's snarky comment, the woman proceeds to explain why this is not your everyday, childhood scavenger hunt. "The goal is to collect as many Clarence Abbot replicas as possible based on clues you will be given. But here's the catch. Each replica has been hidden in a different, discrete location within the Las Vegas city limits. AND, each replica will be closely monitored and not easy to access. You must complete your challenge and face your fears to retrieve each replica."

As she listens, Jinx takes back her earlier verbal disgust. *This competition sounds epic!* She thinks.

The woman continues. "The search for the replicas will cease at 10:00 p.m. sharp each night, at which point all competitors must return to this area no matter where they are in their search. And before you try to continue past 10:00 p.m, the replicas will disappear at exactly 10:00 each night and will not reappear until 10 a.m. the next morning. Also, you will retrieve only one replica per day. The families with the highest number of collected replicas will advance to the next round of competition."

"But how will a member be chosen from the winning family?" Desdemona asks Felix. Felix shrugs, figuring they will find that out if it comes down to it.

The woman glances back at one of the older men of the Society and the man snaps his fingers loudly. "You must be discreet around the humans. You must be prepared to do battle, but anyone who causes chaos in the actual human world WILL be disqualified. The competition begins now. You will now find the first clue in your pocket. Happy searching!"

5

The Anchors each dig furiously in their pants' pockets, searching for the piece of paper to lead them to the first Abbot replica.

"I've got it!" Felix shouts, pulling a ratty scroll of parchment paper from his pocket. Next to them, Kade and Hazel read their own clue.

Unrolling the tan page, Felix reads aloud.

> There's more than meets the eye
> to this tasty treat.
> Peel back the hard outer shell
> to reveal the soft underneath.

"Treat?" Desdemona wonders aloud. "Is it a kind of food?"

Felix shrugs. "I don't know. Where should we start?"

Desdemona butts in. "Real quick before we go! We all have our weapons, right? We might need them." Desdemona motions to her hair clip just as Felix pulls his book from his backpack.

"Yes, Mom," Jinx pulls out her wallet with the photograph tucked safely in the slot. "We've got them."

Jinx, without even glancing at her siblings again, begins towards the staircase they previously came down. Knowing her siblings will follow, Jinx envelopes herself in darkness once more. "Does anyone know anything about what's in Vegas?"

"I came here once with Marcus when I was five," Felix announces. "We had a great time."

"Oh, that's just swell!" Jinx digs at Felix. "I'm so glad you had fun here ten years ago!"

Desdemona hits Jinx on the arm as they continue to climb. "J, we're never going to find this if we can't work together. Remember how we won the Hunt last year? Think of this as the Hunt—just on a bigger scale."

When they reach the top of the stairs, they carefully push aside the velvet curtain to enter the noisy, rambunctious casino. "In the Hunt, we used our powers to find where the Asterian Jewel was hidden," Felix reminds his sisters as they bypass the never-ending array of flashing lights and despairing slot machine losers. "Why can't we do that again?"

"This is on a much bigger scale," Desdemona points out. "In the Hunt, the search was confined to the House and it involved one item. This is an entire city!"

"Mona is right," Felix notes. "We need to find out what's in the city first. Do you think we can get a map?" Without waiting for an answer, Felix zones in on the mind of the flashy male concierge standing behind the front desk. Searching through the concierge's mind, Felix finds his answer.

The maps are directly by the door, Felix reads in the man's mind. Relaying the message to his sisters, the Anchor kids briskly walk towards the main entrance, while trying not to draw too much attention to themselves. They don't want other Asterians catching on to their plan of grabbing a map before proceeding.

When they reach the oversized Julius Caesar statue at the front of the lobby, Jinx spots a wooden stand labeled "City Maps." Noticing a clock above the map stand, she announces, "It's 2:10 here. We have less than eight hours until the replicas disappear."

Just as Desdemona grabs for a map, her hand brushes up against a pale, sweaty palm. Looking up to see who had the same idea as her, Desdemona freezes. Thin, curved nose. Messy, blonde hair. Pale, grey eyes tell the horrors he previously knew.

"Jason Curb," Desdemona murmurs just loud enough for the boy to hear. Desdemona quickly remembers the sight of the timid boy on the Asterian News with Abigayle Rollens from about a month ago. The boy sucks in a shocked breath when Desdemona mentions his name. The sound of his voice sucks Desdemona into a vision of the past.

The brisk, thin air causes Desdemona to gasp for breath. Adjusting to the lack of oxygen reminds Desdemona of only one place: Truchas Peak. Desdemona feels her chest clench as she takes in her surroundings. The rubble of Jane's headquarters on top of Truchas Peak covers every inch as far as the eye can see. On top of the mountain, the chilly breeze forces Desdemona to wrap her arms around herself. As she does, her pasty skin informs her that she is in the body of none other than Jason himself.

She hears a grunt and whips around, realizing she's not alone. Out of the corner of her eye, she notices Margret pulling and tugging on a skinny arm under the rubble. After a few tugs, Margret drops the arm and begins clearing debris from the body. Margret moves the biggest beam and reveals the face of the woman underneath.

The chopped, black hair, striking nose, and almond eyes are unmistakably Jane's. At first, Desdemona feels a twinge of fear as she faces her mother, but lets out a sigh of relief as she recalls Jane died when the headquarters collapsed after Hazel's life-saving earthquake. Jane is dead.

Not wanting to be caught, Desdemona ducks behind a large pile of scraps and watches Margret strip more wood and stone away from Jane's corpse. Once Margret clears the last piece, she grabs Jane's arm once more and gives it a tug. Margret flops Jane upward to a standing position like a limp dog. Desdemona feels a bit of satisfaction at the sight of Jane so helpless, but then grows disgusted as she realizes Margret is holding up literal dead weight.

"C'mon, J," Margret breathes out, making Desdemona cringe at Jinx's nickname being used for Jane. "You've got to help me a little bit here. I can't do this all on my own."

Jane let out a painful, weak groan in response. The blood in Desdemona's veins turns to ice and the oh-so-familiar dread returns. Jane is not dead.

"Mona!" Desdemona hears Jinx yell. "What are you doing? You're wasting time!"

Knowing her vision took only a few seconds in real time, Desdemona snatches a map and returns to her siblings.

"Did you recognize that guy?" Desdemona asks as she struggles to unfold the map with shaking hands. Felix, seeing her struggle, reaches for the map and helps her unfold it.

Jinx shakes her head as they exit the hotel into the city. Stifling and dry, the Las Vegas heat suffocates like a toaster oven. But a little heat will not stop them from finding their first figurine, especially not Jinx.

"I didn't recognize him," Felix answers Desdemona, following Jinx to a secluded corner outside the hotel.

"He was the guy on the Asterian news that one morning. He was the one who spoke out about how awful it was to be under Jane's spell," Desdemona informs them. "And... I had a vision."

Desdemona takes a deep breath, filling her lungs with heat, and tells her brother and sister about her vision from start to finish. Jinx, half-heartedly listening as she searches the Vegas map, snaps her head up when Desdemona tells about Jane's response to Margret.

"Jane is alive?" Felix exclaims, incredulously.

"But didn't Kade check her pulse and tell us she was dead?" Desdemona wonders aloud.

Jinx answers quickly. "A light pulse is easy to miss, especially if the person has just suffered a life-threatening injury of some sort."

Both Desdemona and Felix scrunch their faces up at Jinx, wondering where she suddenly learned these things despite never listening in high school or at the House.

"What? Sometimes I watch documentaries," Jinx snarls at them when she notices their disbelieving looks.

Felix glances between his sisters uneasily. "So... we know Jane is alive, but what do we do with this information? We can't go looking for her."

"I don't think there is anything we can do," Desdemona admits.

"I know something we can do!" Jinx announces loudly. Both Felix and Desdemona look at her expectantly. "Win this contest already! If one of us is a member of the Asterian Council, we could really do some damage to Jane. We need to hurry before the others start finding their first figurines."

Turning their attention back to the map, the triplets study it closely, all looking for some sort of food or candy store.

"There's a cotton candy store a couple of miles from here," Felix notes. "Although cotton candy doesn't really have a hard outer shell."

"Would it be somewhere as generic as a grocery store?" Desdemona asks.

Jinx shakes her head. "I don't think so. We need to think like a tourist! Where would a tourist want to go to buy treats?"

"A bakery?" Felix suggests.

"Tourists, Felix! Tourists don't want to go to a bakery!" Jinx knocks him on the head as Desdemona gives her a look that says 'Be Nice.' "Tourists want to go places that have t-shirts for sale."

Thinking back to his long-ago trip to Las Vegas with Marcus, Felix recalls his favorite place in the entire city. Of course! That's it! Why didn't he think of it before!

"Taxi!" Felix shouts, raising his hand and running to the edge of the sidewalk. A yellow cab pulls over to the side of the road and Felix holds the door open for his confused, bewildered sisters.

"Vere vould you like to go?" the cab driver asks with a heavy Russian accent.

"M&M's World!" Felix shouts a little too loudly. The cab driver floors the pedal, causing the cab to jerk forward. Felix grabs the back of the seat in front of him to keep himself from banging into the side of the cab.

Typical city driving, Felix thinks to Desdemona.

Definitely right about that, Desdemona thinks back. *I hope this ride is short or I'm going to be car sick!*

Jinx mentally hits herself over the head for not thinking of this obvious answer. Tasty treat. Hard shell. Soft underneath. M&M's perfectly fit all the clue's criteria.

"Umm, guys," Desdemona whispers nervously. "Do we have money to pay this cab driver?"

Jinx begins to fish in her pocket, pulling out a wad of cash. After a confused look from her siblings, Jinx explains, "Kade told me I would need money here, for things like this, I guess. He pulled this from the House reserves."

"Speaking of Kade, how are you guys?" Desdemona nosily pokes at Jinx.

Jinx scrunches up her face as the taxi cab comes to a screeching halt. "Mona, this isn't a time to discuss boys! We have a competition to win!"

"M&M's World." the cab driver announces unenthusiastically, as if he's driven thousands of over-excited tourists to locations such as this. Jinx, so excited to begin the search she doesn't even look at the price, thanks the man with a $20, a $5, and a simple "Keep the change."

"Have a good day!" Felix shouts at the man as Jinx pushes Felix out the door. After stumbling out of the taxi, Felix squints into the sun in awe as he takes in the giant M&M packet covering the entire front of the building. The two most famous M&M spokespeople, Red and Yellow, accompanied by their friend, Green, surround the oversized packet. Excited tourists—too many to count—rush into M&M's World with their smiles wide and their credit cards ready.

"I've always wanted to go here!" Desdemona enthuses to Jinx and Felix like a child at Disney World. Although she can't completely shake the anxious feeling caused by her earlier vision, Desdemona compartmentalizes. *We can do nothing about it now*, Desdemona tells herself. Instead, she does her best to simply enjoy a city she's never been to before.

Jinx tugs on Desdemona and Felix's arms, reminding them of the tight schedule. They follow Jinx in through the gigantic entryway, but stop a few steps into the building. M&M's of every different hue line the walls—pink, turquoise, multi-colored, maroon, lime. Children grab t-shirts with the famous M&M spokespeople on them as they beg for a souvenir at every turn. The storekeepers have placed thousands of M&M knick-knacks strategically on sales floor shelves. Turning to a map on his left Felix's eyes go wide.

"This place has four floors?" Felix informs the group, practically in disbelief.

"This place is a glorified gift shop," Jinx sneers at the parents buying their children overpriced t-shirts they will hardly wear after this trip.

"This place is awesome!" Desdemona shrieks, drifting towards the endless wall of colored M&M's.

Jinx rushes towards her, grabbing Desdemona by her tank top to keep her from wandering off. "We can shop after we find the first figurine!"

"But I just want to get a few M&M's," Desdemona whines, breaking from her sister's grip.

Grabbing her again, Jinx tells her again. "Afterwards, okay?" When Desdemona nods in agreement and follows Jinx back to Felix, he catches a glimpse of Jinx's thoughts.

She's like a child! Always distracted! Jinx laments. Felix snickers, deciding not to scold his sister for the mean comment (partially because it was true and partially because he wasn't in the mood to get on Jinx again.)

"Where do we start?" Felix wonders aloud, looking up to the second floor.

Jinx bites her lip in thought. "Didn't the Asterian Society woman tell us it would be a challenge to get the figurines?"

"And that we couldn't get caught by...," Desdemona lowers her voice to a whisper. "Humans."

"Exactly," Jinx agrees, thinking she may be on to something. "There must be some place in this crowded gift shop where we can beat the guard and manage to keep it a secret."

Felix squints at the map one more time. "There's a theatre up on the second floor, I think. But it says it's closed to the public today."

"That's perfect!" Jinx shouts. Without waiting for Desdemona and Felix, Jinx whips around to run up the steps towards the theatre. She turns around to make sure they're following her and as she does, she runs smack into the back of a person in a black sweatshirt with the hood pulled tightly to cover their face.

"Sorry," Jinx apologizes quickly. The rushing Jinx doesn't notice the person remains silent, not acknowledging her apology.

After swerving through crowds at a jog, the Anchor triplets reach the closed theatre on the second floor of M&M's World. The sign above the theatre reads "Amazing Double Feature! Free 3D Movie & Personalized M&M's Printer." Much to the dismay of the patrons in Vegas today, a handwritten sign has been taped to the doors leading into the theatre, informing them the theatre will be closed the entire week.

"Are we sure it's here?" Felix wonders aloud. "If it's not, we'll get in a lot of trouble for entering when the sign specifically says the theatre is closed."

Desdemona shrugs. "We'll never know unless we try."

Jinx slaps her sister on the back, causing Desdemona to jerk forward uncomfortably. "Now you're talking like someone who wants to be in the Asterian Society!"

Looking around to make sure no employees see them, Jinx inches forwards and opens the theatre door. A stubby child around the age of 5 points at Jinx and looks up at her. Unsure how to keep this boy quiet, Jinx slips her finger over her lips in a shushing motion. The boy grins mischievously and quickly turns away from the Anchor kids, back to his unsuspecting mother. Jinx waves her hand, with Desdemona and Felix quickly following behind. The triplets slip through the barely open doorway and into the off-limits theatre.

When they enter, the lights are completely off, shrouding them in darkness. "Guys, is this right?" Felix asks, concerned.

"It doesn't feel quite right," Desdemona responds. Just as Mona opens her mouth to suggest another place, stage lights fill the room with white, hot brightness. A velvet curtain pulled to the side, reveals the bold proscenium stage. Center stage, right under the spotlight, stands a small pillar with a black box poised on top. A small figurine stands at attention on top of the box. Instinctively, Jinx takes a step towards the stage. Felix whips his arm out, effectively stopping Jinx from moving any further, but also clotheslining her in the stomach.

"Ouch! What was that for?" Jinx winces, clutching her abdomen.

Felix squints at the stage, attempting to detect movement from the wings. "It's too easy. The Asterian Society said there will be obstacles protecting each figurine. Remember?"

Jinx shrugs. "Well, we're not going to get anywhere by just sitting here and waiting for something or someone to come at us. We have to make a move."

When neither of her siblings move, Jinx grabs one of each of their arms and tugs them towards the stage. Mostly against their will, Felix and Desdemona ascend the stairs onto the stage. With every step closer to the figurine, Felix's mind irrationally imagines them being eaten by a giant snake. Or worse, a giant insect.

Despite their trepidation, Jinx reaches the figurine with no problem. Her brother and sister come up by her side.

"Now what?" Desdemona wonders aloud. Jinx, hesitating a moment, reaches a handout and grips the head of the figurine in her fist.

Felix practically jumps on Jinx in response to her rash action. "Wait! You don't know..."

Before he can finish his plea, Desdemona holds up her hand in a silent "Wait a second." She places her hand over Jinx's hand and pulls the plastic furiously, attempting to dislodge it from its black captor.

After a few more pulls, Desdemona groans in frustration. "It won't budge."

"What are we supposed to do? It doesn't seem like anything is about to attack us," Felix says. But just after the words leave his mouth, a deep, booming voice fills the empty auditorium.

"I expected to see you here first, Anchors," the voice begins mischievously. Felix, Desdemona, and Jinx look around at one another in confusion before scanning the area, searching for the source. The voice seems familiar.

"Don't be alarmed. The key to this challenge is not a battle, but rather a test of knowing your own strengths and weaknesses. Patience is a virtue, Anchors. The question is, do you know your powers better than we do?" Near the end of the sentence, the voice begins to fade out and a large, clear container falls from the ceiling of the theatre. Before they have a chance to run away, the Anchor kids find themselves surrounded by what looks like a container used to hold lab rats. Inside the container—right next to Jinx – stands a large grandfather clock, much like the one Hilga, their grandmother, used to own. Jinx takes a few steps towards the old, rickety clock before noticing a large chunk of wood has been torn out of its top right corner. This clock doesn't just look like her grandmother's clock. It IS her grandmother's clock.

In an attempt not to be creeped out by the familiar object, Jinx bangs her fists on the plastic, hoping to fight her way out. "Are they serious? I was expecting a clean fight and this is what we get? We're trapped in here like animals!"

Desdemona turns around to the walls as well, but instead of beating them like her sister, she runs her hands over the corners, hoping to find a small opening. After she fails to come up with anything useful she turns back to her brother and sister with a sigh. "I don't see any obvious way out."

"Of course they're not going to make it obvious," Felix mentions. "The voice said we have to know ourselves."

"Know ourselves?" Jinx clarifies. "I think I know myself pretty well, thank you!"

"By the time we get out of here, the competition could be nearly over," Desdemona notes. "It could be days!"

Felix looks up through the plastic towards the black, tall ceilings of the theatre. Slightly to the left, he notices a small, black speaker—probably the one the voice came from earlier. Breathing deeply, he focuses solely on the sight of the speaker, pulling himself up into the mind of the mysterious, unknown voice.

Felix stands in an empty room, wide open and filled with fluorescent light. The ground is flat and feels like tile floor underneath his feet. Deafening silence in the air causes Felix to shift uncomfortably as he stands in the middle of the room.

"You didn't think I would make it this easy, did you, Felix?" the voice speaks once again. Only this time, the voice is not

booming over a loudspeaker. This time, the voice is right behind him.

Whipping around on his heels, Felix finds himself face to face with...

"Mr. Belton? What are you doing here?" Felix asks. Mr. Belton wears a black hoodie.

"I'm surprised you didn't recognize my voice, Felix," Mr. Belton answers in a calm tone. He takes a step towards Felix and Felix sucks in a deep breath, forcing himself to stay rooted to the spot. There is no need to be afraid of Mr. Belton, right?

"If you're wondering why you can't see into my mind, it's because the Asterian Council put up a wall to protect me from intruders like yourself."

Felix scrunches up his nose in frustration. "Then how are we supposed to get out of this box?"

"Use what you know best. Time." Mr. Belton urges him. Not understanding what Mr. Belton means, yet thinking Mr. Belton will say no more, Felix begins to pull himself out of Mr. Belton's mind. But just before Felix escapes completely, Mr. Belton smiles and says, "No time like the future, Felix."

6

Felix opens his eyes to see Desdemona and Jinx each leaning over him, poking him with their bony fingers. The wooden floor of the stage feels cold under his arms.

"Oh good!" Desdemona exclaims, pulling away her perfectly manicured hand.

"I told you he was alright," Jinx nods at Desdemona.

Sitting up and rubbing his head, Felix pulls his legs to his chest. "Why are you guys so worried? You knew I was having a vision."

Desdemona reaches out her hand to help her brother up. "Yeah, but none of us have fallen during one of our visions since training. It made us think something really bad was happening..." Desdemona's voice trails off as she waits for Felix to assure her everything is alright.

Felix reports his vision to his sisters. "We're supposed to use time to help us get out of this box?" Jinx clarifies.

"Maybe he doesn't literally mean time..." Felix mumbles under his breath as he takes a step backward towards the edge of the box. As he moves his foot back, he feels a shooting pain as his ankle collides with hardwood.

"What the...." Felix stops himself as he flips around to catch the culprit of his pain. The tall grandfather clock almost reaches the ceiling. Felix slaps his forehead into the palm of his hand. How did he not think of this before?

Just as Felix opens his mouth to tell his sisters about his epiphany, the looks on their faces tell him they just had the same realization.

Jinx reaches forward to inspect the clock. "Okay, so by time, he meant the clock. But what are we supposed to do with the clock?" Both Desdemona and Felix shake their heads. Neither has the answer.

"Where's Kade when we need him?" Jinx whines. "He would know what to do!"

Desdemona lets her jaw drop practically to the floor. "Wait, you're telling me you need a guy to figure this out? Not even just a guy; your boyfriend, to be exact! C'mon, I thought Hilga taught you to be smarter than this."

When Desdemona mentions Hilga, Jinx feels her stomach lurch. For fifteen years, Hilga took care of Jinx and taught her everything she knows about the real world. Hilga taught her how to make the best blueberry pie. She taught her how to ride a bike, how to say her ABCs, and how to play soccer. Now that Jinx has barely seen Hilga over the last year, it seems as if she has forgotten Hilga's most important teaching of all: how to be independent. Desdemona is right. Jinx will not sit and whine about not having Kade. She *can* and *will* do this all by herself!

Jumping to her feet, Jinx moves over to the grandfather clock to inspect it once more, thinking about Mr. Belton's comments. Looking at the hands on the clock, Jinx opens the glass door encasing the clock face and begins to turn the clock's hands. First, she turns the hands backward from 5:44 p.m. to 8:17 a.m. this morning. Suddenly, a sharp twinge begins to crawl up her body from her toes, through her legs and to her upper body. Panicking, she whips around to see Desdemona and Felix obviously feeling the same thing.

"What's happening?" Desdemona shrieks aloud, rubbing her arms furiously as if she feels bugs she can't brush off. Jinx reaches around to try to turn the clock back to the current time, but before she can manage to do so, the ache continues to stitch its way up her body until it fills every inch. All at once, her body feels tugged, out of her control, in a thousand different directions.

Jinx lands and finds herself seated between Desdemona and Felix. Grey leather slides under her fingertips as she breathes in the cool, compact air of the flight cabin. A skinny flight attendant stands near the door of the plane, holding up a model seatbelt to demonstrate how to buckle and unbuckle, something everyone learns before first grade.

"Flight 1254 with service to Las Vegas is now prepared for take off," a sweet, silky voice announces to every passenger. After a moment of confusion, Jinx realizes where she is. Panicking, she catches the eyes of Felix and Desdemona. They meet hers with a stare just as worried as her own.

"How did we get here?" Desdemona mumbles under her breath.

"The better question is 'how do we get out of here?'" Felix replies in an equally hushed tone.

Jinx nudges Desdemona on the shoulder. "Shouldn't you know, Mona? The past is kind of your thing!" Desdemona shakes her head in frustration as she leans over to look out the airplane window. She feels the plane lurch forward and the ground outside begins whizzing past seemingly at the speed of light.

"Could we just wait until we get back to present day?" Felix suggests.

"I don't think that's going to work," Desdemona replies. "What if time moves at the same speed even though we're in the past. If that happens, we would never catch back up."

The thought of being stuck in the past forever makes Desdemona's stomach lurch. Sure, she doesn't mind seeing the past, but she never wants to live in it!

"You know what they say: 'don't dwell on the past!'" Felix jokes in a failed attempt to lighten the mood. Both Desdemona and Jinx roll their eyes at him. Desdemona, knowing one of them has to take charge, begins to unbuckle her seatbelt. Standing up quickly, the forward movement of the plane going skyward drags her backward. The force slams her back into her seat, causing the back of her head to slap against the headrest.

She looks over and notices Felix and Jinx snickering at her misfortune. Sticking her tongue out at them, she buckles her seatbelt once again. "You know, I think I will just wait until they turn the fasten seatbelt light off."

Crossing and uncrossing her arms against her chest, Desdemona anxiously waits for time to pass. She realizes when she stood up a few minutes earlier, she didn't have much of a plan. In fact, this is one of the first times in her life she doesn't have a plan. No specific route. No certain conversation. No predetermined destination. Although she did not notice this earlier, one feeling is certain. She is scared out of her mind.

For the first time since she harnessed her powers, she isn't in control of her vision. She can't just leave it whenever she receives her needed information. With shaky breath, she thinks loudly and clearly, as if yelling inside her own mind. Felix meets her trembling gaze and nods. He is listening.

When this fasten seat belt light goes off, I have to get up and try to fix this, Desdemona begins. *And I don't have a single clue about what to do.*

Felix smiles softly at her, wrapping his large hand around her small one. *We're going to get out of this. This is just a trick from the Asterian Council, remember? This is just a game.*

Just as Desdemona starts to feel slightly better about their chances, the overhead button on the plane dings, freeing passengers to move about the cabin. Desdemona unbuckles her seatbelt with a shaky hand, continuously saying to herself that it's all a game and they aren't in any real danger.

Shooting up from her seat, Desdemona bangs her head against the overhead compartment with a smack. Felix and Jinx once again try to hide their giggles as Desdemona rubs the crown of her head with the palm of her hand.

"Today... is just not your... day, Mona," Jinx manages in between laughs.

"You're telling me," Desdemona mutters under her breath as she slides past Felix and Jinx into the aisle way.

As she begins to make her way to the front of the plane, a voice comes over the loudspeaker on the plane. "This is your captain speaking. We have officially reached a cruising altitude of 39,000 feet. Please feel free to use your laptops and other electronic devices at this time."

The second the captain finishes the announcement, Desdemona stops in her tracks. The voice of the captain is the same one they heard in the theatre in M&M World! There's no way that can be a coincidence.

Quickening her step, Desdemona rushes towards the cockpit of the plane in hopes of bypassing the flight attendants. Fifteen feet from the cockpit. Ten feet. Five. Three. Just as she puts her hand out to reach for the door handle, a sturdy body steps in her way and knocks her outstretched arm to the side.

"Excuse me, madam," a stocky stewardess sneers. "You can't go in there."

"I really just need to have a word with the captain! I'm friends with him!" Desdemona tells, recalling how Felix said the voice in the theatre was Mr. Belton.

"Sure, and I'm friends with Paul McCartney," the woman says sarcastically. As the woman speaks, Desdemona notices keys jingling from a clip on the woman's skirt. Only then does Desdemona realize the door to the cockpit is locked.

Thinking on her feet and trying to ignore the stewardess' rude comment, Desdemona regains her composure. "Then, please, I just need to use the restroom." Desdemona pushes past the woman on her way to the restroom using all the lessons from Kade on stealthiness and sneak attacks. Desdemona bumps into the stewardess at every possible angle to grab the keys without seeming suspicious. She pulls the restroom door open furiously, trying to drown out the sound of the keys now jingling in her clenched fist.

Desdemona smiles to herself as she closes the bathroom door behind her and opens her hand to reveal a set of three keys. She doesn't have long. It will only be a matter of time before the attendant notices the loss of weight on her already oversized hips.

Screaming furiously in her thoughts, Desdemona calls out *Felix! Felix!*

Felix jumps into her thoughts quickly. *What? Are you okay?*

I need you to create a diversion. I need to get into the cockpit without anyone noticing! Desdemona orders her brother, adding *this is such an adrenaline rush! Let's do it more often!*

Although Felix sincerely hopes this is the last time they find themselves in a situation like this, he replies *alright, give us two minutes.*

Desdemona agrees and turns to look at herself in the tiny airplane mirror. Ratty hair, smeared mascara, and one lost earring. She looks like she hasn't had a shower in days. In a futile attempt to make herself look presentable (but also to make it easier to move quickly), Desdemona pulls her long blonde hair back with a black hair tie. While she's at it, she takes the hair clip out and clutches it in her free hand just in case she needs it.

A quick glance at the watch on her wrist causes Desdemona to realize nearly two minutes has passed since her conversation with Felix. As if on cue, Desdemona hears a loud shouting noise from outside the bathroom.

"I thought I told you this was my bag!" Jinx shrieks in a voice more girlish than Desdemona has ever heard her use. Opening the bathroom door just a crack, Desdemona sees Felix and Jinx playing tug of war with Jinx's shoulder bag.

"HELP! This man is trying to steal something from my bag!" Jinx screams again. At the sound of the commotion, all the flight attendants rush towards the fighting teenagers, leaving the door to the cockpit unguarded. Desdemona looks down at the keys in her hands, wondering which of the three keys will open the door. She definitely doesn't have enough time to try all three keys. Quickly, pushing the bathroom door open, she whispers eenie meenie miney mo and lands on the key on the far right.

Praying the eenie-meenie-miney-mo gods favor her, Desdemona slips from the bathroom door and jams the key into the lock. Twisting furiously she wiggles the key. When the door doesn't budge, Desdemona picks one of the other two keys at random and tries again, glancing rapidly over her shoulder at the pre-occupied flight attendants. This time she feels the lock on the door give and the door opens slightly.

Attempting not to draw more attention to herself, Desdemona slips through the crack in the door. As she closes it behind her, Desdemona knows she doesn't have a clue about what to do next. Her plan stopped at getting to the pilot, and yet, she might be their only hope of returning to the present.

Desdemona turns around to face the pilot and finds her expectations have been met. Mr. Belton calmly sits in the captain's chair, still in his black hood. Desdemona clutches her hand over her heart as Mr. Belton swivels in his pilot chair, laughing.

"Ah, Mona. I suggested to you earlier this is a test of patience, but really I hoped you and your siblings would take the opposing route: control," Mr. Belton tells her.

Still shaken, the words spoken go right over Desdemona's head. Something about patience. Something about a test. Something about control. Trying to regain her composure, Desdemona forces herself to listen to the principal of the House.

"Lucky for you three, more than one solution to any given problem exists in the Asterian world. Instead of waiting for the flight to land to approach the cockpit, you took the situation into your own hands. Patience is a virtue, but members of the Asterian Council weigh courage with just as much importance. For that, I praise you and part one of your task is completed."

The feeling of stretching and pulling fills the room once more, starting at Desdemona's feet and shooting its way up to her head. Just when she feels like she can't be pulled any further, the feeling subsides. Desdemona opens her eyes to find herself once again encased in a box made of plastic.

7

"We did it!" Desdemona shouts as she flips around to find Felix and Jinx hesitantly adjusting to being back in the present.

Jinx examines the box still surrounding them. "No... it doesn't seem like we did. If we did what they wanted us to do, we would have the figurine and be on to the next clue."

Desdemona shakes her head in frustration, thinking back to what she experienced in the cockpit of the plane. She focuses on Mr. Belton's words.

"Part one of your task is completed," Desdemona murmurs under her breath.

"What did you say?" Felix asks. "We couldn't hear you."

Desdemona clears her throat and repeats, "Part one of your task is completed. That's what Mr. Belton said to me just before we came back to the present."

Jinx approaches the grandfather clock once more and examines the hands. They have returned to present and only about twenty minutes has passed since they time traveled back to the airplane. Suddenly, she wonders what will happen if she turns the hands on the clock forward just a smidgen...

Instead of clearing it with her brother and sister (mainly because she knows they will not approve of her experimentation), Jinx impulsively pulls both hands of the clock past midnight twice and to the 8:00, making it 8:40 p.m. tomorrow evening. Once again, she feels her skin pulled tight around her bones and cringes at the feeling rushing through her veins.

"Jinx!" Desdemona yells in a weak voice. "Why did you do it again?"

Jinx has just enough time to shrug in response before they are pulled out of the plastic box and into the future.

The air stifles with heat within concrete walls surrounding the Anchor triplets, causing them each to cough as they take in their surroundings. Felix rubs his eyes and allows them to adjust to the darkness. Light streams through metal bars at the front of the room, providing little visibility. In the corner of the room sits a small, rusty toilet.

Shock rolls through Felix's entire body. "Guys... we're in a jail cell!"

"What did we do this time?" Jinx snorts, seemingly unfazed by their imprisonment. She walks calmly from one end of the small cell to the other and examines its holdings: an unappealing bed with a torn blanket, a nightstand to match, and a half-shattered sink with a dripping faucet.

"What DID we do?" Desdemona wonders, the tone of her voice hinting at panic.

Jinx chuckles lightly. "Guess we'll find out sometime tomorrow!"

"How can you be so calm about this?" Felix slaps Jinx on the shoulder, gesturing to the concrete cell. "Apparently we're going to be arrested sometime in the next twenty-four hours!"

"Don't forget, Felix. The future can change anytime. And besides, this is all just a Council game. The only question now is how we get out of here and back to the theatre," Jinx says methodically, seeming wise beyond her years.

"Shouldn't you know, J? The future is kind of your thing!" Desdemona snarls, throwing Jinx's earlier comment back in her face.

Without even turning around, Jinx responds passive aggressively. "This isn't like my visions and you know it."

Felix steps between his sisters to calm the storm before they stand in its eye. "This isn't a time for fighting, and you guys know it. This is just another part of the competition and we have to work together to win."

As Felix finishes speaking, a voice from down the hall interrupts their conversation. They have grown very familiar with this voice over the past year and the past few hours, specifically.

"Their guardian is supposed to come bail them out within the night, but he said he might wait until tomorrow to 'teach them a lesson.'" Mr. Belton's voice vibrates through the concrete walls. He, along with two other guards, halt their procession just outside of the Anchor's cell.

"Guardian? Who would be our guardian?" Desdemona wonders aloud.

Felix shrugs. "Kade, maybe? He's the only one I can think of who would know about this."

Desdemona feels shivers run through her veins. "I sure hope we can change this future. I don't want Kade coming to bail us out! He'll kill us!"

"Nah," Felix laughs. "All we have to do is get Jinx to give him a kiss and we'll be off the hook!"

As Desdemona snickers along with Felix, Jinx whips around and punches Felix hard in the shoulder. "What?" Felix jokes. "It's true!"

"I don't care what it is. Don't you have bigger things to worry about than my love life?" Jinx shoots back, turning around again to inspect the bars holding them in the cell.

Is she alright? Desdemona wonders to Felix. *Is everything with her and Kade okay?*

Felix, wondering the same thing, responds *I don't know. I imagine we'll find out eventually... Just like we always do with J.*

Desdemona agrees with a slight nod and sighs audibly. Their sister remains guarded, particularly when it comes to matters of the heart. When Jinx and Kade first connected, Jinx denied their relationship for nearly a month. Even now she hardly mentions him. Desdemona, always longing for a sister as a built-in best friend, can't help but hope Jinx will open up sometime soon.

Maybe someday, Mona, Felix reassures Desdemona.

Desdemona turns to face Felix directly. "Hey! Don't go into my mind unless I say so, remember? And there's no excuse you can't control your powers because we all know you can!"

Felix holds his hands up in surrender and apologizes just as Jinx calls out, "Aren't you guys going to help me get us out of here?"

"Get out of the cell or get out of the future?" Desdemona asks Jinx as she walks up next to her sister. Reaching out her hand to touch the bars of the cell, she feels the cool sting of metal under her fingers.

Jinx thinks for a second, unsure. "I don't know. Both, I guess."

Felix, hoping to gather information from the guards in the hallway outside the cell, pushes into the first guard's thoughts. *I hope Kathleen makes pot pies tonight... I could use a good pot pie after this rough day at work.*

Useless, Felix notes. Knowing Mr. Belton won't let Felix into his mind, Felix skips Mr. Belton and looks into the second guard's thoughts. *Where did I leave those keys? Maybe I left them in my office.*

The first guard opens his mouth to announce, "I am going to check my office for the cell keys. Keep an eye on these three for me, okay?" Felix hears footsteps as the first guard leaves the hallway and follows him mentally.

Not in this drawer, not in this drawer... Nope. Not here. Not in my desk... Not on the nightstand... Just like that, the guard's thoughts seem to stop for a second. Felix remembers Kade teaching him that when the stream of consciousness halts suddenly, something important has been remembered.

THEY'RE IN THE NIGHTSTAND! The guard shouts to himself. Felix next hears footsteps running back down the hallway.

"The nightstand?" Felix says aloud, unsure what nightstand the man is talking about.

"Nightstand? This one?" Desdemona responds, gesturing to a crooked nightstand. Despite having only three legs, the table still manages to stand just enough to make it functional. The top of the stand has a small knob leading to a drawer. Felix hears the guards rustling with a large, bulky set of hundreds of keys. Thinking this must be the master set of keys, Felix knows he doesn't have much time before the guards enter their cell.

Felix darts over to the nightstand and yanks open the drawer. The drawer slides out easily, so easily it comes off its track and falls to the hard, concrete floor. The Anchors hear a clanking sound as the silver keys to the cell tumble out of the drawer and onto the ground. Triumphant, Felix grabs the keys just as the other guards open the cell from outside. Felix whips around to see three burly muscle men standing where the metal bars used to be.

Panicking, Felix glances at his sisters, wondering how they plan to get past these guys and out of the cell. Jinx pulls her wallet from her pocket and taps the photograph three times fast. Instantly, her knives, along with her belt, appear perfectly fitted to her waist. Similarly, Felix taps his book and it morphs into his sword and Desdemona taps her hair clip, feeling her bow appear in her hand and her arrow sheath appear on her back.

This is for sure the coolest thing the Council has ever done, Desdemona enthuses next to him as Jinx stares directly at the guards. Faster than anyone watching can comprehend, Jinx slings the knives at the guards from left to right—1, 2, 3—just missing each one's right ear by a matter of inches. The guards' faces morph from power to fear. As if choreographed for a dance, the stunned guards duck in unison under tables outside the cell.

While Desdemona and Felix stand stunned, Jinx orders "What are you waiting for? We don't have all day!" Jinx jumps quickly over the ducked guards with her brother and sister tightly at her heels. Overhead, a loud alarm begins to sound, alerting all guards on duty of a prison break in progress.

"Now what?" Desdemona shouts over the alarm. "They've got the whole building running after us!"

"We need to find Mr. Belton," Felix yells as they continue running. "That's how we got out of the plane earlier!"

"But... how do... we find... him?" Desdemona pants as they continue sprinting. Suddenly, she rues the day she ever slacked off in PE both in high school and at the House. Understanding why Kade pushed them so hard during training, she makes a mental note to thank him for all the times he yelled at her and to apologize for all the times she said she hated him for it.

"I know where we can find him," Felix tells his sisters, firmly and calmly (because he actually followed Kade's fitness plans!). Thinking back to earlier when he went into the guard's mind, Felix remembers Mr. Belton walking in between the two guards. Mr. Belton even followed the guard as he went to look for the keys to the cell. Putting the pieces together, he makes a sharp turn down a concrete hallway, following a sign pointing them to "the offices."

Desdemona presses her feet hard into the ground as she follows closely behind Felix and Jinx, trying to ignore the gaining sound of footsteps behind her. The footfalls remind her of being taken by Jane's minion down into the abandoned mineshaft on Truchas Peak. Running her fingers over the faded scar marring one eye and her nose, she shudders, remembering the devilish look on her mother's face as Desdemona began passing out from blinding pain.

Desdemona snaps back to reality when she notices she has fallen more than a few steps behind Jinx and Felix. The guards are nearly upon her as she starts to sprint faster than she ever has before to catch up with her siblings. Just to be safe, she grabs for her bow, loads it quickly and flings an arrow slightly to the right of the guards. Although she doesn't hit them, it slows their progress.

She catches a glance of them pulling open a door and Felix yells back at her. "Mona! Hurry!" Forcing her feet to move even faster, Desdemona flies through the open doorway and hears it slam behind her. It locks with a click. Sliding her back against the closed door, Desdemona breathes heavily and runs her hands through her hair in exasperation.

"Next time we're in a competition, let's make sure there's less physical activity involved," Desdemona manages once she catches her breath.

Felix laughs. "I'm sure this isn't the last time we will be running Mona."

Jinx notices a large chair sitting behind the desk, with its back to the room. "Guys," she stage-whispers. "I don't think we're alone."

The chair spins around in a flash to reveal a tall, bearded man. All three Anchor kids flinch before realizing that the man is none other than Mr. Belton, the man they have been looking for this entire time.

Mr. Belton begins to laugh. "I've always wanted to do that!" he jokes, referencing his spin around in the chair to startle the Anchors. "You should have seen your faces!"

Desdemona stands up from the floor and brushes off her pants as Jinx snaps at Mr. Belton. "What is this? This is the lamest competition I've ever been in. Didn't the Council say we would get to fight someone?"

"Ah, but Jinx Anchor, you did fight someone," Mr. Belton points out.

Jinx groans out loud and faces to her siblings. "Why do adults always do this? They beat around the bush and make everything a riddle instead of just telling us straight out!" She turns around to direct her attention to Mr. Belton. "And no, we didn't fight anybody! I didn't get to use any of the skills I learned in training except when I threw those knives. I didn't even get to use my damn powers!"

When Felix places his hand on his sister's shoulder, Jinx shoves it off roughly. Knowing not to take it personally, Felix decides to let Jinx have her space.

"Calm down, Miss Anchor. If you haven't forgotten, I am still your superior," Mr. Belton reminds Jinx in a tone smoother than water. Jinx seems to visually deflate in front of him, having gotten her fill, and Mr. Belton elaborates. "What I meant was that you fought yourselves. This first part of the competition flipped your Asterian gifts on you, forcing you to find a way to battle through challenges your own powers present. The Council used your powers to transport you into visions of the past, present and future. Sometimes, we are our own worst enemies and as a result, we need to learn to fight our own powers at times. And you did battle through them. You found a way. You fought back."

"So that explains why I was pulled into the vision in your mind," Felix says excitedly.

"And why we were taken back to the plane even though I didn't take us there," Desdemona hits herself on the head as if she should have figured this out before.

"And why, right now, we're sitting in the future in an office of a jail having just escaped from a group of security guards trying to mob us," Jinx adds with a twisted chuckle.

Mr. Belton continues. "The three of you chose to take control of the situation, quite as I suspected, instead of waiting. Your internal struggle is strong, and yet this time, working together, you prevailed."

Desdemona feels a chill go up her spine as she remembers they're still in the future right now. "Wait... This time? Does that mean in less than twenty-four hours we're going to end up in jail?" Her breathing quickens at the thought of being in that jail cell.

Felix rushes over to stop Mona from embarrassing herself, but much to his dismay, he is too late. Desdemona runs to Mr. Belton and gets on her knees, pleading. "Mr. Belton, I don't think you understand! I can't survive life in prison!"

Mr. Belton lets out a belly laugh and motions for Desdemona to get up. "Don't you worry, Miss Anchor. You underestimate yourself. You all are stronger than you think." And with that, the feeling of stretching returns to the Anchors' limbs, running from their fingers to their toes.

They spin back to reality, finding themselves back in the M&M world theatre. Only this time, the large plastic box has disappeared. Standing tall on a podium, center stage with a large spotlight illuminating it sits the prize they've been searching for this entire time: the figurine of Clarence Abbot. And under this figurine is a small, folded piece of parchment—their next clue.

Jinx sprints over to the podium, feeling competitiveness and excitement well up in her stomach. Snatching the figurine, she throws it back to Desdemona to keep in her purse as Jinx unravels the next clue, not wanting to waste a single second. They find more of a personal letter than a short clue.

Congratulations, Anchors! You have completed your first task. Each day, you will complete only one task. As a result, you must return to the Ironwell for a good night's rest. Dinner will be served at 7:00 p.m. Tomorrow morning, you may begin your search early at 8:00 (breakfast will be served at 7:00 a.m.). You have the remainder of the night to ponder your next clue

Underneath the personalized letter is a clue much like the first one.

> Only the birds appear to reach these heights
> Don't be afraid, however.
> This place will leave you saying "O!"

8

Desdemona and Felix groggily climb out of the taxi in front of Caesar's hotel, hungry and excited to catch up on some much-needed sleep before continuing the competition tomorrow. Jinx, however, battles a racing mind. Jinx finally considers her vision on the plane where Margret appeared to have the Asterian Jewel and might even be working for Jane in Vegas. Much to her dismay, Margret and Jane don't appear to be totally out of the picture.

"J, are you okay?" Felix asks, concerned, as they enter the hotel and walk through the casino. "You've seemed off ever since we finished the task."

Jinx brushes him off. "Yeah, I'm fine. Just thinking about the clue." Lies. Despite knowing she should tell Mona and Felix about the vision, Jinx tells herself she doesn't want to distract them from the competition at hand. Jane wouldn't dare mess with the work of the Asterian Council. They're safe... at least until they leave Vegas.

Not in the mood for Friday night casino hustle and bustle, the Anchors pass through without so much a glance at the people throwing their money away. Jinx shoves through the velvet curtain, just as their escort did when they first arrived.

After climbing down through darkness for what again feels like forever, they finally reach the imitation lobby underground and approach the elevator to change for dinner.

As Desdemona clicks the elevator button, Jinx feels a tap on her left shoulder. She turns that way, only to find the space on that side entirely empty.

"Over here, gullible," Kade laughs as Jinx flips around to her right with a scowl on her face. Quickly realizing Jinx is not amused, Kade tries to suppress his chuckle.

"*Not* in the mood, Kade," Jinx admonishes him in an icy tone.

Kade holds his hands up in surrender when the elevator bell dings, indicating its arrival to the lobby floor. Before Jinx steps in, Kade brushes his hand on her arm and stops her. "Hey, I'm sorry, J. Let me make it up to you. Meet me down here in thirty minutes wearing something nice?"

Jinx snorts at him as she steps into the elevator. "Yeah, in your dreams!"

Desdemona slaps Jinx roughly on the arm and screams out to Kade in a girly, excited tone just before the elevator closes. "She'll be there!"

When the elevator door shuts tightly, closing Kade off from the conversation, Jinx gives Desdemona a disapproving grimace. "There is no way I'm going there. Not tonight, Mona."

"Oh c'mon, J," Felix edges her on. "The guy is trying to be sweet and take you out. Have you never been on a date before?"

"Of course not! And I DO NOT plan on changing that tonight."

When they reach their floor, even further underground than the lobby itself, Desdemona attempts to reason with Jinx. "Don't you like him, Jinx?"

Jinx mutters something unintelligible under her breath as she shoves the room key into the lock on the door.

"Excuse me, what was that?" Desdemona asks, pushing her even further.

"I said," Jinx whips around to face her sister. "That yes, I do like him!"

"You sure have a weird way of showing it," Felix adds. When they get into their bedroom, Jinx runs into the bathroom and slams the door behind her. Desdemona shoots Felix a look saying 'let me handle this.' Felix nods and goes to lie down on the bed, happy to let the girls do their touchy-feely girly things.

Desdemona knocks lightly on the bathroom door. Not hearing any response, she turns the doorknob, praying Jinx isn't half naked and about to get in the shower. Peeking an eye in, she sees Jinx sitting on the tile floor, looking dejected. Desdemona gets down next to her sister, sitting criss-cross next to the sink.

"Jinx, I know you like Kade. And I know he brings out a goofy side of you that nobody else can seem to get... He makes you happy." When Desdemona sees Jinx glance at her, showing she is listening, Desdemona continues. "I'm not some kind of relationship guru, but I learned enough from Stacy to know relationships are all about give and take. He wants to grow closer to you and you keep pushing him away. You have to give him something to grab onto, or you're going to lose him."

Jinx tucks her legs up to her chest like a child. "I don't want to lose him..."

"Then go," Desdemona pleads. "Go with him tonight. And who knows? You might even enjoy it!"

Jinx's frown turns into a slight smile and Desdemona knows she has prevailed. Jumping up from the bathroom floor, Desdemona drags Jinx up and shrieks, "You know what that means! Makeover!"

"Oh no, don't you even...." Jinx begins as she struggles against Desdemona's iron grip. Desdemona pulls harder and pushes Jinx down in a chair in front of the mirror next to the TV, not taking no for an answer. Finally, Jinx gives in and decides to let Desdemona play fairy godmother for tonight.

A full thirty minutes later, Jinx walks out of the bathroom in the most girly thing she brought. Black like the color of her straightened hair, the slightly form-fitting dress contrasts her pale skin exceedingly well. The red lipstick Desdemona insisted on adds a pop of color. It feels cakey and heavy, making Jinx smack her lips together to free them from their ruby prison.

"You look so beautiful!" Desdemona shrieks as she throws a pair of black heels at Jinx. Jinx shakes her head, gesturing to the heels. "Oh no, this is where I draw the line." Jinx throws the heels back at Desdemona and instead, digs out a pair of red and white converse.

"But...." Desdemona begins to argue.

Pick your battles, Mona, Felix advises in Desdemona's mind. *She already let you go this far.*

Visibly deflating, Desdemona sighs. "Alright, alright, I guess you can wear those."

"You really do look stunning, J," Felix praises. Jinx snorts, but smiles shyly at Felix, appreciating the comment even though she doesn't want to admit it.

Desdemona claps her hands together in excitement. "You've got to get upstairs! You're going to be late and Kade is going to think you actually decided not to show."

"I'm fine, Mona," Jinx reassures her. "He's not going to leave." Desdemona smiles as Jinx references their earlier conversation; Mona finally begins feeling like she has a sister, a sister who actually wants to be a sister.

Tonight is a big step, Desdemona thinks to Felix as she waves goodbye to Jinx.

I know, Felix responds. *I just hope she doesn't relapse anytime soon.*

Outside the room, Jinx tip-toes nervously towards the elevator, wondering the whole way up to the lobby how tonight will go. How do girls usually act on dates? Do they giggle when the guy says something that's not really that funny? Do they pretend to drop something so they could show off their butt in their jeans? Whatever they do, Jinx plans on doing the exact opposite.

When the elevator dings, breaking Jinx from her inner panic, the door opens to reveal Kade—but this Kade is dressed nicer than Jinx has ever seen. The black suit with a red accent bowtie fits him impeccably, while simultaneously matching Jinx's outfit choice. In his linen-clad arms lies a clear box containing a red and black corsage.

Not knowing how to react to this level of romance, Jinx defaults to what she knows best: teasing. "Where are we going? A lame high school prom?"

Kade lets out a laugh, brushing off the brooding facade he usually keeps in front of most people. "Something of the sorts." He pries open the box and pulls out the wrist corsage, spreading the stretchy bracelet to fit Jinx's wrist snuggly.

"It's..." Jinx pauses, trying to find a description for the over-priced miniature bouquet sitting on her wrist. "Beautiful?"

Kade laughs again and this time Jinx chuckles along as she feels the worry of the day fade away. Kade takes her hand and leads her up from the Ironwell to the lobby of Caesar's Palace. In awe of the casino's lights and colors, Jinx almost misses a soft, feminine voice in her ear.

"Hello, Jinx," the voice whispers seductively. Instantly, Jinx feels her blood run cold as she recognizes the voice of Margret. Flipping around to identify the source of the voice, her eyes come up empty and she sees no one.

"Are you okay J?" Kade questions, obviously concerned about her sudden stop.

Jinx shakes her head. To brush it off, her voice comes out higher pitched and excited than she intended. "Yeah, let's go!"

Kade shoots Jinx a curious look, but continues walking. "You know, if there's anything you need to talk to me about, you can."

"I said, I'm fine," Jinx curtly responds.

Kade, always knowing when to back off, nods and continues leading her out of the hotel. When they exit the large gold double doors, Jinx sees a tall man in a pinstripe suit much like Kade's standing near a jet-black Mercedes.

"Mr. Defrates?" The man asks in a thick Russian accent. Jinx instantly recognizes the man as their taxi driver from earlier in the day—the one who drove them to M&M World. She didn't know that the man drove both a taxi and a house car!

The man opens the door to the backseat and Kade motions for Jinx to get in first. "After you, m'lady."

"What has gotten into you, Kade?" Jinx asks when they are both in the car and the man shuts the door behind them. "Since when are you the perfect gentleman?"

"Since I realized you are the perfect girl," he answers, smooth as ever. Jinx fights the tug on her heartstrings and she can't help but smile at his cheesy compliment.

"Where are you taking me anyhow?" Jinx asks as the driver pulls the car out onto the busy Las Vegas strip. Horns honk from every direction and the wind blows lightly from the cracked windows of the car.

Kade laughs. "Always impatient, aren't you? You'll find out in about five minutes."

Jinx groans outwardly, but inwardly she feels the full effects of being wooed by Kade Defrates. The guy who every girl at the House fawns over behind his back. The guy who appears cold and mysterious on the outside, but who has a gooey inside like no other.

In what feels like an instant, the car pulls into the driveway of yet another hotel. In less than 12 hours, they have already been to two hotels and Jinx is beginning to believe Vegas is all about the hotels. Only, this one initially stuns Jinx more than the rest. With a large replica of the Eiffel tower guarding the entrance, it seems as though someone must have pulled the Paris Hotel from a storybook set in France itself.

"Okay," Jinx says as the driver opens the door on her side, letting her out. "But why would someone pay to go to Vegas and see the Eiffel Tower, instead of going to the real Eiffel Tower in France?"

Kade follows her out of the car and wraps her hand in his, sending unwanted shivers through her arm. "It's for people like us! People who can't go to Paris right this very minute."

As Jinx walks hand in hand with Kade into the glistening lobby of the breathtaking hotel, she says, "Well, I guess this is the next best thing."

Kade and Jinx step on the elevator along with another couple. The girl hangs on the guy's arm like a leech and Jinx can't figure out what this guy sees in her. Blonde, pin-straight hair, a short miniskirt with heels too high for anyone in their right mind: a classic Vegas drunk girl. The guy takes the girl in his arms and starts kissing her right then and there in the elevator.

"Umm... What floor?" Kade clears his throat and asks.

When the couple doesn't respond, Jinx leans over and hits the guy on the arm. "Hey!" She shouts. "What floor are you guys going to?"

"Six," the man mutters to Jinx, ignoring her slap on his arm. When the elevator dings on the sixth floor, the couple stumbles out, giggling.

"Oh gosh!" Jinx laughs when the elevator door closes. "Promise me we will never be THAT couple!"

Kade nods furiously. "Oh, I definitely promise."

The elevator stops on the eleventh floor and the door opens to reveal the most stunning restaurant either of them has ever seen. With floor to ceiling windows on all sides, every table and booth has a stunning view of the colorful fountain shooting skyward outside the window. The dim lighting sets a romantic tone, accented by soft music playing lightly above the quiet chatter of other diners.

"Table for two for Defrates," Kade tells the hostess standing behind a marble counter. The hostess smiles, picks up two menus, and begins to lead them to their table. Jinx sees only one empty table in the whole restaurant: a table right in the corner where two giant glass windows meet. A table with a perfect view of the outside fountains.

Oh, there's no way that's our table, Jinx thinks to herself as she follows the hostess. But lo and behold, the woman glides to the corner table and sets their menus down.

"Henry will be your server tonight and he will be with you in a few moments," the hostess announces, walking away. Jinx reaches for her chair to sit down, but Kade stops her by putting his hand on hers.

"Let me get it," Kade says endearingly, pulling her chair just wide enough for Jinx to sit down, then pushing it back in after she sits.

"What was your challenge for today?" Jinx asks Kade once they settle in.

Kade groans. "It was the worst thing ever! They turned our powers back on us."

"Oh us too," Jinx relates unenthusiastically.

"The clue led us to the Madame Tussaud's," Kade tells her. When Jinx responds with a confused look, he elaborates. "You know, that place with all the wax figures of celebrities?"

"What? That's a real thing?" Jinx exclaims, appalled. "That's so creepy."

Kade nods in agreement. "It got even creepier when the Council turned Hazel and me into wax statues of Baby and Johnny from Dirty Dancing. They took away all of our senses, just like I usually do."

"Now you know what it feels like! Not fun, is it?" Jinx claims, happy he's finally getting the karma he deserves for using his powers on them so many times during training.

Jinx takes her time explaining her crazy afternoon to Kade as the waiter comes over in a pleated tux to take their drink order. After he hands them a fancy leather menu, Jinx and Kade fall silent as they decide on their meal. Jinx's eyes scan the page and she realizes she doesn't know half of the dishes on this menu. Tartare, Foie Gras, Escargot, Grenobloise! What are these? Hilga, her grandmother (and legal guardian until she turned fifteen), rarely took her out to eat. And when she did, it definitely wasn't to a place where the cheapest thing on the menu is a cup of soup for $22!

"Oh no," Jinx whispers to Kade under her breath. "If I can't pronounce it, I'm sure as hell not going to eat it!"

Kade meets her panic with an equal look of concern. He obviously isn't sure about this food either. "I think I see some chicken under the meat section."

The waiter comes over once again and gets out his pad, asking if they are both ready to order.

"Would you two like to start with an appetizer tonight?" the man asks in a husky tone.

Jinx shakes her head furiously. "I think we would just like to go on to the meal." The man nods and Jinx continues. "Umm... I think I'll take the Caesar salad without the anchovies, croutons, or capers. Also, can I swap out the vinaigrette for some ranch?"

The waiter pauses, giving Jinx a strange look before regaining his composure. "So, you would just like lettuce and ranch dressing?" Even though Jinx realizes how silly she sounds ordering that at a restaurant like this, she nods. Much to her relief, the waiter moves on to Kade.

"I would like the chicken, but without the shallots and mushrooms, please," Kade orders. Nervously, he adds, "Actually, can you just give me a plate with plain chicken on it?"

The waiter again tries to hide his surprise, but abides and leaves Jinx and Kade to their drinks.

The minute the waiter leaves, Kade begins to laugh. "I think we're in a little over our heads here."

Jinx agrees, but doesn't laugh along. "I'll say. Did you know anything about this restaurant before you got a reservation?"

"No!" Kade admits. "I just asked the concierge what the nicest restaurant in town was and he sent me here. I know it's crazy, but you just wait. After dinner, the real magic begins."

Jinx grins. "Oh, I'm not sure how much more magic I can do tonight.

Silence falls over the table as Jinx and Kade turn their attention to the fountain outside. Water shoots up from holes in the ground, lit up by a rainbow of colors—blue, green, pink, red, yellow. You name the color; it's in that fountain. It falls back to the tile floor with a splash just as another stream flies into the air. The waiter drops by quietly and places their simple dishes on the table, not wanting to interrupt their thoughts.

"Do you think any of us actually has a shot at winning this competition?" Jinx asks when the waiter leaves, breaking the silence.

Kade looks away from the mesmerizing fountain and shrugs. "I guess we've got as good of a shot as anyone else."

"But if one of our families were to win, only one of us could be a part of the Council. And how do they decide which one?" Jinx asks. Even if she shows little affection towards her brother and sister, she still can't imagine having to go head to head. "I mean, isn't the whole point of the House to teach us to work as teams? This is pitting us against one another."

Kade raises his eyebrows at Jinx. It's very unlike her to want to turn down a challenge to one-up her siblings. "They have to pick someone one way or another." When Jinx doesn't respond, he questions. "What's wrong?"

Jinx takes a deep breath before revealing what she hasn't even had the guts to tell Desdemona and Felix yet. "I'm concerned Jane or her followers may be here in Vegas...."

Kade's eyes go wide and his head begins to reel with memories from Truchas Peak, memories of his own sister being prepared and willing to kill him before he managed to talk her out of it. Reuniting with Hazel has been a dream come true, and there is no way he will let Jane take her again. "How do you know?"

Before Jinx can answer, a tall man in a pinstripe tuxedo approaches. "Hello, I am the manager of the Eiffel Tower Restaurant," he says with a heavy accent. "How is everything tonight? Is the food to your liking?"

A chilling feeling goes up and down Jinx's spine as she recognizes the man standing in front of her. It is the same man who drove their taxi this morning; the same man who drove them to the Paris hotel just an hour ago.

"It's delicious, thank you," Jinx tells him with a glance down at her untouched salad. The man smiles dazzlingly at Kade and Jinx and wishes them an amazing evening. The minute he moves out of earshot, Jinx leans in close to Kade. At the same moment, Kade veers toward Jinx and they bang their foreheads together

"Ouch!" Jinx shouts a little too loudly for this romantic restaurant. The couples sitting around them turn their heads at the noise and stare uncomfortably.

"Oh like you've never done it!" Jinx retorts to the staring people. Each feeling awkward, they whip their heads back to the food and return to their conversation. Jinx remembers the man's familiar face and feels ice run through her. Something is definitely off.

"You recognize him too," Kade says. It's not a question; it's a statement. Kade knows Jinx wouldn't miss a thing like this. "Should we get out of here?" he asks.

"Can we eat a little bit first? We won't get dinner if we don't," Jinx reminds him.

Despite the situation, Kade laughs. "It's always about the food with you!"

"Hey," Jinx defends herself as she shoves a spoonful of salad into her mouth. "Is da fruit ovf life!"

They both finish their meals in silence, rapidly chewing bite after bite. Plates cleaned, Kade doesn't wait for the check. Instead, he pulls out enough money to cover the food and tip and slides it under the flower vase in the middle of the white cloth table.

"Is that money from the House reserves, too?" Jinx teases, recalling how he had given her a whole wad of cash before their trip. Kade puts his finger up to his lips, shushing her with a smile. Jinx and Kade quickly and quietly exit the restaurant, avoiding the attention of the so-called "manager."

When Kade presses the up button on the elevator, Jinx corrects him. "We have to go down to get to the lobby, silly."

"I know," Kade winks at Jinx, taking her hand in his. "I'm not going to let some sketchy man ruin our entire evening. I told you the real magic starts after dinner."

"It's dangerous though!" Jinx argues. "I told you. Jane might still be alive and after us!"

"Danger?" Kade laughs. "Danger was when we climbed a mountain to fight the most evil woman the Asterian race has ever seen."

Jinx smiles at him as they step into the elevator. "Yeah, you're right. We can handle one wimpy man."

"Plus, I've got a girlfriend who has a wicked knife throwing arm," Kade smirks, but Jinx feels her heart stop. Girlfriend? Kade has never called her that before—at least not out loud! Jinx knows their relationship has already been established, but never formally. She tries to suppress the butterflies in her stomach; she hates the gooey feelings she gets around Kade. When she's around him, she is like a cookie just out of the oven. Solid on the outside, but runny and melted on the inside. She can't shake the feeling and maybe, just maybe, she doesn't want to.

The elevator ride seems long, causing Jinx to wonder where in the world they will end up. She doesn't have to wonder much longer before the walls of the hotel fade away, revealing the colored lights of the Las Vegas strip. Jinx watches large metal poles whiz by her head through the elevator's glass walls.

"Where are we?" Jinx asks. The elevator continues to fly upwards.

"Weren't you paying attention when we came in?" Kade asks. Jinx nods, racking her brain to remember the look of the hotel's entrance. It only takes her a few seconds longer to realize the metal poles whizzing by are Eiffel tower's support beams!

Finally, the elevator stops at the tower's observation deck. Kade and Jinx step out hand in hand. For the first time in her young life, Jinx finds herself speechless. A giant, illuminated Ferris wheel sits to the right in the skyline, lifting as high as Caesar's Palace. Lights of every color burst from buildings all around: hotels, theaters, attractions. Other people, mostly couples, whisper around them, each writing their own love story hundreds of feet in the air. Having never really been anywhere besides her hometown and the House, it's the most incandescent thing Jinx has ever witnessed.

Kade leads Jinx to the edge of the observation deck and Jinx put her hands on the cage encasing them in the sky.

"I know we're not in this city to sight-see, but I want you to see all of the sights. Why not just knock out all them in one view?" Kade enthuses. Jinx feels her heart melt as he begins to point at each building in the skyline, naming it and explaining why it's famous.

"Those fountains over here," Kade points to the left at a group of perfectly synchronized fountains next to a strange rock formation that appears to be a volcano. "Are in front of the Mirage Hotel. On most nights the volcano erupts and they have this whole big show. It scared me to death as a child, but most people love it."

"Have you been here before?" Jinx enquires when Kade stops for a breath.

Kade nods. "Once when I was really young. I think I was five. It was before Hazel got her powers and went away to the House."

"And you remember all of this?" Jinx asks incredulously, breaking her eyes away from the stunning skyline to stare at him.

Kade laughs. "Well... not exactly. But I did do some research before we left."

Jinx smiles at him, thinking back to just a few hours earlier when she didn't want to consider coming on this date with Kade. She makes a mental note to thank Desdemona for practically shoving her out the door.

"You look stunning, you know?" Kade admits to her. He nervously shoves his hands in his pockets, reminding Jinx he's just as clueless as she is about dating. Jinx blushes and feels her pulse throb as she watches Kade's eyes shift from her eyes to her lips and back to her eyes again. He leans in to kiss her softly and for a few seconds she lets him, before pulling away and clearing her throat.

"So... what's that building?" She asks, pointing to the Mirage, even though he named just a few seconds before. He laughs and pecks her on the cheek. Jinx feels the blush rise rapidly again to her face in the lights of the city. If she weren't so awkward, this could be a scene out of a fairytale. To avoid Kade's intense gaze, Jinx turns away, only to see their stalker, the man who has seemingly been following them everywhere since they arrived in Vegas. When Jinx catches his eye, he raises his eyebrows. Jinx tugs on Kade's coat sleeve, trying to slyly get his attention while acting natural.

"Sweetheart," she whispers in a voice so sweet that Kade instantly recognizes it as an alternate message. She flicks her eyes over her shoulder and leans in close to Kade's shoulder. "I think we need to be getting home. It's getting... chilly... up here."

Jinx sees Kade's face go blank, the lights reflecting in his pupils before regaining his composure. "Wouldn't want my girl getting cold, would we? Let's head out." He pulls Jinx tightly against his arm, upset someone has once again tarnished their moment. But, is it Jane's fault?

Kade hears footsteps behind them and realizes they are still being followed towards the elevator. Kade knows that he can't let this man and Jinx together in a close, confined space, but before he can act, Jinx beats him to the punch.

"Can I help you?" Jinx stops in her tracks and asks the man.

"Maybe you can," the man speaks. Before Jinx can reply, he crumples to the floor and Kade pulls Jinx into the door of the open elevator without taking his eyes off of Jane's minion. He furiously pushes the close door button, leaving them as the only two in the elevator.

"Hey!" Jinx tears her arm away from Kade's and stomps to the opposite corner of the elevator. "You didn't have to take his senses away! I could have handled that!"

Kade is unfazed by Jinx's attitude. "Is that your way of saying thank you?"

Jinx huffs and puffs, wanting to say more, but knowing he's right. She doesn't know the potential or power of this man.

When they step off the elevator into the hotel lobby, Kade leads Jinx out to taxis pulling up by the dozen. He knows he can no longer let Jinx ride back in the car they came in. Not with that man.

He raises his arm to hail a taxi when Jinx questions, "I've been in a moving vehicle with that man twice today. If he wanted to kidnap us or kill us or whatever, why didn't he do it when we weren't suspecting anything?"

Kade shakes his head as the pair climbs into the taxi. Jinx has him stumped with this one. Perhaps the stalker seeks information, not blood. Instead of verbalizing his thoughts, Kade stays quiet. Jinx is a fighter. If he's not careful with what he says, Jinx will go out looking to take this guy's life.

9

Desdemona opens her eyes sleepily to a pitch-dark room, with Felix snoring softly on the pullout couch. She shoots up in bed, momentarily forgetting where she is. Furiously glancing from side to side, Desdemona takes in the surroundings of their Ironwell room, sighing when she remembers they're in Las Vegas. She sees Jinx in the other queen size bed, splayed out in all different directions. Desdemona racks her brain to remember when Jinx returned from her date last night, but figures she was already asleep by the time Jinx got back to the room.

"If you have a question, why don't you just go ahead and ask it instead of staring at me?" Jinx says. Desdemona flinches, not realizing Jinx was even awake and leans over to turn on the light.

"Woah, that's too bright and it's too early!" Felix groans from the couch, smashing his face into the pillow to block out the artificial light.

Desdemona laughs. "It's not even that early. 8:00 a.m., that's it!"

"Eight a.m., that's it?" Jinx moans. "Eight a.m. mornings were created by Jane herself."

Desdemona leans over to Felix and grabs the pillow from his head. "You two were the ones saying we have a competition to win!" At the reminder of the contest, Jinx perks up long enough to lift herself out of bed and go to the bathroom to brush her teeth. Her foot brushes a soft, silky fabric and her eyes look down to meet the dress she wore last night with Kade. Her heart swoons at Kade's sweet gesture, but then stops as she remembers the man who followed them yesterday.

"Gus, I haf somefing to vell you," Jinx mumbles through a mouth full of toothpaste.

"What was that?" Felix laughs from the edge of his bed, pulling his feet around to hit the floor.

Jinx spits quickly and walks back into the bedroom. "Something happened last night."

Desdemona perks up with excitement. "Something happened?? Like what? Where did he take you? Did he kiss you? Was he the perfect gentleman?"

"Woah, slow down. It's too early for your excitement." Jinx orders, rubbing her temples with her fingers. When Desdemona sits down and snaps her mouth shut, Jinx continues. "It's not like that... Well, I guess it kind of is. He took me to the Paris hotel for dinner and then up to the top of the Eiffel Tower to show me the city, but something happened."

"Just tell us, J," Felix urges her. "You're never one to beat around the bush."

Jinx spills the events of the previous night, focusing on the man who continued to appear throughout the date.

"The same man drove us to M&M's World?" Felix clarifies, shaking his head, hoping she could be wrong. When Jinx nods, Felix feels anger well up in the pit of his stomach. He notices the large, faded scar running through Desdemona's left eye and it takes him back to when Jane gave her the scar. On that day Felix swore he would never let Jane hurt either of his sisters again. When they defeated Jane on top of Truchas Peak, Felix thought he succeeded. He thought the only memory of Jane would be the fading scar on Desdemona's face, but now, he isn't so sure.

When Felix looks at his sisters again, he sees a tear slide down Desdemona's cheek and his anger flares up once again. He wraps his arm around Desdemona's shoulders and feels her shudder.

"Mona, it's going to be okay..." he states halfheartedly, hoping she doesn't hear the uncertainty in his voice.

Mona shakes her head, wiping the tears from her eyes. "I thought we were done with her. It feels like I am back where I was a year ago, scared and helpless."

Felix opens his mouth to console his sister, but Jinx surprisingly beats him to the punch. "But we're not scared and helpless anymore. We're different people than who we were before we went to Truchas Peak. We're a different family."

Felix feels Desdemona hiccup in surprise at Jinx's words and watches as her tears turn into a smile brighter than the sun. "You called us a family..."

Jinx shakes her head, brushing off her words. "It's not...." But before she can even finish her sentence, Desdemona breaks free from Felix's arm and wraps Jinx in a bear hug.

"Oh gosh, don't do this again," Jinx pushes back a bit, but Desdemona clings like a bug.

"Hey, don't we have a competition to win?" Felix blurts out, attempting to save Jinx from suffocation by Desdemona's tiny arms.

"But what are we going to do about Jane?" Desdemona wonders aloud, a twinge of worry oozing from her words.

"Desdemona's right. We need a plan. We can't just act like sitting ducks," Felix notes as, after dressing, the triplets gather their bags for the day.

Jinx stops in her tracks, dropping the water bottle she just picked up from her bag. "Or maybe that's exactly how we should act."

"What?" Desdemona asks, dumbfounded.

"So we know Jane—or someone on Jane's side—is probably after us, right?" Desdemona and Felix both nod. "But she doesn't know we know. We wait. We wait for her to make the first move and we counterattack."

"But isn't that kind of what we did last time?" Desdemona asks. "We fell right into all her traps on the mountain and we see how that turned out..." Desdemona's voice trails off as she looks down to the ground, hiding the faded scar marring her otherwise perfect skin.

Jinx sighs, uncharacteristically feeling sympathy for her sister. Even though each of them carries something from that mountain, Desdemona's something is out in the open for everyone to see. There's no hiding it, not from herself or anyone else.

Trying to move everyone's mind off the elephant in the room, Felix suggests, "Should we tell Kade? He always seems to know what to do."

"We won't see him again until tonight after the competition is over for the day," Jinx reminds them as they begin to walk out of their room for breakfast. As she steps out of the doorway, she stops mid-step. "Everyone has their weapons, right? We might need them for more than the competition."

Felix checks his bag and Desdemona motions to her hair clip, nodding, as they fall in step with Jinx. "Besides, what can Jane do to us while the Asterian Council is here?"

"And don't forget, thousands of other Asterians will also be on our side," Felix adds. Even though he means to console Desdemona with these words, all three of them need to hear it.

"Are you all as nervous as I am?" Felix rubs his hands together, trying to wipe the sweat beads forming on his soft palm.

Desdemona agrees. "Hey, but at least we're all nervous together, right?"

Jinx rolls her eyes at her siblings. "Enough with the sappy family crap. We have a competition to win, remember?"

The voices of other Asterians grow louder, filling the empty space as the Anchors approach the breakfast area. The hotel walls curve suddenly, leading the trio to the over-sized, over-stated lobby. The statues stand tall and proud with water rushing from every side, splashing over the stone surrounding it with a whoosh. Close-knit families of Asterians huddle together, laughing and discussing strategies as they make their way to a buffet-style restaurant. Just below the ceiling, bright white letters read GORDON RAMSAY PUB AND GRILL.

"Who is Gordon Ramsay?" Jinx asks, stopping to read the flamboyant title.

Desdemona gasps as if she's just seen a ghost, covering her mouth with her hand. "You don't know who Gordon Ramsay is?"

"Oh, give me a break." Jinx raises her eyebrow at her sister, waiting for Desdemona to explain why this guy deserves such an over-the-top reaction.

"He's one of the most popular chefs in the world! And his food is TO DIE FOR! I heard a woman once passed out after taking a bite of his steak because it was just. That. Good." Desdemona pauses between words for added (and unnecessary) emphasis.

"But this may not be his restaurant," Felix notes as they make their way in. "I checked out a book about the Ironwell last night while Jinx was out with Kade. I read they attempted to make a near replica of Caesar's Palace, just underground. Which means that the real restaurant with the real food could only be upstairs."

Desdemona visibly sinks as she realizes he must be right. Suddenly a low voice comes from behind them, interrupting her pouting.

"But I also heard that they have a chef here who can replicate Ramsay's dishes down to the last parsley leaf," the voice tells her. Desdemona turns around to identify the source of the voice and finds herself face to face with the all-too-familiar messy blonde boy, Jason.

Desdemona has no idea how to react to Jason. Panicking, she does what comes most naturally—flirting. She laughs and tosses her hair over her shoulder. "Well, if I pass out, then maybe you'll have to be the one to catch me!"

Desdemona instantly knows that that was NOT the right thing to say and she whips around, tugging Felix and Jinx by the wrist behind her. Desdemona rushes so quickly she almost misses the restaurant's creative Las Vegas feel. They pass a wall made entirely of colorful, empty beer kegs dividing the restaurant from the pristine, yet noisy white kitchen. Red leather booths line the sides of the black walls and red tables with black chairs sit on a multi-colored floor.

Desdemona finally picks a table in the back corner of the restaurant, right under a giant oil painting of Gordon Ramsay himself.

"What the hell was that?" Jinx asks with a ragged breath, running her hand through her hair. She looks over her shoulder to see Jason relatively unfazed by the interaction.

Desdemona, her eyes focusing on anything besides Jason, answers, "What do we do about him?"

"What do you mean 'what do we do about him?'" Jinx responds. "Just because he made a bad decision doesn't mean he's suddenly some psychopath. Hazel was in the exact same position as him."

Felix leans his head in close, whispering. "I mean I feel like we can use him to help us. He is one of Jane's closest survivors. If he knows Jane is alive, maybe he knows her plan."

Jinx's eyes light up with surprise. "Hey, you might actually be onto something!"

Felix sticks his tongue out while Jinx laughs before letting him continue. "Seriously though, that might help us here. We have Hazel on our side, but she left Jane before Jane lost power. Jason, on the other hand, stayed until the end. He might know more about why her body is apparently not rotting on Truchas Peak right now."

Desdemona nods. "But how will we go about asking him? It's not like we can just go right up and ask him about the time he tried to help an evil woman overthrow the entire world."

Desdemona, seeing Jason has chosen a seat all the way across the restaurant, picks up her plate excitedly. "Can we figure this out over some omelets and sausage biscuits? My mouth is watering just looking at it." When her brother and sister hesitate, she continues. "I mean, c'mon, it's GORDON RAMSAY!"

Felix chuckles at his sister as they follow her up to the buffet. Felix has always loved Desdemona's resilience in the face of something horrific. For someone who grew up in a home where everything came easy, she adapted well to Asterian life. Even though she was the princess in high school (and pretty much the princess at the House), she never backs down from a challenge.

Felix sees Jinx file in behind them as they begin to pile as much food at they can carry onto their plates. When they return to their table and begin to eat, Desdemona takes the first bite of her French toast, causing her eyes to roll back in her head.

"It's even better than I imagined it would be!" She squeals with a mouth full of half-chewed bread and syrup.

"What? Is it so good you're going to—oh, I don't know—pass out, maybe?" Jinx teases Desdemona with a wink. As both Felix and Jinx laugh at their sister's expense, excitement begins to grow in their stomach about the upcoming competition.

"Has anyone thought of anything for the next clue?" Felix asks, rustling through his backpack for the small slip of parchment telling them about their next hidden location. "'Only birds appear to reach these heights.' What do you think they mean by that?"

"Last night, Kade took me to the top of the Eiffel Tower in front of the Paris Hotel." Jinx hides her smile and her blush as she remembers her wonderful date with her uncharacteristically sweet boyfriend last night. "Could they mean there?"

"But it says this place will leave you saying 'O,' right?" Felix checks, glancing down at the paper. "And normally the view from up there would make someone say "oh," but this is the letter O without an H. It must mean something more specific."

Jinx starts to rack her brain for answers, for a place where the letter O would be significant. After about a minute with no ideas, and just when she begins to become frustrated, a thought pops into her head.

"Love." The word spills out of Jinx's mouth before she can stop it or even think about where it came from.

"Love?" Desdemona repeats.

"Love. There's a sculpture in the Palazzo where the word LOVE is spelled out in big red letters. My gut tells me that's the 'O'," Jinx wonders aloud. Felix and Desdemona both nod as they clear their plates.

"Is it tall? Because it says that only birds can reach those heights," Desdemona asks Jinx.

Jinx nods. "Oh yeah, it is. I don't think its giant, but it's definitely oversized."

"I don't know," Felix shakes his head in frustration. "I'm just not sure that's what they mean."

"I can't think of anything else though," Desdemona admits. Jinx silently agrees with her as she piles up her napkin and silverware onto her now empty plate. Felix and Desdemona follow her lead, knowing they have a long day ahead of them and need to get out into the city.

Other Asterian families begin to stir around them as well, moving towards the exit of the restaurant and going up the stairs into the real hotel. Not wanting to get a late start, the Anchors follow their lead and rush through the stunning lobby into the darkness of the stairwell. The stairwell is dead silent; each Asterian knows any word so much as whispered to another will be heard by every other person. Nobody wants to be the one to give away their family's strategy. When the Anchors exit the stairwell into the already packed casino, Felix turns to Jinx.

"Hey, why did you think of the LOVE sculpture anyway? Have you seen it somewhere before?"

Jinx shrugs her shoulders as they continue walking. "I don't know, actually... I must have heard someone talking about it yesterday or something."

Although Felix thinks it's odd Jinx can't remember, he decides to let it go. Any lead is better than no lead. When they exit through the large double doors, bright sunlight hits their faces instantly warming their skin.

"Oh my gosh, it is going to be a hot one today," Jinx complains aloud, moping.

"It's Vegas, J. It's always hot!" Desdemona reminds her, pulling out her Ray Bans and flipping them over her baby blue eyes.

Suddenly a familiar voice behind them interrupts their conversation. "It won't be hot if I have anything to say about it!"

The Anchors turn around, finding themselves face to face with Kade and Hazel. Desdemona pulls Hazel into a big hug while Kade and Jinx greet each other with an awkward, yet sweet peck on the cheek.

"I didn't know you were able to be in the competition! I thought you were over the age limit," Felix asks Hazel. He suddenly realizes that sentence might have made it sound like he didn't want Hazel here and he quickly backtracks. "But don't get me wrong! I'm glad that you're here!"

Hazel chuckles and shakes her head. "They said I'm allowed to come help Kade compete because he doesn't have any other siblings, but I can't actually win the spot on the Council for myself."

"Then as long as you're here, can you really make it a little cooler out here?" Jinx asks, fanning her face with her hand. Hazel laughs and twitches her finger only slightly, causing a cool breeze to fly through the air. "Oh that's so much better already!" Jinx sighs with relief.

"Where are you guys going?" Desdemona asks Hazel and Kade as she pulls her blonde hair into a tight, high ponytail.

"The Paris Hotel," Kade answers, winking at Jinx. Jinx feels the blood rising rapidly to her cheeks and coughs into her hand, the perfect excuse for lowering her head. When she looks up again, she sees Desdemona with a wicked smile and a glance from Kade.

"Umm... Shouldn't we get going?" Jinx fumbles for a way out of this interaction.

"Jinx is right," Felix adds. "We don't want to be the last ones to get our replica for the day!"

Felix, Desdemona, and Jinx wave goodbye to Hazel and Kade. When Felix and Desdemona turn around to leave, Jinx feels a hand on her arm, willing her to stop for just a second.

"Try not to get yourself killed, kid," Kade whispers in Jinx's ear. Jinx smirks at him quickly before following her brother and sister, all the while trying to hide her smile. Ahead of her, Felix and Desdemona decide it would be safer for them to walk instead of getting into a taxi cab with a potential ally of Jane's. Jinx silently agrees and falls into step with Felix and Desdemona.

During the fifteen minute walk to the Palazzo, the Anchors fall silent, each one individually taking in the city. Tourists speaking many different tongues pass, excitedly mentioning Vegas attractions. Hazel's breeze has left them as the intense Vegas sun slaps their skin, causing Desdemona to complain about the need for sunscreen. Buildings, each paired with a fluorescent sign of every shape and color, rise towards the cloudless blue sky. Although the city remains stunning by day, Jinx knows it is at sundown when it truly becomes the city of lights.

Before they know it, the golden Palazzo hotel stands directly in front of them, rising to what appears at least 50 stories.

"Does anyone else think this looks exactly like Caesar's Palace?" Jinx wonders aloud, noticing their roughly similar shapes and colors.

Felix nods in agreement. "Yes, but the Palazzo Hotel was built in 2007, while Caesar's Palace opened in 1966."

Desdemona raises her eyebrows up at him in question. "Where did you learn that?"

"The library," Felix shrugs as they walk into the extravagant resort. "I was just trying to do a little research to help us win this competition! You all should be thanking me."

"And yet I was the only one with even a suggestion on this clue!" Jinx reminds her brother as they enter the hotel lobby. From the minute they walk into the brightly lit, Roman inspired room, the sound of a rushing water fills their ears. Turning towards the sound, the Anchors find themselves face to face with the object of their search: a larger than life art installation of the word LOVE in bold red letters. Behind the word an indoor waterfall splashes from the second story down to a tile pool on the main level. As the Anchors walk closer, they feel small water droplets escape from the pool and fall onto their skin.

"It's beautiful!" Desdemona trills. "Can we get a picture by it?"

Jinx slaps her sister on the shoulder. "No, we're not tourists! We're here for one reason and that reason is to get the replica."

"There's no need to be so bossy, J. We're in Vegas for free and you know how the saying goes... 'When in Vegas!'" Desdemona runs over to the oversized letters and sits in the opening of the O, crossing her legs in front of her.

"Isn't the saying 'when in Rome?'" Felix whispers to Jinx. Jinx nods and starts to walk over to Desdemona before Felix puts his hand on her arm, stopping her.

"Hey... Does something seem weird to you?" Felix asks. "Shouldn't our challenge have appeared by now?"

Jinx thinks back to their time at M&M World. When they found the right place, their challenge presented itself almost immediately. And this is the right place. Jinx expects a giant troll or something of the sort to burst out from behind the waterfall at any moment to try and keep them from getting the replica.

But a moment passes and nothing happens.

Felix lets his mind begin to wander, listening to the thoughts of the people around him, looking for anything out of the ordinary. Using his Embellishment, Felix hears one voice louder than the others, letting him know that this particular person stands close to him.

All you need is love... Isn't that a Beatles song? The voice thinks. Felix turns his head towards the familiar voice, which confirms his suspicion. There, by the L in LOVE, stands Jason, staring at a small slip of parchment in his hands.

"Is he following us?" Jinx asks.

Felix shakes his head. "He has a different clue than us, I think. His clue quotes a Beatles song. All you need is love."

Desdemona suddenly notices Jason standing just a few feet from her and spins around in the O, exiting from the back to evade his attention. She walks quickly yet naturally over to Felix and Jinx before not so naturally pulling them by the arms behind a yellow stone pillar.

"What is he doing here?" Desdemona whisper yells. "I can't handle another moment of embarrassment in front of him!"

"He's here looking for the replica just like we are. But he doesn't have the same clue as us, which means-"

"Which means we're not in the right place..." Desdemona finishes Felix's sentence.

"How did you think of this place anyway, J? Really, really think," Felix orders Jinx.

Jinx shakes her head, practically confirming Felix's suspicions. "I truly don't know. It just popped in my head."

"And you've never heard of this sculpture before?" Felix asks again, rubbing his hands together nervously. Felix begins to wonder about their safety. Something is going on.

"I never even heard of this hotel before I read about it last night."

Desdemona picks up on what Felix is saying. "Do you think Jane put this place in Jinx's head?"

"Or maybe..." Felix peeps around the pillar towards Jason, who has moved to sit in the O, just as Desdemona did a few minutes ago. "Maybe it's someone *with* Jane."

All at once, Jason's head flicks up, staring straight at Desdemona as she peers around the pillar. He makes eye contact with her, not breaking it until she whips around to move out of view behind the pillar once more.

"We gotta get out of here, guys. This isn't the right place," Desdemona whispers with a raggedy breath. "But we can't go out the front. I don't trust this guy one bit."

Jinx and Felix nod in agreement and begin to tiptoe from pillar to pillar, doing everything in their power not to be noticed more than necessary. When they get to the edge of the waterfall, a small hallway leads them under the water, allowing hotel guests to cut through to the back exit.

Felix lets his mind wander to Jason once more as they walk through the hallway. *Where are they going? Should I follow?* Felix feels fear grip his chest and his pace quickens. When they push through the double doors into the pool area, the smell of chlorine immediately hits their nostrils. "I wish we had time to swim. It's so hot out here!" Jinx laments as they walk past the joyful, bikini-clad guests. Waiters bring out plates full of hamburgers and french fries, carrying them to pool-side tables along with fruity alcohol drinks.

Felix shakes his head at Jinx, quickening his pace to a jog. "We DEFINITELY don't have time for that. Jason is thinking about following us!"

As the thought settles into Jinx's mind, Jinx spots a familiar tall man in a waiter outfit. The man meets her eye and winks before turning away from her. Even though he doesn't say a word, he gets his point across. They have to get out of here.

Ignoring the pool sign which reads "NO RUNNING" in red capital letters, Jinx increases her pace to a full out sprint. Her siblings match the pace. They fly through the gated exit to the pool area and find themselves around the back of the Palazzo Hotel. Breathing heavily, they make the short trip back to the busy Vegas strip before catching their breath. Jinx leans over, putting her hands on her knees to catch her breath.

"We need to keep walking," Felix tells them, pulling Jinx up and weaving through the crowded sidewalks.

After a few minutes of silence, Desdemona speaks quietly from the back of the group. "What are we going to do now...?"

"We have to keep going," Jinx orders them all without so much as a glance back. Even though Jinx doesn't look at them, Felix knows she has a face of pure determination. Trying to decipher her thoughts, Felix pushes just a tiny bit into her mind.

Now it's personal, Jinx thinks. The second Felix hears that sentence, Jinx whips around to face him.

"Hey! Stay out of my mind. We've been over this before!" Jinx growls at Felix, both stopping in their tracks. People on the wide sidewalks turn their heads to stare at Jinx making a scene. Usually Felix would be bothered, but right now he's had it with Jinx lashing out at them.

"What do you mean 'it's personal?'" Felix confronts Jinx.

"Can't you just stop being nosy for once, you bonehead?" Jinx raises her voice again, causing more people to stare.

"No," Felix answers. "I won't. Because I know our lives are on the line here." He takes a step closer to Jinx, making the height difference between the two more noticeable. Despite Felix's height, the way Jinx carries herself makes her appear nearly as tall.

Jinx stops to contemplate, and for a split-second, Felix thinks she's going to back down. By this point he should know Jinx never turns away from an argument. "She's in my mind, Felix! I've never even heard of the Palazzo Hotel before and yet; it was my suggestion. Jane must be putting thoughts into my head and the last thing I need is for someone else to go around digging through my brain!"

Just as Felix opens his mouth to respond with something about how it's all for her own good, he hears a high-pitched yelp. Felix knows that squeaky sound could come from only one person.

"Oh. My. Gosh," Desdemona spits out. She lifts her hand to her shoulder and when she pulls it away, it comes back covered in a white paste. Instantly, Jinx breaks out into a cackling laugh. Felix, realizing Desdemona is okay, begins to chuckle as well.

Of course, the only one who isn't laughing is Desdemona herself. "There's bird poop on my favorite t-shirt!" She whines in a piping voice that makes her sound like a grumpy child. As soon as the words leave her mouth, she realizes how silly she sounds and her glum face lifts towards a slight smile.

"Las Vegas, you just keep getting better and better!" Jinx guffaws at her sister's misfortune, putting all the fighting with Felix on hold at least for the moment.

"On a real note," Felix adds when the laughter dies down. "What are we going to do next?"

"I think we should start by getting me a new shirt. You know how much I love those tacky souvenir t-shirts!" Desdemona informs them gleefully, pointing to a semi-sketchy tourist shop. The Anchor siblings walk side by side past the excitable and busy Vegas visitors down the block towards the shop. Another fluorescent sign advertises the tourist shop as OPEN as they walk through the wide double doors. Instantly, the muggy smell of vape cigarettes and too much cologne hits their nose. Desdemona turns her head to the side, coughing into the shoulder not covered in bird poop.

"Okay, I'm going to get a shirt and get out of here," Desdemona says in a hushed, pained tone. "Gosh, I can't stand the smell."

Desdemona wanders to the back where Las Vegas shirts have been stacked by the hundreds on the racks. She fans herself with her hand and the heavy, moist air sits without any movement. It's obvious they don't have AC in here. Up front, Felix and Jinx have drifted to look at a side table filled with classic tourist collectibles like shot glasses, lighters, and fridge magnets. Desdemona shifts through a couple of racks, looking for her favorite color and style of shirt. She pushes towards the back rack, just about to decide on a baby blue "I heart Vegas" shirt, when she notices a half ripped, damp flyer advertising Cirque Du Soleil hanging from the wall. On the cover of the flyer stands a man in the middle of a large golden "O" ring, seemingly in the middle of the ocean. Above him, women in leotards hang from the ceiling by multicolored ropes and strings.

At first, the colors on the flyer mesmerize Desdemona, but then she realizes something more. This is it! This is the answer to the clue! Grabbing her blue shirt and ripping the flyer from the plaster wall, Desdemona sprints up to where Felix and Jinx are waiting.

"Guys. I found it!" Desdemona unfolds the flyer rapidly and holds it so close to Felix's face he can't read it. He pushes Desdemona's hands away and allows his eyes to focus on the flyer. At the same time, recognition crosses his face.

"Excuse me," Desdemona yells to the back room of the store, leaning over the glass counter filled with knick-knacks. "Is anyone here?"

At the sound of her voice, an old man stumbles out from the back room, twirling his long beard in his left hand. "Can I help you?" The man mumbles in a grumpy voice.

"Yes, actually you can. First, I'd like to buy this shirt," Desdemona puts her shirt on the counter, causing the hanger to hit the glass with a bang. She ignores it. "Second, can we buy tickets for this show here?"

The man nods slowly, grabbing her shirt from the counter and ringing it up behind the register. "Yes, but there are only two tickets left for tonight's show."

Desdemona nods furiously. Felix opens his mouth to stop her, but he is too late. "We'll take them!"

IO

Jinx slaps Desdemona on the shoulder as she struts out of the store with the tickets clutched between her fingers. "There are three of us and only two tickets! Are we just going to split up or something?"

"Oh no," Desdemona shakes her head as she flags down a yellow taxicab. When the cab pulls up to the curb, the sun reflects blindingly off the windows, making it impossible to see who is behind the steering wheel.

"J, can you use your Embellishment to make sure this man isn't the one who keeps following us?" Felix suggests to his sister. Jinx stares straight at the cab and lets her power wander thirty seconds in the future, enjoying every minute of using her Embellishment for something amazing. Last year when they were facing Jane on Truchas Peak, Jinx's finally received her first Embellishment. Her particular Embellishment allows her at times to see into the immediate future without the passage of current time, and it's quite possibly her favorite thing about Asterian life.

Jinx finds herself in the stuffy backseat of the Las Vegas cab with Desdemona and Felix pressed tightly against her side. The grey cloth feels scruffy under her fingertips as she leans forward in her seat, catching a glimpse of the driver. It is a woman, her brown hair kissing the top of her shoulders. Instantly, Jinx knows this isn't the man. Even if this guy can change his appearance, they don't have time to walk all the way to the Bellagio where the show is held daily and they need this cab.

Letting herself fall out of the future, Jinx swings back to the present and opens the cab door. "It's safe," she tells her brother and sister. Desdemona climbs in first with Jinx behind her and Felix last. The tall, flashy buildings of the strip blur by as the driver weaves in and out of the crazy traffic. Jinx can't help but notice the ridiculous Vegas traffic and feels a sigh of relief at the idea she doesn't have to learn to drive in a wild city. With their sixteenth birthday rapidly approaching, each Anchor hopes to soon get their driver's licenses. That is if Asterians can get their licenses at age sixteen. Jinx makes a mental note to ask Kade about driving in the Asterian world.

"What is your plan for getting all three of us in when we only have two tickets?" Felix whispers to Desdemona just loud enough for Jinx to hear.

Desdemona waves her hand dramatically over her face and pretends to fan herself with a colorful array of feathers. "Cheer squad, plus four months of dance lessons at age five are finally going to pay off!"

"Oh my gosh, you're not going to try to be in the show, are you?" Jinx asks. Usually, she would be all for her sister stepping out of the box and taking risks, but the stage fright of being in a show terrifies Jinx.

Felix shakes his head. "You don't even know the steps, Mona. How do you expect to keep up with those professionals?"

Desdemona rolls her eyes at her siblings' silly questions. For once, she has it all figured out. She keeps her voice very low, making sure the driver can't hear this part of the conversation. "I can see the past, in case you've forgotten. If I can play the vision in my head while I'm on stage, maybe I can mimic what I am seeing."

Jinx raises her eyebrows in question. "But won't you be running into people on stage if you can't see because of your vision?"

Ok, so maybe she didn't have it all quite figured out. "Well... That sounds like a problem for when I am actually on stage."

Felix raises another valid question. "How do you plan on getting a costume? And how are you going to get backstage in the first place?"

Okay, so maybe she REALLY didn't have it all figured out. Desdemona racks her brain for a solution to the problem, but comes up short. "That... also seems like a problem which can be solved in the future."

"Mona, you're stressing me out here! You hardly have any plan at all." Felix huffs.

"This would be so much easier if we had the power of looking like other people," Desdemona slaps her hand over her mouth, realizing that her voice has been raised to a near yelling level and the driver can hear every word coming out of her mouth. She exchanges an anxious glance with Felix and Jinx just as Jinx slaps her on the arm yet again.

"Nice going, little miss 'I've got this,'" Jinx sneers at Desdemona in a hushed whisper.

The woman sitting behind the steering wheel glances at the triplets in her rearview mirror before joining in with a brittle voice. "You three don't have to worry about keeping your secret from me. I'm very aware of the competition."

Felix's attention snaps from the passing city towards the driver. "You're an Asterian?"

The woman laughs. "I wish! My husband used to be an Asterian."

"Used to? What happened?" Jinx asks.

Now it's Desdemona's turn to hit Jinx. "J, you just can't go around being nosy like that."

The woman takes her eyes off the road just long enough to turn up the AC in the car. "Oh, don't worry about it. I don't mind telling the story." As the Anchors wait patiently to hear what happened to her husband, she continues. "My husband and I met when we were both twelve before he knew about his powers. Of course, he knew his parents had powers, but he never told me about it. When he turned fifteen he got his own powers and went away to Jararcks, I was heartbroken."

Felix politely interrupts her to ask the question they were all wondering about. "What's Jaracks?"

"It's the Asterian school closest to Vegas. We both grew up here," she pauses to let the information sink in. "Well, when he finished Jaracks and left to work as a messenger for the Asterian Council, he got into my cab one day. And from the moment he sat down, I knew I wanted him to be a part of my life again."

"Did he become a part of your life again?" Desdemona eagerly asks, leaning forward in her seat as if she is watching a thriller movie.

The woman smiles. "Yes, he did. The day he proposed to me was one of the best days of my life, but he did it at the cost of his powers. When the Asterian Council found out he wanted to marry me, they said he had to choose. Me, or his powers. Apparently, that's what happens when an Asterian marries a human."

All three Anchors sit in stunned silence. None of them had any idea about the consequences of falling in love with a human, but apparently, it has an ultimate price; giving up your life as an Asterian. Even though none of the Anchors originally enjoyed the idea of Asterian life, they have grown to love it and now can't imagine their life any other way.

"I didn't know they did that..." Desdemona let her shaky voice trail off.

"It seems a little harsh to me," Felix adds.

The driver nods. "They told us they didn't want any humans heavily involved in the Asterian World."

"That kinda makes sense, if you ask me," Jinx inputs. When her siblings shoot her angry looks, she backtracks. "Of course, it's awful it had to happen like this, but think about it. If some humans are involved, what's stopping all of them from finding out about our world?"

The cab pulls up to the curb in front of the Bellagio with a screech and Felix looks at the clock in the front seat to find it's

3:00 p.m. They have four hours before showtime to figure out how to pull this off.

"Thanks for the ride," Desdemona digs in her purse and pulls out enough money to cover the ride plus nearly a ten dollar tip. She feels like it's the least they can do for the woman who simultaneously shared her heart-breaking story and taught them about Asterian life.

The woman thanks them graciously for the tip and hands them her card. "If you ever need a ride during your time in Vegas, don't hesitate to call. I'm always available."

The Anchors spill out of the cab onto the hot, concrete sidewalk as loud, upbeat dance music fills their ears. Turning around, they find themselves face to face with yet another out-of-this-world golden Vegas hotel. Fountains splash ferociously in front of the hotel, rising nearly five stories before falling back down to the pool below. Yellow and red lights illuminate the entrance to the hotel as limos and Mercedes swerve up to the overarching entryway. Guests in lace dresses and suits flow out of exotic automobiles. Others sip on martinis and fruity cocktails.

"Okay, there's no way this is all necessary," Jinx declares as she spots a woman fanning herself with an array of colorful feathers. They fall in behind the fancily clad group and enter the most imaginative hotel lobby they have seen yet. Easily the size of the lobby in Caesar's Palace, the room has an enormous, ornate rug spanning nearly the entire length of the floor. Three giant tables garnished with bouquets of flowers space evenly on top of the rug. Directly above the rug, hundreds of colorful works of hand blown glass adorn the ceiling. Light hitting the glass creates a rainbow of colors on the walls and floor of the lobby. It is truly breathtaking.

"This is the most extra of them all." Jinx states, being her usual uninterested self and hardly even glancing up at the ceiling. Jinx makes a beeline for the concierge desk and puts her palms on the hardwood of the desk. "Excuse me," she gets the attention of the woman behind the desk. "Where is the theatre for "O?"

The woman, whom Jinx imagines spent way too much money on a hospitality degree at a prestigious university, declares, "It's down the hall and to your left, sweetheart."

Jinx shoots the woman a look of disdain with raised eyebrows. *Sweetheart?* Jinx thinks to herself. *Ew.* Despite feeling frustrated, Jinx knows it isn't worth a second thought as she waves her siblings forward and steps quickly in the direction the woman pointed. A large golden archway silhouettes red double doors. To the right of the doors stands a large play poster hung on the wall. Jinx looks down at the tickets in her hand and notices the picture on the poster. The ticket is the same—a man riding an oversized yellow "O" through the stormy sea.

"Alright, where do you guys think the back door is?" Desdemona leans in quietly and asks, looking around suspiciously for anyone who might be within an earshot of their conversation. "Like where do you think the dancers go in?"

Neither Jinx nor Felix answer. They don't see any other entrances except through a small, unattended ticket booth. A door sits to the right, leading into the small area behind the window. All three triplets exchange a glance as if to say "should we do it?

Jinx takes this as her cue to look just a few seconds into the future and allow herself to slip beyond the present.

Jinx sits from afar as she watches herself, Desdemona, and Felix fiddle with the lock on the ticket window door. Desdemona pulls a yellow bobby pin out of her golden hair and picks the lock like a pro, obviously having practiced it before. Jinx leans to the side and watches as they go into the booth. She hears a surprised yelp from an unrecognizable voice, which could mean only one thing. There's someone else in the booth.

Jinx pulls herself back next to Felix and Desdemona and relays the information to them.

"I bet if we reason with her, she will let us in" Desdemona nods surely and struts over to the door where, just as Jinx saw in her vision, she pulls out a bobby pin and snaps the lock open almost instantly. Felix and Jinx rush to catch up, not accustomed to following at Desdemona's heels. Just as Jinx heard only a few seconds earlier, a shriek fills the air when the door flings open and hits the wall behind it. At this point, Jinx can see the source of the scream; a young blonde woman in a red velvet suit jacket with a black lanyard strung around her neck. Attached to the lanyard is a name tag with a grainy, low-quality picture.

Perfect, Felix hears Desdemona think. Before he can ask her what she plans on doing, Desdemona takes two quick steps towards the seated woman, raises her arm behind her head, and rears her fist at the woman's face with all her might. The impact creates a loud cracking sound and the woman slumps over the back of the chair, her tongue lolling to the side of her mouth.

Jinx, hardly fazed, has the presence of mind to reach back and close the door quickly. Desdemona doubles over in pain, clutching her right hand in her left.

"Holy Asterian, that hurts!" Desdemona wails in a hushed voice. She slowly turns her attention to the knocked-out woman and her heart begins to beat in her chest, the pain in her hand temporarily forgotten. "Oh my gosh, what did I just do?"

Jinx raises her hand for a high five. "You just got us into the show, Mona!"

Felix slaps Jinx's hand out from the air. "While J has a point, it isn't good to high five over punching someone! Also, this is a bit of a disruption in the human world, which is something the Council said could affect our chances in the competition."

"Do you think she's okay? I wasn't planning on punching her! I was just going to talk to her and convince her to let us in. I don't know what came over me!" Desdemona begins to freak out, rushing over to the woman and checking for blood. "What if I hurt her brain—or maybe her jaw—or what if I broke her nose? No, her nose would be bleeding more. But there could be internal bleeding in her brain! What if I broke a cheekbone? Oh, I can only imagine the pain she must be in!"

Jinx laughs aloud and the scene has become so comical Felix even smiles along. "Mona, I promise that your tiny fist did not do any serious damage," Jinx reassures. "Just grab her lanyard and jacket and go in the back door over there." Jinx gestures to a door Desdemona assumes leads to the stage.

"You're not coming with me?" Desdemona asks as she removes the jacket from the woman and slips it over her Vegas shirt, leaving the woman in a black button up. Luckily, the red velvet hides the bright blue fabric of Desdemona's Vegas shirt perfectly. Desdemona throws the lanyard around her neck and takes a minute to examine the picture. Thanks to the low res photo, she can pass for the attendant.

"How can we come in with you?" Felix asks. "We wouldn't be allowed in. We don't have an ID or a jacket. But, don't worry, I'll be with you the whole time you're back there," Felix reminds Desdemona, knocking on his forehead to let her know he'll be in her mind.

Desdemona takes a deep breath. "Alright, I've got somewhere between two and three hours to learn every step in this show."

"Piece of cake!" Jinx encourages her sister. "And you know when the actual challenge comes around, we'll be there to help. I'm sure it will involve all three of us one way or another."

Desdemona nods and hugs her brother and sister goodbye. They bid her good luck before slipping unnoticed back out of the door to the ticket booth. In the theater, Desdemona realizes anyone who walks in the ticket booth will immediately know something is up when they see the unconscious girl, Desdemona struggles to grab her by the feet. Desdemona winces when the woman's torso hits the floor. "Oh my gosh, I am so sorry." Desdemona reflexively apologizes before she remembers that the woman can't hear her at all. Laughing at herself, she opens the closet in the ticket booth and finds herself face to face with hundreds of old posters and signs advertising past shows. Desdemona uses what little strength she has in her upper body to prop the woman up against the closet wall.

With a pang of guilt residing in the pit of her stomach, Desdemona closes the closet door and exits the ticket booth into the theatre. Like everything else in this city, the decor and architecture make Desdemona's jaw go slack. Red fluffy, spongy chairs fill the large space in front of the stage. Golden arches like the ones surrounding the doors of the theatre kiss the top and sides of the stage, framing it like a pristine, serene landscape.

The dimly lit theatre seems unoccupied until Desdemona listens very closely. Muffled, far away voices begin to fill her ears, trailing from the wings of the stage. Desdemona finds herself hoping the voices belong to actors and actresses. Maybe she can pick up a few tips from them before the show starts.

How's it looking in there, Mona? Felix asks in Desdemona's mind. His voice in her mind brings her back to Truchas Peak when Jane kidnapped Desdemona and hid her in an old abandoned mine shaft. Her brother's voice in her head kept her sane. Desdemona reaches subconsciously to run her fingers down the length of her scar and shudders.

Mona? You there? Felix asks again, jolting Desdemona from Truchas Peak back to the theatre in Vegas.

Oh, yeah! Desdemona responds with a little too much enthusiasm. She takes a deep breath and continues. *It's beautiful in here. I hear some voices backstage and I am going to go check them out.* Felix makes a noise of agreement and Desdemona begins to tip-toe backstage, not wanting to draw too much attention to herself. As she does, the lanyard hits against her forearm, reminding her she doesn't need to hide anymore. She works here, right? Right. Straightening up, Desdemona walks up the back steps leading to the stage and, for a moment, Desdemona pauses center stage.

Looking out at the empty patron seats in front of her takes Desdemona back to high school when her cheerleading squad competed for the national title in front of an audience at least ten times as large as this one. She remembers butterflies eating away at her insides as her teammates lifted her into the final pyramid. For a split second, she misses her high school and her squad. How easy was everything back when her biggest worry was if the cute boy with spiky blonde hair liked her back?

Desdemona pulls on the sides of her suit jacket, reminding herself where she is. She has a competition to win for her brother and sister, especially after she claimed to have this all under control. If she messes this up, Jinx will NEVER let her hear the end of it.

As the voices projecting from backstage become louder, Desdemona lets herself drift towards the sound. She can make out female voices, no doubt. Forgetting about the sound of her footsteps, Desdemona disturbs the ladies as she walks backstage. The talking ceases.

Knowing she can't hide anymore, Desdemona steps completely into the backstage area, having no idea how she will explain her random appearance. Two classic show makeup mirrors sit side by side, surrounded by bright light bulbs. Two women stare into the mirrors, powdering their noses with fluffy brushes.

"Oh, thank goodness you're here!" A woman in a black leotard and white pantyhose enthuses, tossing her hand over her forehead in relief. Desdemona begins to panic, not knowing how to respond to this woman who has apparently been awaiting her arrival.

When the woman sees the blank, stunned look on Desdemona's face, she elaborates. "You're here to fill in for Selena, right?"

Desdemona nods hurriedly, seeing this as her perfect way to slip into the show without too many questions. "Of course... Thank you for calling me here... by the way." Desdemona raises her voice an octave, playing along with the women.

The other girl, dressed in a similar white leotard with black pantyhose, joins in with an apologetic tone. "We hate that we had to call you in on such late notice, but you know how leads are. Dramatic as ever!"

"Dramatic is an understatement!" Black leotard laughs. "She has been a nightmare this whole show!" Desdemona laughs along, pretending she knows what these women mean. Inside, however, Desdemona's heart does backflips as she realizes that the woman said "lead." As in *she's* playing the lead? And she's supposed to be memorized? At least in high school drama class she got to read the script!

White leotard turns back to the makeup mirrors. "For a second, we were worried you weren't going to show. Gerry asked us to get here a little early to run through the steps with you once more. We know it's been a while since you've rehearsed."

Desdemona laughs uncomfortably. "I've been keeping up with the steps. I'll be alright!" Desdemona's mouth spills out the words before she can bite her tongue.

Why did I say that? Desdemona mentally slaps herself. *I should have said I needed a lot of help!*

What's going on, Mona? Felix jumps in on Desdemona's mental war, sensing her change in tone.

I'm apparently stepping in for the lead. This should be really...interesting, Desdemona fills Felix in as Black Leotard grabs Desdemona a similar costume in vibrant blue. She turns around and flings the leotard at Desdemona, along with white pantyhose. It hits Desdemona in the face and when she grabs it, she notices it's covered in sparkles. So much for trying to blend in on stage.

Desdemona begins to panic as she realizes she doesn't know where the dressing rooms are. But if she asks these women, she will blow her cover! She gives them a nervous laugh and rushes past them, hoping to wander in the right direction. She makes a left through black curtains and breathes a sigh of relief when she finds a door labeled "costume closet." It may not be the dressing room, but it's close enough.

When she opens the door, the musty smell of dust and hairspray fills Desdemona's nose as her eyes meet rack after rack of show costumes. Everything from princess dresses to peasant rags seems to be hanging on these racks, causing Desdemona to wonder how many shows have been produced in this theatre.

Desdemona slips into the room and figures she better give Felix another update before he begins to worry. *Felix,* she thinks loudly, knowing he will be listening.

Everything going okay? He asks almost immediately. Desdemona doesn't know why he asks that. No doubt he's been listening intently to all her thoughts.

Yeah, I am going to get a "refresher" on all the steps from two of the cast members, Desdemona tells him.

Felix's voice lights up in her mind. *Hey, that's good, right? They can teach you.*

Well... the thing is I kind of maybe actually told them I knew the steps pretty well and just needed to be reminded a little.

Felix pauses before replying. *Jinx says you've officially met the dumb blonde standard. I say that you've become about as dumb as Bella from Twilight.*

You've read Twilight? Desdemona laughs at Felix as she finishes struggling to squeeze into the thin pantyhose and flashy leotard.

Psshh... no... Desdemona can practically feel the blood rush to Felix's face as he tries to defend his manhood. Desdemona laughs out loud as she throws her hair into a ponytail and bids Felix goodbye for now.

"Are you ready?" Black leotard shouts once she hears Desdemona's footsteps around the curtain. Desdemona makes a noise of affirmation and when she gets back to the wings of the stage, she notices the theatre has become a flurry of motion. More and more actors file in as they grab costumes off nearby racks and chat excitedly with their cast mates.

Desdemona exits the crowded stage, closely following Black and White Leotard. She feels her stomach turn in knots as she watches the way the women walk; their legs bend as gracefully as silk. Their toes point like a sharpened pencil and they haven't even started dancing yet!

"In the real show, obviously, you'll be in front of us, but you can stay behind us for now. Just so you can get the steps back into muscle memory," Black Leotard suggests Desdemona. Before Desdemona can say anything, Black Leotard begins counting. "And a 5—6, a 5—6—7—8."

Desdemona studies the women carefully, trying to follow their steps. After twelve years of cheerleading and a few months of dance class, she figures this can't really be that different. Right? She appears to be getting the hang of the simple sidestep until they turn into a quick spin. Flustered and clumsy, Desdemona spins also, but unlike the professionals, her butt makes hard contact with the wood of the stage.

"Ow!" The word escapes her mouth before she can stop it as pain shoots through her tailbone. The women twirl around gracefully with identical looks of concern.

"Are you alright?" White Leotard asks as she extends her hand to help Desdemona up.

Desdemona takes her hand with a shaky laugh. "Maybe I'm a little more rusty than I thought." The women laugh along and wave off her worry before returning to the mini-dance lesson.

For the following thirty minutes, Desdemona trips over her feet time and time again. Usually, the stumbles are subtle enough to go unnoticed by her trainers, but as more members of the cast and crew arrive at the theatre, her nerves build as tall as skyscrapers.

After what feels like an endless array of missed steps and rolled ankles, the women finally stop dancing, wrapping it up with Desdemona.

"And then there's the acrobatic sequence during the second act, but I'm sure you remember what to do," Black Leotard says with a smile and an affirmative nod. Desdemona's nods quickly back, trying to hide her gasping breaths. The only time she had sucked wind like this was at cheer practice when they ran sprints.... And that wasn't very often!

Black and White Leotard strut off stage, leaving Desdemona alone as she stares into the stage lights. She begins to panic. *Felix, I am in WAY over my head. I can't do this.* As she relays this message, Desdemona jogs in her soft ballet shoes towards the stairs leading into the audience.

No, you've got this, Felix reassures her. *Have you tried your original plan? Visualizing last night's show?*

Desdemona mentally hits herself over the head. With the impromptu dance lesson and sparkly leotards, she completely forgot about her plan. Thanking Felix quickly, Desdemona bounds back up the steps, re-energized with a mix of excitement and apprehension. She makes her way back to the costume closet in search of a quiet place where she can try to summon a vision of last night's show. As Desdemona makes her way past the stage wings, a young man wearing red skinny jeans, makeup sponge in hand, stops her.

"Oh, good! I've been looking for you," the man lets his hand cover his face in the act of relief. He grabs Desdemona by the arm and drags her into the wings towards the makeup mirrors. "If we don't get you started on hair and makeup now, you won't be ready for curtain!"

Desdemona nods, flustered, wishing she understood why he spoke about a curtain as if it were a time of day. Just as she begins to panic about not having the chance to use her powers to see the show, the man squirts some foundation onto the sponge and begins to smear it on Desdemona's cheek. He then whips out an eyeshadow palette seemingly full of hundreds of different shades of blue, grey, and green.

"This palette matches your costume so perfectly. I just love it!" the man enthuses as he dips a feathery brush into the powder. When the sound of his voice reaches Desdemona, that familiar feeling warns her a vision is coming in full force.

Oh no, not right now! Desdemona thinks to herself. Just as Desdemona braces herself to practically blackout in front of this man, the feeling suddenly subsides and the strangest thing occurs. As she expects, the vision of last night's show appears in her mind, but it only appears behind her right eye. Like a split screen television, her left eye focuses on the man's red skinny jeans. Meanwhile, her right eye catches a woman in a leotard identical to hers leaping through the air, doing everything from pirouettes to handsprings until she lands in the arms of a hunky man with flowy yellow locks.

Desdemona watches in disbelief, focusing on both sides, with the ability to sharply see both at the same time. Wanting to test the limits of her newfound vision, Desdemona decides to give it a go.

So….Have you been a makeup artist for many other shows?"Desdemona asks hesitantly. Her heart seems to leap in her chest and the words flow out just as they normally would. Meanwhile, she continues watching last night's show. The main character uses her feet to hang onto a silk rope fifteen feet in the air.

Not even listening to the man's answer, Desdemona calls to Felix with more excitement than she's had all day. *Felix, I think I got another Embellishment!*

Seriously? Felix's voice is mingled with surprise and enthusiasm. Felix pauses as he relays this information to their sister. *Jinx is upset she didn't get her second Embellishment first, but what else is new?*

Desdemona holds back a laugh as she projects a facade of interest in whatever the makeup artist says. Desdemona feels halfway bad about not listening because he seems like a sweet guy, but this is a huge deal! An Embellishment! And just in time, too.

During the next hour, Desdemona sits in the chair watching last night's performance. Finally, the makeup artist waves his hand with a flourish and sings, "All finished!" He steps to the side and allows Desdemona to see herself in the mirror. What she sees completely shocks her. Her pale skin has been covered with a blue tint and her scar has been hidden by an array of sparkly, teal fish-like scales. Her hair has been tied into a messy ponytail of curls and braids with a tint of blue hair dye coloring, obscuring her blonde updo.

"Oh wow!" Desdemona enthuses, running her fingers lightly over the scales. She begins to tear up as she realizes that with this makeup no one can see the scar. Nobody will ask what happened to her and nobody will look at her with an expression of pity when she tells them.

Suddenly feeling like she can win this competition with her brother and sister, Desdemona jumps out of the makeup chair and hugs the man with renewed enthusiasm. The man staggers back at first, not expecting the excitement, but then gives her a tight squeeze. "Break a leg!" He chatters as she lets him go.

A man with a hardy clipboard and a stressed effect shouts "Places everyone, places!" Even though Desdemona doesn't know what he means by "places," she notices everyone rushing on stage behind the closed curtain. She follows their lead.

Through the split screen vision playing behind her right eye, she sees the lead gliding towards stage left to pose gracefully against a large, styrofoam rock spray-painted gray.

Flouncing across the stage with newfound confidence, a glint of gold catches Desdemona's eye from the black ceiling in the rafters above the stage. She doesn't even have to look all the way up to know what it is: the replica. For a moment, Desdemona forgot the purpose of this whole fiasco. Remembering now, she quickly fills Felix in.

Found it, she tells Felix. *It's dead center stage, hanging from the ceiling by a short string.*

How are you going to get it? Felix asks her.

Desdemona arranges herself appropriately on the rock for the start of the show. She realizes she has done nearly everything to get them this replica. *Hey, I can't do this all by myself. I need you back here to help me.*

Felix pauses for a moment. *Okay, but how do you expect us to get back there?*

You have tickets. Go through the ticket booth like I did. The show will be starting soon anyway. Desdemona responds.

Jinx wants to know where Kade is when we need him! Felix tells Desdemona with a worried tone. Desdemona agrees with him and begins to pray for a plan to come to her to retrieve the replica – and fast. To re-group, Desdemona suddenly jumps off the rock and runs across the stage into the stage wing.

"Hey, where are you going? It's three until curtain!" A cast member shouts as Desdemona rushes by him. Ignoring his comment, Desdemona pushes her way past thick black curtains and exits the wing into a small hallway leading into the house, where the seated audience now chatters excitedly about the upcoming performance. She peaks her head out of the curtain dividing backstage from the audience and sees a theatre employee standing guard, preventing people from entering the stage area. She taps him on the shoulder quickly. Confused, he turns his head from side to side. When his eyes meet Desdemona's, she waves him into the hallway with a swish of her hand and he follows.

"We're all out of water backstage. Can you please go get some more?" Desdemona asks in a voice sweet like honey. Even with the wild stage makeup and halfway dyed hair, her beauty and charm radiate as brightly as ever.

The man nods rapidly. "Of course, of course. I will get someone to cover my post and put the bottles on the makeup counter."

As the man hurries quickly out of the theatre, Desdemona knows she doesn't have much time. *Felix, come to the right side of the stage, your right, and pretend to take a picture together. And hurry too!*

Alright, on the way. Felix responds. Desdemona doesn't risk poking her head out again to watch. She knows her brother and sister will come through. After about twenty seconds, Felix reports, *we're here.*

Come into the hallway behind the curtain to your right. Only a second after giving this order, Felix and Jinx burst through the curtain into the dimly lit area. Happy to know she doesn't have to do this alone anymore, Desdemona throws her arms around Felix and Jinx in a big group hug.

"Agh!" Jinx howls in disgust as she squirms out of the hug. "You guys know physical affection is not my thing."

"But it is your thing when you're with Kade!" Desdemona teases. She feels the scales on her face crunch as she laughs, but then it hits her. She is supposed to be on stage right now! "I'm leaving the rest of this up to you guys." Not knowing what else to say, Desdemona offers, awkwardly, "Break a leg!"

Felix and Jinx watch as Desdemona runs back out through the hallway and onto the stage. Jinx waits a few moments before moving towards the backstage area. Felix grabs her arm, halting her progression.

"Hey, we can't just walk in there! Somebody will wonder what we're doing backstage," Felix anxiously whispers.

Jinx waves him off and confidently enlightens him. "No, they won't because we're the Bellagio's newest interns." Her conviction is contagious. Even though they don't have much of a plan, they stride backstage and walk to the edge of the curtains to get a good look at the replica.

"How are we going to get up there?" Jinx whispers to her brother. Before Felix can answer, music begins to blare from the speakers scattered around the auditorium and the curtain begins to rise, revealing the actors behind. Lights shine as bright as the sun to illuminate the stage. Desdemona, with a semi-blank expression, glides off the rock and leaps across the stage. Though unnoticeable by the audience, Desdemona dances along to last night's performance while simultaneously interacting with the stage and actors in real life. Inwardly, Felix hopes he gets a similar Embellishment. He knows it will be useful if Jane has truly returned.

Jinx points up into the dark rafters and taps Felix. "Look! Look up there!" Felix turns his eyes towards the ceiling and sees a man walking across a catwalk near the lights. The catwalk soars above the stage, just barely out of the audience's sight. He reaches up to twist a dark bulb and with a flash, a green beam of light springs out.

"How do we get up there?" Felix wonders aloud as they both watch the man walk back from the way he came, moving out of view. Jinx and Felix turn away from the stage and as they do, Felix decides to pass along some encouragement to Desdemona.

You look great out there. Keep it up! Felix invigorates. When he hears no response, Felix assumes that she is deep in concentration, but he knows she heard him anyway. After only two or three minutes of wandering, they arrive at a staircase spiraling up towards the rafters.

"There's only one place this can lead," Jinx says. Felix nods and heads up the staircase. When they reach the top, he hears Jinx's footsteps stop and feels her stiffen behind him. He turns around to find a very startled, panicky Jinx.

"What's wrong?" Felix asks. He has never seen Jinx like this before, not even when they faced death fighting Jane on Truchas Peak.

Jinx takes a deep, shaky breath before answering. "It's just a bit... a little... really high."

"Wait," Felix raises his voice over the growing noise of the thundering orchestra. "You're afraid of heights?"

Jinx nods her head in affirmation as she tries to keep her eyes off the ground and focused on the ceiling.

"But you weren't afraid at the canyon in the mountains when we were walking down a thin path right next to a hundred foot drop-off?" Felix asks in disbelief.

Jinx swallows hard. "I hardly knew you and Desdemona. There was no way I was letting you know about my fear of something as stupid as heights."

Felix smiles at his sister, enjoying the moment of vulnerability—even if it is slightly passive aggressive. He extends his hand to her. "C'mon, I'll help you. We need to do this for Mona."

Instead of accepting his hand, she waves it off and latches both of her hands onto his shoulders so she can follow closely behind. "If I fall, you'll be here to soften the landing." At first, Felix thinks she is joking, but she doesn't laugh. Felix walks forward, feeling Jinx's rickety breath against his neck until they stand right above center stage. Below them, Desdemona rather clumsily tries to keep up with the professionals in a quick, physically demanding acrobat routine.

"There it is," Jinx whispers in Felix's ear, mustering enough courage to reach one hand off his shoulder and point downward. Felix sees something he hadn't noticed from the ground. Instead of sitting on the catwalk, the golden statue dangles from the walk by a thick rope attached to its bottom. Another thick rope hangs from the ceiling above the catwalk. Knowing Jinx won't get anywhere near the edge, Felix pries his sister's hands from his shoulders and gets down on his knees to reach in between the bars of the handrail. Grasping wildly his hand comes up just slightly short of the rope.

"I can't reach it," Felix sighs.

Jinx's replies in a breathy, nervous voice. "I'm shorter than you. If you can't reach it, then I definitely can't. So, you know, there's absolutely no point in me even getting near the edge."

"Unless..." Felix lets his voice trail off as he stands up and reaches for the rope hanging above them. This time, his hand meets the rope and when he gives it a quick tug, it cascades down onto his head. "I don't think you're going to like this." He closes the gap between him and Jinx and wraps the rope around her small waist. As Felix pulls the rope into a strong knot, Jinx catches onto his plan and pushes against his hands.

"Oh no, there is no way I am letting you dangle me over the edge. I refuse," she states with an unsteady conviction.

Despite her complaints, Felix resists her pushing and finishes tying the knot. "Don't worry; there's no way you're going to get hurt!"

"What? There are a thousand ways I can get hurt! What if the knot gives out? What if you drop me? What if the rope breaks?"

"J, the knot won't give out. Marcus had me in Scouts until I was twelve and I was the best knot tier in Troop 15," Felix says, attempting to reassure her.

Jinx lets her mouth hang open. "A few years of Boy Scout Camp doesn't make me feel better at all!"

Felix grabs Jinx by the shoulders and turns around to get behind her, lightly urging her to move forward. When she resists, Felix says, "Hey, just take two steps." When she finally does, he lifts one hand to point to the stage below. About fifteen feet below the catwalk hangs a layer of netting to catch falling objects (or in this case, possibly people).

"Okay, but I'm still not doing it. What if the net breaks?" Jinx continues to protest, wishing with every part of her she can somehow get out of this.

"J, I've been trusting you and your visions for almost a year now. Maybe now it's time for you to start trusting me," Felix urges her with the utmost sincerity. After a moment more of hesitation, Felix feels her shoulders deflate and then she nods doubtfully. Felix's eyes light up with excitement and his heart swells at her show of trust.

They walk towards the very center of the catwalk, directly above the Abbott replica. Blood rushing through her veins, Jinx takes an indecisive step up onto the cold, metal handrail and pulls herself up while Felix holds tightly onto the rope. Jinx readjusts herself to sit on the rail and slowly begins to slide off, her arms shaking in fear.

After (by far) the worst minute of her life, Jinx propels in the air, held only a piece of fabric and the strength of her nerdy brother.

Below her, the show must go on. Desdemona, its star, glances up to where Jinx hangs and offers a supportive, over-excited wave. However, the wave causes Mona to take her eyes off the stage and she ends up stumbling over the dancer next to her. Desdemona throws her arms in the air to depict the stumble as part of the act. Wading through her muddy and distracted mind, Jinx remembers why she dangles forty feet in the air. She spins around to face the replica. Reaching her arm out, Jinx finds the replica still slightly out of reach.

"Did you get it?" Felix whisper yells.

Just when Jinx thinks this can't get any worse, she realizes what she must do to reach the replica. "Swing me a little, but ONLY A LITTLE!" Felix begins to swing the rope forwards and backwards as he grips with all his might. Jinx slowly begins to rock back and forth as she extends her arm and tries to take deep, calming breaths. Her fingers brush the plastic of the replica. On the next pass, her hand grasps around it, freeing its bonds.

"I got it!" Jinx begins to prematurely celebrate. As soon as Jinx tries to get Felix's attention, the thick rope snaps as if someone cut it with scissors. Immediately panicking, Jinx screams and quickly prays for a quick, painless death.

In her terror, Jinx forgets about the net designed to catch anything falling from the catwalk. Instantly, the netting catches her back for a soft landing, graceful even, with the replica clutched between her fingers. Still shaking, Jinx crawls up to her hands and knees to whisper-yell to Felix, who leans over the edge of the catwalk with a look of concern. Once she meets his eyes, he points furiously down to the stage and then towards the audience. Jinx shakes her head, confused.

Eventually, he gives up on his game of charades and yells at her. "The audience can see you!"

Jinx whirls her head around and stares into the blinding stage lights. After her eyes adjust to the lights, she can just barely make out a few of the audience members, many of whom point to something in the sky—pointing at her, to be exact. Meanwhile, Desdemona slows her pace and looks skyward, watching the whole debacle unfurl, abandoning any pretense of matching pace with the professionals.

Knowing they have to get out of here, Jinx gives up on her whole act of secrecy and screams down to the stage. "Mona, let's go!" Even though her pulse races faster with every inch, Jinx crawls across the netting to find her footing on the same stairwell they came up. Desdemona, always the people-pleaser, waves in character to her love interest in the performance before awkwardly leaping off the stage into the wings where she reunites with her siblings.

II

"I can't believe we got out of there without anyone trying to stop us! We just ran through the hotel and nobody said anything!" Desdemona beams as she walks alongside her brother and sister in her showgirl costume down the brightly colored strip. The walk from the Bellagio to Caesar's Palace will be a short one, with plenty of time to make it back before the competition ends for the night.

"Nobody tried to stop us," Felix admits. "But you did get some pretty weird stares!"

Looking around at the tacky tourists and crazily dressed street performers, Jinx chuckles out, "Lucky for us, you fit right in with the people on the strip!"

Desdemona sticks her tongue out at Jinx and holds her hand out, asking for the replica wrapped in Jinx's fist. Jinx hands it over to her and Desdemona inspects it carefully, running her fingers over the name "Clarence Abbot" engraved on the front.

Safely out of danger, Jinx now has plenty of time to roast her brother. "Okay Felix, explain to me what *that* was?"

Felix tilts his head to the side. "What do you mean?"

Jinx throws her arms up in the air in mock horror. "Oh, you know what I mean. The strong rope and the good knot! You said it wouldn't break and I wouldn't fall."

Felix looks at her earnestly. "J, I really don't know what happened. I swear that rope was more sturdy than any rope I saw in all my years of Scouts."

"All two of them," Jinx whispers under her breath. Felix had five years of Scouts, but he doesn't comment on her snark. "It's like someone cut that rope with a giant pair of scissors. I didn't see it ripping or tearing at all. It just snapped."

"Unless it didn't," Desdemona adds. "I watched from the stage and noticed the same thing. And, look what else I noticed." Desdemona points across the street towards the opposite sidewalk. There, among the concentration of people moving towards the Bellagio, stands Jason. Slouched over with his hood pulled loosely over his face, he starts towards Caesar's Palace, just like the Anchors.

"It was him. He made the rope break," Desdemona nods with certainty.

The Anchors quicken their pace to stay parallel across the street from a briskly walking Jason. Felix disagrees with Desdemona. "Mona, that doesn't make any sense."

"Yeah," Jinx scoffs. "If his power is really as lame as cutting ropes from afar, we definitely don't have anything to worry about from him."

Desdemona pleads with her brother and sister. "No, guys, I have a really bad feeling about this guy. Once a follower of Jane, always a follower of Jane."

Felix stops dead in his tracks. "Desdemona. Think about what you just said." Instantly, Desdemona feels guilt flood through her as she realizes the weight of her statement. Hazel, the girl who practically saved their lives up on Truchas Peak, also followed Jane. Desdemona might as well just have accused Hazel of continuing to work for Jane.

Desdemona sighs. "Agh, I'm sorry, guys. I don't know what's gotten into me tonight. I guess I'm just a little on edge." Desdemona reaches up to touch her scar, but is slightly cheered when her fingers meet the scales applied by the makeup artist at the theatre. After all, she did become a showgirl tonight, even if for only one awful performance.

Felix nudges her arm with his shoulder. "It's okay, we're all on edge and there's nothing wrong with being cautious. It helps keep us alive."

The Anchors continue to move directly across from Jason as they make their way back to the hotel in relative silence. The city's excitement surrounds them with a noisy roar.

"Hey, where's the next clue?" Jinx wonders aloud. She holds her hand out, asking for the replica back from Desdemona. Desdemona hands it back to her with a shrug. None of them know. The last clue appeared on parchment carefully placed below the first replica.

Jinx turns the replica from side to side before finally noticing a tiny compartment on the underside of its base. Jinx attempts to pry it open with her fingers, with no success. She hands it to Desdemona, who pries it open with her long, painted fingernails and reads the clue.

Trust is a vital component of a Council member.
But how many fears can you face
from 550 feet above the city?

That familiar feeling of panic grows in Jinx's stomach. Five hundred and fifty feet above the city? Jinx has no interest in being 550 feet above anywhere.

"Five hundred and fifty feet above the city," Jinx repeats as if saying it out loud will make the problem disappear, which of course it doesn't. "Count me out of this one, guys. Good luck."

Desdemona raises her eyebrows in confusion. "What do you mean? You're the most competitive of us all!"

While we were on the catwalk, I found out that Jinx is afraid of heights, Felix fills Desdemona in through his thoughts. It's better to save Jinx the embarrassment by avoiding repeating it out loud. Desdemona doesn't catch Felix's drift and chuckles, covering her hand with her mouth. Jinx crosses her arms angrily over her chest, causing Desdemona to stifle the laughter and comfort Jinx.

"Hey, we each have our fears. You're afraid of heights? So what? I'm afraid of tight spaces," Desdemona admits to Jinx as they enter the flashy Caesar's Palace hotel.

People of all ages mull around the hotel. Adults over twenty-one enjoy their time in the casino, losing way too much money on slot machines and blackjack games. Families of all sizes fill the shops, purchasing everything from wax candles to fridge magnets. Others sit to eat at one of the many unique restaurants located within the hotel.

"I'm not afraid of anything!" Felix states proudly as they make their way through the hotel towards the red curtain. Instantly, both girls break into laughter. They are 100% sure this statement is a load of bull.

"Okay, alright, whatever. Because I TOTALLY don't remember you asking me to kill the stink bug in the room last night!" Desdemona pokes fun at her brother.

"Stink bug? You were afraid of a stink bug?" Jinx tries to clarify as they pass through the curtain and make their way down the pitch-dark stairs. Their senses heighten, causing the low murmur of Asterians and the strong scent of delicious food to drift their way.

Even though they can't see him, Felix holds his hands up and offers an awkward defense, "It's not just stink bugs! It's insects and spiders and everything with more than four legs." Felix shudders at the thought of ghost insects crawling on his skin. Finally, they reach the end of the dark stairwell and enter the lobby under the lobby. The low murmur they heard earlier has morphed into a roar as Asterians return from their daily tasks, some with closed fists clutching Abbott replicas and others with bitter, hanging heads. Jinx holds their replica a little tighter and makes a mental note to put it on the nightstand next to their first one.

"I'm hungry. Let's go get dinner with Gordon Ramsay," Desdemona drools with hearts in her eyes. Just as they move towards the restaurant, someone pushes Desdemona forward from behind.

Desdemona whips around to tell the person off, but stops in her tracks when she finds herself face to face with Jason. Time stands still as they stare at one another, neither knowing what to say. Desdemona opens her mouth to ask him to apologize before shutting it with a snap. She opens it again to ask him why he's been following them, but again, she chickens out. After a few more painful, silent-filled seconds, Desdemona lets out a small squeak before turning on her heel and moving away, tugging Felix and Jinx with her.

"What is up with you and this guy?" Jinx says a little too loudly. Desdemona shushes her quickly, but once out of earshot and seated in the restaurant, Jinx continues. "I've never seen you speechless with anyone before!"

"I just don't trust him, okay?" Desdemona admits. "I may not know exactly what it is, but I know *something* is up with him."

A waitress comes to their table from the kitchen and asks them if they would like to eat from the buffet or order from the menu. When Felix turns to answer, Kade and Hazel rush up seemingly out of nowhere and interrupt.

"Hi, we're going to join them," Hazel proclaims bluntly. The waitress nods in stunned silence as Kade and Hazel squeeze into the booth on both sides of the triplets.

Kade looks at Jinx with all seriousness. "We need to talk to you, guys."

Felix, hearing this, makes an executive decision for the table and tells the waitress they all want to order from the menu. The waitress offers them more time to look over the menu and quickly moves away.

"What's going on?" Jinx asks Kade and Hazel with a solemn tone. Kade never looks at Jinx like this unless it's something serious. Hazel begins shuffling through her purse and pulls out a paper filled with hastily scribbled symbols and signs.

Felix identifies the letters in only a moment of examination. "Are those runes?"

Hazel nods quickly. "Yes, but neither Kade nor I can read them. We found the runes with our replica today. I took that class while I was at the House, but that was a long time ago."

"And I never took it," Kade adds. "It wasn't a required class for my power type and I'm definitely not crazy enough to take it as an elective."

Hazel speaks over Kade as if he isn't here. "And we were wondering if you can read them."

Finally, Hazel's talking pauses and Kade adds. "We know you only had about a month of Asterian Runes, but we figured you could do a better job than either of us."

Desdemona and Jinx exchange a shaky glance before turning their attention to Felix. While at the House, Felix excelled in most classes, but he particularly enjoyed Asterian Runes.

"Why are you looking at me?" Felix asks when he notices his sisters' stares. Finally, their reasoning sets in. "Okay, but you guys have to help me as much as you can."

"I can't help you. I slept through the majority of that class anyway," Jinx admits. She's always disliked foreign languages; in high school, she hated Spanish. At the House, she just transported her hatred to a different language, Runes.

Desdemona and Felix disregard Jinx's statement and begin to study the Rune very carefully. While they do this, Jinx remarks, "If we're in the same city as the Asterian Council, why can't they just read the message for us? Why be all secretive about the rune and stuff?"

"That's just how it works, J," Kade tells her, trying to hide his smile at her sarcastic comment. He tries not to encourage her snide remarks, but they're part of a personality he loves.

After a few minutes of studying, Felix announces. "It says 'Be wary of not only former enemies, but of yourselves.'"

When she hears this, it transports Jinx back to Truchas Peak, when she became emotionally vulnerable to someone besides Hilga for the first time in her life. She confessed to Kade her fear of becoming Jane. Shortly after Jinx first realized she looked like Jane's mini-me, for a brief moment everything inside her yearned to join Jane. A similar, fleeting feeling twists her stomach into knots, but this time she knows she can beat it. With Kade's help, she defeated it last time and she fully intends to do it again.

"What?" Hazel questions. Everyone at the table but Hazel knows Jinx's story and her connection with Jane on Truchas Peak. Hazel, of all people, should understand Jinx's struggle. Even so, something inside Jinx that wants to keep this between as few people as possible.

A moment of tense silence passes before Desdemona breaks it by talking about the competition. "So... how did you guys do today?"

Hazel and Kade's faces light up at her question and Hazel launches into an explanation of their day's adventures, not sparing a single detail about their expedition to the Coca-Cola Museum, where they fought a real life, oversized polar bear to retrieve the replica from inside a large coke bottle. As Hazel tells her story, the waitress comes over to take their dinner order.

The worries of the Anchors slip away for the next hour over dinner. Their fears about Jane's followers, their stalker, Jason, and now this Rune, temporarily fade as they laugh about the crazy escapades this competition has brought into their lives.

"This is so much better than taking classes at the House," Jinx announces. "We're getting way hands-on experience here instead of being stuck in those classrooms!"

"What? You didn't enjoy training with me?" Kade opens his mouth in mock offense before his expression sputters into a laugh. Jinx joins along, all the while knowing she will cherish the memories of Kade's training sessions for many years to come.

"Okay, now I gotta ask," Hazel begins. "What's with the makeup and costume?"

"Oh! It's a funny story actually," Desdemona answers. She jumps into the story of their wild shenanigans, telling Kade and Hazel everything from their time at the Palazzo to their escape from the Bellagio theatre. Desdemona rises and acts out her epic knockout punch in slow motion. She swings her fist exaggeratedly towards Felix's face and he flops his head dramatically to the side.

The waitress brings their food from the kitchen and all five dig into their meals. Each skipped lunch in search of the replicas, leaving them hungrier than they can remember.

A large voice booms over an intercom, interrupting their happy conversation and delicious meal. Jinx recognizes the voice as belonging to the woman who introduced them to the competition on their first day at Caesar's Palace. "All Asterians competing in the tournament for the spot on the Asterian

Council please report to the lobby and surrounding area for a brief announcement."

The Anchors and Defrates leave their half-empty plates at the table and wander towards the edge of the flamboyant restaurant. Other Asterians eating in the restaurant follow their lead, chatting excitedly about the possible message. From the doorway, they can see the marble ceiling casting a milky white glow on the immense lobby floor. Just as it did last time, the ceiling opens to create a gaping hole above them. The group of eleven Asterians, the Asterian Society, dramatically descends from the opening. The woman Jinx remembers as the leader, the same voice on the intercom, speaks boldly.

"Asterians! For those of you who have forgotten or don't know, I am Eileen Tary, Council liaison, member, and representative. I hope you had an exciting competition thus far," she beams at them from above. Smiling, she notices some carrying replicas and others empty-handed. "We know it has been a very emotionally and physically draining week, and that is why tomorrow will be the final day for the first stage of the tournament."

Asterians congregated in the lobby gasp in response, prompting Eileen to raise her hand and silence the crowd. Quiet falls instantly as the competitors hang on her every word. "Tomorrow at 10:00 p.m., any family with three or more replicas will continue to the second round of our competition. Any family with two or less replicas will leave Las Vegas and return to their home schools."

"Oh no, there's no way I'm going back to the House when I can spend more time in Vegas!" Jinx pleads with her brother and sister. At this point, Desdemona and Felix can't help but agree with her. They enjoy most of their time at the House, but nothing can beat a city as exciting and bustling as Las Vegas.

Felix nods his head in firm agreement. "We've been given an amazing opportunity here and we can't waste it."

Eileen again silences the excited crowd with a flick of her hand. "The specifics of the second round will be announced tomorrow, along with the names of the families still eligible to compete. Good luck and happy searching!"

The ceiling closes, once again hiding the council from view. Jinx turns to Felix and Desdemona and they walk briskly back to their table. "Okay, we have to get this replica tomorrow, or we won't move on."

"Do you think you can do it, J?" Felix asks in all seriousness. Despite the way they poke fun at one another, Felix knows Jinx's fear of heights is real and he knows they will need her help to succeed tomorrow.

Jinx responds. "Of course. I'm not going to miss this." As she answers, Jinx looks down at her watch and finds it's almost eleven. "We should be getting to bed. We'll need to get up early tomorrow to make sure we have plenty of time to get the replica."

Desdemona and Felix agree, finishing their meals quickly alongside Hazel and Kade. Like the Anchors, Hazel and Kade have two replicas and they need just one more to advance to the second stage. After seeing the full extent of Kade's abilities on Truchas Peak, Jinx knows they will get what they need to stay in the competition.

"We should get going," Desdemona announces. Plates cleared, she slides out of the booth with Felix close behind. Hazel and Kade both get up to let Jinx out. Kade stays, standing to give Jinx a small peck on the cheek before she goes. At first, she shies away, but then she smiles lightly as his lips meet the skin of her cheek.

Before he pulls away, he lingers by her ear to whisper in a deep tone. "I had a great time with you last night."

Jinx smiles a more girlish grin than usual, uncharacteristically star struck by Kade. He continues. "Let's do it again sometime."

And with that, he pulls away from her face, again leaving her insides a puddle of melted goo. Her heart flutters at the thought of their next date and she mentally punches herself in the gut. This so isn't her! It's Desdemona's job to swoon over boys, not Jinx's. She continues to wrestle with her lovey-dovey mushy-gushy feelings as they make their way past the lobby to their room. When they reach their door, Felix opens his wallet to look for the room key, giving Desdemona just enough time to see Jason striding down the hallway towards them.

"Hurry, Felix," Desdemona shakes Felix's shoulder with a firm hand, urging him to find the key.

"I'm looking as fast as I can, Mona," Felix brushes her hand off, not noticing Jason growing nearer and nearer. She shakes his arm one more time and Felix finally looks up to find Jason upon them. Jason passes them slowly before he stops at the door right next to them and begins to fumble for his key just like Felix.

"I didn't know you guys were my next-door neighbors," Jason utters in a nervous voice without even glancing up at them.

When nobody else responds, Desdemona takes the reins. Panicking, she fumbles over her words in a trembly voice. "Ha, yeah, guess we are."

Finally, Felix finds the key in his wallet and shoves it hurriedly in the door handle. It opens with a resounding "click" and the door gives way under Desdemona's pressuring hand.

"Good luck tomorrow," Jason calls as they pass through the doorway out of his sight. The minute Jason's voice hits her ear, Desdemona feels a familiar sensation in the pit of her stomach. Because she hasn't mastered her Embellishment just yet, she knows this vision will take all her eyesight. Moving over to sit on her firm bed, the vision overcomes Desdemona's senses.

Darkness fills the area where Desdemona stands. The stench of musty walls and dead animal carcasses reaches her nose, forcing her to cover her face with her hand and cough to clear her lungs. Her legs feel wobbly on the floor, and only then does she realize she is barefoot on nail-filled floorboards. The thought of accidentally stepping on a dead animal or a rusty nail turns her stomach into somersaults, but she forces herself to move forward as she desperately looks for the light switch. Her legs shake. She feels like a toddler just learning to walk. Her arms seem to hang limply by her side.

A squishing sound reverberates from under her right foot. Fur, wet with water or—heaven forbid—blood, brushes against her bare skin. Where in the world am I? Desdemona thinks to herself. She reaches one of the walls of the room and uses all her might to raise one arm and fumble for the lights. Torn wallpaper and chipped paint smash under the weight of her weak arm until she clicks the lights on. Although she expects the power to be out, light instantly illuminates the room. The second she can fully see the room, she wishes she hadn't. The feeling of dead rats under her feet was no better than the sight of them, beady eyes open and jaws dangling loosely on the torn up floorboards. Just as she always does when she has a vision, Desdemona reaches her hand up to her head to feel and look at her hair. Her fears are confirmed. Black, short, jagged. Jane.

Trying to keep her eyes off the revolting room, she begins to inspect Jane's body. She first notices the innumerable scars, cuts, and bruises covering her legs and arms. Some of the scars have faded as if they first occurred many years ago. Others are caked in blood as if they happened no more than a few hours or, at most, a few days ago. Some bruises have newly formed, blackened with blood, while others appear old, yellow and blue.

Why have some injuries faded while others are fresh? Jane had no scars or bruises on Truchas Peak before the arena walls crumbled down upon her. The old bruises could be from that day, maybe. But how did Jane get the new cuts? Unsteady legs, shaky arms, trembling lips, and scars galore. Something is definitely wrong with Jane Anchor.

Desdemona snaps out of her vision to find herself sitting on the comforter. Both her siblings go about their normal activities; Felix, of course, has his nose stuck in his newest book obsession while Jinx flips through the television channels, searching for anything good to watch. They seem to be completely ignoring her, but the minute she stands up from the bed, they realize her vision is over and jump up to interrogate.

"What did you see?" Felix asks in a concerned voice. Felix always makes sure to be gentle with her after visions. He knows how badly the interaction with Jane on Truchas Peak affected Desdemona mentally and he's always worried a vision will cause her to relapse. Jinx, on the other hand, chooses not to be gentle with Desdemona. Yet again, Jinx isn't gentle with anyone. "Did you see something about Jason?"

Desdemona shakes her head and spills her vision to her brother and sister, who, as always, listen with full attention. "Jane isn't herself, but I don't know why."

"Why is she like that?" Felix asks. He understands her vision perfectly and yet he can't wrap his head around how the world's strongest Asterian can be on the brink of a weak death.

Jinx racks her brain for a reason, but only one comes to mind. "It has to have something to do with the epic beatdown we put on her. Think about it. She was almost dead, so close to death that Kade couldn't even detect her pulse. That's gotta make her weak."

"But that still doesn't explain the new cuts and bruises," Desdemona points out with a half-smile. Something inside Desdemona enjoyed the sight of Jane so weak, so helpless, so injured. Jane has finally received some of the payback she so rightfully deserves.

"Do you think that's why she has sent other people to do her dirty work? Because she's weak?" Jinx wonders aloud. Desdemona shrugs.

"Like who?" Felix asks Jinx. Wanting to cut out the distractions, he grabs the remote to turn down the television all the way.

Jinx begins to list off the names, putting up one finger after another to denote their existence. "Margret, Jason, Maxine, that creepy stalker guy... And I am sure there are more we don't even know about yet."

"But we aren't sure any of those people are working against us." Felix counters. "Except for Margret. We know for sure she's on Jane's side."

Jinx, thinking of Felix's misguided infatuation with Margret on Truchas Peak, snorts. "You don't say."

They all let out a little, half-hearted laugh before Jinx continues. "Okay, but seriously. A few days ago, I saw Maxine in a vision with Margret. Jason *coincidentally* has the room right next to ours, and that other guy is literally stalking us."

Desdemona's heart starts to race as she allows her mind to scatter. "It feels like the entire Asterian race is against us," she blurts out.

At once, both Felix and Jinx feel the weight of the world on their shoulders. They know how she feels. Felix wraps his arm around his sister's shoulders and even though Jinx doesn't join in on the hug, she nods her head in a weak attempt to comfort from afar.

"Yeah, I know," Felix agrees. "But we've got people on our side. Kade, Hazel, Mr. Belton, even the Asterian Council!"

Jinx pauses for a moment, taking a deep breath to mentally prepare herself for the excited reaction she's sure to get from this comment. "And most importantly, we have each other."

Desdemona's long face instantly turns into a wide grin and she pulls her sister into the already existing hug. They really do have each other.

Jinx bears it for a few seconds before pushing against them. "Alright, alright, that's enough."

12

"I can't believe you did this, Kade," Jinx tells Kade at breakfast the next morning. The clock above the entryway of the Gordon Ramsay restaurant says 6:30 a.m. Normally, Jinx would want nothing more than to be curled up in bed under the covers, asleep in the darkness.

But this morning is different. Jinx wasn't expecting anything special from Kade, especially not after their amazing date at the Paris Hotel. She figured the ball was in her court, but when she heard a loud knock on the door at 6:00 a.m. and opened it to find Kade, with his smoldering eyes and messy brown hair, she figured she was wrong.

"Come with me," Kade had asked her. At first, she couldn't understand why he just wouldn't wait until later in the day, maybe at night, to do this. But it only took a few minutes of coaxing for Jinx to agree. He always knows how to make her cave.

As it turns out, he made reservations for breakfast before the buffet opened to the other Asterians, and as a result, they have the entire restaurant to themselves.

"Why didn't you wait until after the competition like we did the first night?" Jinx asks. She knows whatever he says will satisfy her question.

Kade instantly responds. "I was going to wait until night, but then the Council said they would be naming which families continue on and I knew you wouldn't want to miss that. No way." Jinx nods, handing it to him for planning ahead, as he continues. "And I know you hate waking up early, but I also know that you can't wait to go get that third replica. I had to be early so I wouldn't have to share you."

Jinx responds with the sweetest 6:30 a.m. smile she can muster, but then asks a serious question puzzling her since their date at the Paris Hotel.

"Kade..." She pauses, not exactly sure how to word this. "Why are you suddenly being so sweet to me?" When he gives her a confused look, Jinx clarifies. "I mean, you've always been sweet to me behind closed doors, but now it's all of the sudden like you want to be public about our relationship. You took me to a fancy restaurant; you planned a breakfast date, you kissed me in front of other people. It's just not like you. What's going on?"

This time, Kade's answer isn't so quick. He takes a bite of his eggs before meeting her gaze with a serious look. "Why don't you come with me for a walk?"

Jinx shoves a mouthful of pancakes into her open jaw to make a statement. "Imph not dfone eafing yef," she mumbles with a full mouth. It is one thing to wake her up earlier than 8:00 a.m., but it is another thing to pull her away from a giant plate of syrup-drenched, butter coated, chocolate chip pancakes.

This lightens Kade's mood a little and he smirks at his girlfriend's quirky tendencies. After waiting for her to finish the pancakes, they pay the bill and leave a very generous tip (because the restaurant opened early just for them). Hand in hand, Kade leads Jinx through a part of the Ironwell she has never explored, its shopping mall on steroids. Shops filled with nearly every product imaginable stretch as far as the eye can see. Fountains with trim more ornate than Buckingham Palace occupy every open square. Soft music accompanies them as they walk under the ceiling painted like a sky. With all the storefronts closed, something about the empty shopping mall puts Jinx and Kade both at ease. They are, for the first time, truly alone.

"J, you know things aren't going to be like this forever," Kade informs her. Instantly, her heart sinks. This isn't the direction she hoped the conversation would take.

As much as she hates to admit it, he has a point. "I know. I've been thinking the same thing."

He squeezes her hand a little tighter. "Imagine if one of us wins this Asterian Council spot. We would have to move to spend time in Vegas and at the other headquarters."

"But you know there are hundreds of Asterians fighting for that spot. The odds are slim."

Kade considers her point and agrees silently. "I think... I don't think I want to spend the rest of my life as a mentor in the House."

Jinx stops walking and turns to face him with a serious expression. "Honestly, I don't expect you to. You can help so many humans with your powers and I know you want to do that."

When he hears Jinx say this, his heart fills with gratitude. She understands. They begin to walk again and for a few minutes they find an easy silence. That is until Jinx breaks it by asking the one question Kade has been hoping to avoid.

"So... where does that leave us?" She questions in a trembling voice. Although she asked the question, she isn't quite sure she wants his answer. "Are we going to try to make it work even if you're far away?"

In a weak attempt to avoid the question, Kade stops and kisses Jinx harshly. At first, she melts into the kiss, forgetting momentarily about their soon-to-be argument. But then, she remembers her question and slaps her hands on his chest to push him away. "Kade, you can't just not answer me. I need to know... Am I wasting my time or not?"

Kade's face twists up in confusion. "Wasting your time?" He repeats in an incredulous voice. "I didn't know you thought this relationship was a waste of time."

At first, Jinx begins to backtrack. This is definitely not the first time words have come out of her mouth before thinking. "It's not that it's a waste of time. It's just..." She pauses, considering her earlier question and choosing her words carefully. "Kade, when you date someone, you have only two possible endings. You're either going to marry them or break up with them. If there isn't a future in this relationship..." Jinx stops again as she feels tears well up in her eyes as she realizes where she is going with her sentence. This is *not* what she thought would happen this morning. "Then what are we doing?"

Instantly, Kade becomes angry. So angry that he can hardly think straight. In a tempestuous voice, he yells "I am loving you! That's what I'm doing!"

Jinx's heart skips a beat in her chest. Yesterday, during dinner at the Paris Hotel, for the first time Jinx knew she loved Kade. And at that moment, she almost told him... before one of Jane's minions rudely interrupted them. She's dreamt of saying it to him and hearing him say it back.

But like this, with his eyes ablaze and lips pursed, is not how she wanted to hear it. For a moment, dead silence comes between them, until a romantic, smooth tune fills the shopping gallery. Kade's anger fades to sorrow and he waits anxiously for Jinx to say something, to respond with words he wants to hear. With a kiss. With a hug. He'll even accept a punch. Anything to break the silence.

"I love you, J," Kade repeats in a breathy rasp.

A single tear rolls down Jinx's cheek. Instead of making a move to wipe it away, she stares straight at Kade, hoping to sear her glare into his memory. Without a word, Jinx turns on her heel and walks away.

Felix hears the door to the hotel room slam and watches a shadow stomp from the entryway to the edge of the bed, where it sits upright and rigid.

Why is she already back? I thought we were meeting her in the lobby, Desdemona thinks to Felix. She doesn't dare break the silence.

Felix nods, even though she can't see him from across the room. *Yeah, that's what I thought too...* He trails off.

I wonder if something happened, Desdemona thinks. *We should get up.*

Following his sister, Felix flips on the lamp next to his bed and Desdemona does the same. The illumination reveals Jinx's expression: a mix of anger, confusion, and absolute misery.

And now the usual question arises when Felix and Desdemona struggle with Jinx. Do they try to drag feelings out of her and risk making her more angry, or simply let her shut them out and wallow in her feelings?

Attempting to find a happy medium, Desdemona hesitantly sits down next to her sister, making sure to leave a good amount of space between them. "Were you with Kade this morning?" She asks, waiting with apprehension. In response, Jinx stands up from the bed, walks into the bathroom, and bangs the door closed behind her.

Desdemona turns to Felix with a long face. "At least we tried."

Felix sighs and sits down in the spot Jinx vacated. "I still think she'll come around."

"She might not," Desdemona shrugs, leaning her head against Felix's shoulder. "I think she's one of those people who tries to work things out before telling anyone else."

"Oh, she definitely is," Felix responds. "But how do we figure out what is going on? We need to know so we can stop it from affecting the competition."

Felix and Desdemona dress quickly to get ready for the day. Preparing for what promises to be a long one, they dress comfortably in clothes allowing movement. Because Las Vegas is by far the hottest place they've ever been.

Felix chooses basketball shorts and a t-shirt. Desdemona wears running shorts and a tank top.

Desdemona knocks lightly on the still shut bathroom door. "J? We'll be upstairs getting some breakfast if you want to join us."

Hearing no response. Felix adds, "I figure we should leave kinda' early to go find the replica. If you don't want to eat with us, we'll meet you at the entrance to Caesar's Palace at 9:00 a.m.."

Once again, Jinx doesn't respond. Desdemona shares a desperate look with Felix before walking out of the hotel room. "We just have to hope she was listening. If it's 9:20 and she's still not there, we will have to go on without her."

At the elevator, Felix notices his pockets feel lighter than before and he realizes he forgot his wallet back in the room. "One sec, Mona. I have to go grab my wallet to pay for cab rides," Felix informs Desdemona. She nods and turns to push the elevator button, which lights up a dull yellow.

Suddenly, a slight tap on Desdemona's shoulder interrupts the silence. Always on edge, Desdemona spins around to see Jason standing right behind her. With arms folded in front of him and his back slouched apprehensively, Jason's nervous eyes shift back and forth.

"There's something I want to tell you," Jason blurts out to Desdemona. Behind her, the button dings, signaling the arrival of the elevator.

"Um, I-" Desdemona stutters out. She searches for an immediate escape route. He is blocking the hallway in front of her and the stairwell is on the opposite side of the hallway, which only leaves one option. The elevator. "Ah, I have—um—to—um—go now." She mumbles and turns to enter the open elevator.

At first, Jason stops and slumps even further with an expression like a dejected puppy. But then, receiving a surge of energy, he follows Desdemona into the elevator.

Panicking, she calls to her brother. *Felix! Hurry! Jason is getting in the elevator with me!*

Mona, give the guy a chance, Felix thinks to her. At first, she wants to argue. Everything silently screams for her to run as far away as possible from Jason.

If I die in here, it's all your fault, Desdemona snaps back at Felix. She tries to backtrack and run out of the elevator, but much to her dismay it closes quickly. Desdemona finds herself locked in a moving elevator with one of Jane's previous followers.

"Desdemona," Jason begins. His deep breath is shaky and hesitant. Desdemona discreetly reaches for her hair, grabbing for her clip in case she needs her bow and arrow. She has to be ready if Jason suddenly decides to try to attack her. "I think you're absolutely beautiful."

Desdemona stops in her tracks, letting her hand fall from her hair down to her side. "You what?" Desdemona lets her jaw go slack and her eyes widen.

Jason pauses and averts his eyes from her face. For a second, it seems he might not say anything more. But then, he hesitantly clarifies. "You're the most beautiful girl I've ever seen."

At first, Desdemona doesn't know how to react. Twenty seconds earlier she had been planning to fight him in the elevator, and now here she is accepting his compliments. But maybe... Maybe she shouldn't be accepting his compliments. The Anchors aren't exactly developing a great track record with relationships. Margret pulled the ultimate trick on Felix on Truchas Peak, Kade appears to have dumped Jinx, and now Jason could be trying to fool Desdemona into letting her guard down.

But she will not be deceived again.

The elevator dings one last time, signaling its arrival on the main floor. With a brief smile, Desdemona acknowledges him curtly. "Thank you." She steps out of the elevator, leaving Jason stunned, nervous and alone.

You better get down here now so I can kick your butt, Desdemona thinks to Felix in as angry a tone as she can manage inside her head.

Felix laughs. *Hey! You're alive!* He jokes. When she doesn't respond, he gets serious. *Alright, alright, I'll be right down.*

It only takes a minute for Felix to meet Desdemona by the fountain. When he arrives, he finds her sitting on the lip of the water, flicking her hand into the pool. Her eyes meet his and she runs over to him before slapping her hands on his chest.

"Don't leave me like that! He could have killed me in there!" Desdemona yells at Felix. A few young Asterians mulling around turn to look, wondering about all the commotion. Felix shushes Desdemona with his finger and looks at her with disapproving eyes.

"What did Jason say to you?" Felix asks.

Desdemona relays Jason's compliment to her, but crosses her arms over her chest. "He wasn't genuine. He is just trying to trick me."

"I really don't think Jason is a danger to us. Especially not when we have all these other Asterians around us," Felix reasons.

"Jane won't try anything with the Council so close."

"When has the Council stopped Jane? They didn't stop her on Truchas!" Desdemona argues. She pauses for a second before divulging something she's been thinking about for a while now. "Sometimes I think you're too trusting, Felix."

Right after the words leave her mouth, part of Desdemona wishes she could take them back. Felix's face falls instantly as the weight of her statement hits him. Felix, never the one to snap back, searches her expression in silence.

Desdemona hates hurting her brother, but he needs to hear this. He might not like it, but isn't family there to tell you what you need to hear, not what you want to hear? "Nine months ago, our trust almost killed us. If it weren't for the Asterian Jewel, we wouldn't be here. We would be lying dead somewhere in New Mexico. Did you learn *nothing* from that?"

Felix stares at his sister with a blank expression. He gives her no satisfaction of a reaction.

Desdemona continues, voice raised. "Jane isn't something or someone who will just go away. We thought she was gone for good, but she's not. And to be honest, I'm not sure she ever will be. If we keep trusting everyone, we're going to get ourselves killed—for real this time."

Felix gives Desdemona a few more seconds to fix her words. But when she holds her ground, he brushes past her, hitting her shoulder with his and exiting through the stairwell to the main hotel.

When he moves into the already bustling casino, Felix fumes from all angles. Angry tears begin to well up and he wipes furiously with his sleeve. The last thing he needs is someone calling him a wimp because he cries when someone yells.

Not paying attention to anything or anybody in the hotel, Felix stomps toward the doors and attempts to rationalize his emotion. He can hardly believe Desdemona – his sister and his closest friend—said that to him. Of all people, Mona and Felix have to support one another. Maybe her success yesterday with the "O" performance to get the replica went to her head. Maybe she's cocky because she got her second Embellishment before anybody else. Maybe her natural beauty has finally given her the ego everyone else thinks she has.

Felix hails a taxi without knowing where he's going. The competition begins in fifteen minutes. Why not just go ahead and begin searching for the replica? If he finds it without his sisters, maybe Desdemona will stop acting so full of herself. Or maybe Jinx will get over her boy troubles and realize what's really important.

When he gets into the cab, Felix is thrilled to find the same cab driver from yesterday, the woman whose husband was an Asterian. He pulls out his wallet and checks the name on the card. It reads "Lilianna Hurtz, Vegas Cab Company."

"Where to?" The woman asks Felix. She glances at him in the rearview mirror and her face lights up in excitement. "Ah, the boy from yesterday! What's your name, son? I never caught it."

"Felix," he answers curtly. Even though it's nice to see a familiar face who can help him, he isn't in the mood for small talk. Answering her earlier question, he responds, "Take me to the highest point in the city. Wherever that is."

The woman nods. "The Stratosphere it is!" She pulls the yellow cab out into the busy Vegas traffic with a screech and a red light immediately stops them. She groans in frustration. "Agh! The traffic today is awful. Usually, it's busy, but this is as busy as Christmas week."

Too occupied thinking about Desdemona's uncharacteristic nerve, Felix hardly hears the cab driver. When he doesn't reply, the woman speaks again. "I hear there was a competition plot twist last night. That today is the last day of the first round."

"Mhhm," Felix mumbles back to her. Attempting to focus on something other than his family, he stares out the window at the passing buildings. They head to a part of the strip Felix hasn't been to before and it causes him to wonder if the strip ever ends! Flashy lights and oddly-shaped buildings seem to go on forever, with a different sight in every direction. Felix sees a completely upside-down house to his left. A museum memorializing the

Coca-Cola company resides across the street, adjacent to yet another ostentatious hotel stretching to the heavens.

Lilianna glances back at him through the mirror again and notices his long, pensive expression. "Where are your sisters, Felix?"

Felix sighs heavily from the backseat and tears his attention away from the street. "Somewhere back at the hotel, I think."

"And why are they not with you?" Lilianna asks. "Isn't this supposed to be a competition about teamwork?"

"Why don't you tell them that? I'm don't think they understand the 'teamwork' part because they just do what they want to do and they don't listen to me whatsoever," Felix rants. Before he can stop himself, the morning's events spill from his mouth onto a woman he met only once before. The taxi stops, then veers into the traffic, jerking Felix and causing him to slur his words slightly.

"And now we don't seem to be talking to each other. I won't talk to Desdemona and Jinx won't talk to either of us, which means nobody is talking to anybody," Felix finishes. He turns his eyes back towards the busy street, seething with anger and frustration.

The brake lights of the cab in front of them light up bright red and Lilianna stops. She turns around, putting her elbow on the passenger seat, and looks Felix directly in the eye with an airy gaze. She doesn't at all seem concerned or sympathetic to Felix's plight.

"Felix, do you ever think Desdemona might have a point about you being too trusting?" Lilianna asks.

Felix shakes his head. "There is nothing wrong with being trusting. Asterians are supposed to help humans and each other. All I'm trying to do is accomplish what I was made to do."

"But not all Asterians are like that and you know it," Lilianna reminds him. "The ones who forced my husband to give up his powers sure weren't."

Felix has to hand it to her on that one; not all Asterians follow their calling like he is trying to do. "But even they had the best interests of our race in mind."

"You don't believe Desdemona might have a point at all?" Lilianna asks again. The car in front of them finally begins to move, but Lilianna doesn't step on the gas. Instead, she continues to stare at him. But this time, her glare takes on an otherworldly quality.

Tension builds within the cab. Felix's gut twists, screaming at him to get out as fast as he can. But high tailing it out of this cab based on only one look would go against his point about trust. Yesterday Lilianna's story was so genuine... so real. It taught them something new about the Asterian world. And yet the way she asked him the same question twice makes him wonder if he gave her the wrong answer. Does she want a particular answer? Felix finds himself wishing Desdemona were here to help. For a second he debates going into her mind to ask her, but he decides against it. There's no way he will give in this soon.

"Shouldn't you..." Felix pauses, gesturing to the traffic moving around them. Cars behind them blare their horns furiously before angrily swerving into the lane beside them. "Go?" Felix finishes.

"Oh no, people can just go around me," Lilianna responds, still turned around and looked directly at him.

Felix knows he can't take this anymore. He unbuckles his seatbelt and reaches for the door handle. He glances backward and notices traffic in the next lane has momentarily cleared.

He opens the door and leans back in to get the last word. "You know, I really don't think I am too trusting." Felix slams the door shut behind him and sprints across the street, thanking God the crazy traffic cleared a path. When he reaches the busy sidewalk, he veers off to the side in front of a fountain.

What now? He thinks to himself. Usually, Jinx is the one who would know what to do next. She would be the one pushing them to just jump to the next step. Occasionally, her recklessness gets them in trouble, but right now it might be better to leap without looking.

Lilianna said he needed to go somewhere called The Stratosphere. He could get in another cab and ask the driver to take him, but he would have to risk getting into a car with someone he doesn't know. It's the tallest point in the city. How hard can that really be to find? Felix looks towards the sky and sees a sky needle that appears to stretch to the heavens. Could that be it?

Hundreds of tourists pass him on this busy day, some pointing towards buildings as they pass and others with their nose stuck in a city map. A couple walks slowly while their young children jump around at their feet. The father holds up a map in one hand and holds onto his son with the other.

I can trust them, right? Felix wonders to himself. The family reminds him of his own family with Marcus and his mother—well, step-mother. *I can trust them.* He concludes. On a whim, he gets off the stone and approaches the family. When he reaches them, he taps the wife on the shoulder.

"Excuse me," he begins. The woman turns around and flashes him a smile. "Do you happen to know where The Stratosphere is?"

The woman leans over to her husband. "Daniel, can I see your map?" Her husband hands over the map and picks their daughter up, waving her around before placing her on top of his shoulders.

Momentarily distracted, the woman gazes adoringly at her husband and the way he interacts with their children. In a moment she switches back to reality and leans over the map alongside Felix. She points to a tiny stick on the map. "That's the Stratosphere. It's just a mile and a half from here."

Felix thanks the woman and before he leaves she stops him. "And in this traffic, I think it will be quicker to walk."

Felix says thank you once again before bidding the happy family goodbye. He begins his walk through the Las Vegas sauna and wishes he had his sisters with him.

No, don't think that, Felix mentally hits himself. He is supposed to be mad at Desdemona, not wishing she were here.

Well... Felix begins to reason with himself. *Maybe I can just see what Desdemona is thinking. Then he'll know where she is and she won't even know he's snooping.*

He hits himself a little harder this time. He needs to learn to be independent of his sisters. He can't just keep going to them

147

whenever he gets lonely. He's a man, a man who can protect himself and others. Maybe.

With a heavy sigh and a heavy heart, Felix makes his way to the Stratosphere, fully prepared to win this competition all by himself.

"Jinx! Jinx!" Desdemona bangs on the bathroom door as she yells. Even if everyone within the Las Vegas city limits can hear her, it doesn't matter. "Get your butt out here right now!"

After a few more screams, the lock on the bathroom door clicks and Desdemona's heart lifts. Jinx cracks the door to the point where Desdemona can see just one of her dark eyes. It isn't a lot, but it is enough.

"J, Felix ran away," Desdemona informs her.

Jinx raises her eyebrows in question. "Ran away? What is he? Five years old?"

Desdemona brushes the comment off. Jane is out there somewhere and as a result, Felix could be in danger. "I said something to him that he didn't like and he stormed away. I don't know where he is."

After hearing this, Jinx opens the door entirely. Her puffy eyes and flushed cheeks make it obvious she has been crying. Mona wonders if she should try to comfort her, but decides it will have to wait. Felix's safety takes top priority.

"What did you say?" Jinx asks. She is still wearing her nice jeans from her "date" this morning.

"I told him he is too trusting," Desdemona tells Jinx. Normally she would feel guilty and distraught after making Felix upset, but right now she doesn't. He needed to hear that.

Jinx blows a raspberry with her lips. "He is!"

Desdemona throws her hands up in the air. "Thank you! I knew I wasn't crazy!" In the midst of her frustration, Desdemona remembers why she came to Jinx in the first place. Felix could be in danger and she's standing here ranting about him! "Okay," Desdemona refocuses her attention on the task at hand. "We need to find him. I've tried talking to him through my mind, but he can't hear me. Either that or he's just not listening." Desdemona bets that the latter is true. Even when Jane captured Desdemona on Truchas, Felix could hear her. He's never not been able to hear her.

"Do you think he went looking for the replica?" Jinx brainstorms. Her puffy eyes have flattened and red cheeks have whitened throughout this conversation. From now on, she plans to focus 100% of her efforts and attention on this competition.

"Yes," Desdemona responds. "But how do we know where he went? We never even talked about where the replica is."

Jinx brainstorms as she changes out of her nice clothes into stretchy ones. She expects this day to be one filled with an excruciating amount of walking and maybe even a little running. Desdemona suddenly hears a voice sounding like Felix inside her head.

Mona! Help! I'm in trouble! Felix shouts. Desdemona's heart races and she panics. This is exactly what she feared!

What's wrong? Desdemona asks in an anxious voice. She waves her hands around frantically, urging Jinx to hurry.

Felix's voice comes back so shaky he almost doesn't sound like himself. *Something's happened. Someone took me!*

Desdemona's mind flashes back to the way she felt when Jane kidnapped her on Truchas Peak. Right now Felix must be feeling the same way. Whether Jane or one of her followers bears responsibility for Felix's precarious position, the weight of the dangers are equal. And heavy.

Where are you? Desdemona asks. Without a clue on Felix's location, the rescue will be entirely impossible.

Felix pauses and Desdemona feels her pulse under the skin of her neck. *I'm at the top of the Stratosphere.* Felix pauses again. *Hurry!*

"J, we have to go. Now," Desdemona urges Jinx. Jinx slips her shoes on and for once, she doesn't argue with Desdemona. As they run out of the hotel room, Desdemona fills Jinx in on Felix's whereabouts. Lucky for them, the lobby is mostly empty as most families hunt for their replicas and they run up the pitch-black stairwell without disturbance. With a heightened sense of touch, Desdemona and Jinx hold onto the handrail feeling the next step until they reach the casino lobby.

"Should we get another taxi?" Desdemona asks Jinx. Both wonder the same thing. Who can they trust? Anyone, no matter how innocent looking or acting, can be one of Jane's followers in disguise.

"Hold on, I'll figure out if this next taxi is safe," Jinx answers with confidence. She uses her powers to try to see roughly a few minutes into the future. Coming out of her short vision, hardly any time passes in the real world. "It's safe."

Desdemona thanks the Asterian Gods for Embellishments as they push each other into the first taxi they see. Because of this extension to Jinx's powers, they can finally feel safe, even if only for a few minutes.

"Can you talk to Felix?" Jinx asks Desdemona. Her voice trembles slightly and Desdemona's heart warms as she realizes that Jinx is worried about Felix. Finally. Some positive emotion.

Desdemona nods in affirmation and tries to think to Felix as the cab pulls out into the Las Vegas Strip. *Felix? FELIX?* She yells at him. She waits for a moment, but hears no response. She calls his name again, but again hears silence. Felix usually has his powers turned on at all times.

Desdemona relays this message, or lack thereof, to Jinx as the cab skids to a halt. The sudden stop flings the sisters forward and they both slap their hands on the back of the cloth seat cushions. Desdemona lifts her head and sees lines and lines of break lights illuminated in front of them.

"What is going on?" Desdemona says to the cab driver.

With a heavy Southern accent, he responds, "It looks like there is a traffic jam, ma'am."

Desdemona curls her face up in an uncharacteristic expression: a snarl. "We don't have time for a traffic jam," she snaps. Before the cab driver can respond, Desdemona continues. "Our brother is in serious danger right now and if we don't get to him soon, he could die."

The cab driver, momentarily confused, responds. "I'm sorry, ma'am, but this traffic is going to take quite a long time."

Desdemona and Jinx share an anxious look. Both wonder

which will be faster—getting out and running or staying in the car and waiting.

"How far is the walk to the Stratosphere?" Jinx asks the driver. When the driver tells them it is only about twenty minutes, Jinx looks confidently at Desdemona. "Let's make it in ten."

After quickly thanking the driver and tossing money towards him, both girls begin running, panting in rhythm, all the way to the Stratosphere. They weave in and out of street performers and touring families. They pass countless churches designed for impromptu Vegas weddings and elaborate museums that charge way too much for their "one of a kind" exhibits.

In just nine minutes they arrive at the base of what they believe to be the Stratosphere, a sky-high needle connected to yet another hotel and casino. Above the entrance to the hotel, glowing red letters inform them it is, in fact, the Stratosphere Hotel.

Jinx speaks in a shaky voice as she points to the sky needle. "Do you think Felix is... up there?"

"It only makes sense," Desdemona answers, following the line of Jinx's finger towards the tippy top of the needle. "The clue says the replica is hidden 500 something feet in the air, right?"

"Yeah... But I was kind of hoping that was all just a fun little joke," Jinx laughs curtly in a pitiful attempt to ease her nerves. It doesn't work in the slightest.

"We have to go, J. Felix needs us," Desdemona says to Jinx in a serious tone. As Jinx feels her pulse racing in her chest and blood pumping in her veins, she knows Desdemona is right. If she faced her fear yesterday to help Desdemona, she can do it today for Felix... Right?

Desdemona grips Jinx's arm in an iron fist, not taking no for an answer, and tugs her into the hotel. The simple entryway to the Stratosphere hotel sets it apart from other Vegas hotels. No fountain, and only one statue—a medium sized golden lion perched in front of the reception desk. It's obvious this hotel isn't known for it's lobby. Instead, the main attraction of this hotel is the tower itself.

With Jinx in tow, Desdemona rushes over to a desk and

asks the receptionist how they can get to the top of the tower as quickly as possible.

"There's an elevator arriving for the Stratosphere tower in five minutes," the receptionist answers without so much as a glance up. She continues typing on her computer as Desdemona turns to Jinx in frustration.

"We can't waste any more time!" Desdemona shouts, throwing her hands in the air. As soon as she does, she realizes her words came out a little louder and more shrill than intended. Some of the other hotel patrons stare at her with nervous eyes before Jinx waves them off. This time, Jinx grabs Desdemona's arm and pulls her towards the elevator.

"Hey," Jinx begins in a soft tone. For once, the snark in her voice has entirely disappeared, leaving behind a voice of comfort and reason. "I know you're worried, but freaking out isn't going to make it any better, okay? We're getting to Felix as fast as we can."

Jinx's words of consolation have the opposite effect on Desdemona. Tearfully, and loudly, Desdemona rages on, "J, this is all my fault. If I hadn't been so hard on him, he wouldn't have just torn out of the hotel like that and he wouldn't have come looking for the replica and he wouldn't have put himself in any danger and I would still be able to hear his voice in my head and we would still be able to see him and talk to him and win this competition with him. It's all my fault!"

Jinx pauses for a moment; she doesn't know exactly what to say. Awkwardly, she puts her hand on Desdemona's back and pats it lightly. Desdemona continues to cry, wiping her runny nose with her hand and brushing off her tears with her fingers. Looking around hurriedly, Jinx realizes the true source of her unease. Felix, not Jinx, *always* does the comforting. They are at their best together, but without Felix, Jinx knows she has to step up, or at least try....

"Mona..." Jinx figures this is a good place to begin. "It's not all your fault."

Desdemona begins to cry even harder, informing Jinx this definitely was *not* the right thing to say. Jinx tries again, this time with Plan B. "We don't need to worry about whose fault it is because... everything is going to be alright. When we finally see Felix again, he'll be fine. I bet he will even make some dumb book reference!"

Desdemona's tears stop momentarily and she smiles softly at Jinx. "You really think so?"

Jinx nods as the elevator button dings and a man in a flamboyant bellhop uniform steps out of the empty elevator. With a flourish of his hand, he waves the gathered group into the cramped area.

"We're going to be with him in a minute, you'll see," Jinx comforts her again. At this point, Desdemona's tears seem to have stilled entirely, but she continues to sniffle as the group files in and the doors close behind her. The noise of the elevator creaking up to the top of the tower reminds Jinx of her date with Kade at the top of the Paris Hotel. She feels a lump in her throat before biting her lip to keep her emotions where they belong, under tight lock and key.

The competition. The competition. Focus on the competition, Jinx repeats over and over. Maybe this will be the only way she can force him out of her head.

After what seems like an eternity, the elevator reaches the top of the tower and its doors open slowly. People standing in front of them shuffle out at a snail's pace. Desdemona resists shoving her way through the crowd to get to her brother. Guests mill about in a pleasant, even joyful, mood. The viewing area is much larger than Jinx imagined from the ground. Just to their left is a casual dinner restaurant with tables set up against the glass, allowing guests to enjoy the view of the city along with a nice buffet. On the opposite side of the observation area, Jinx notices hundreds of people lined up, waiting for something.

Jinx hears thrilling screams and the sound of a coaster on a track. As the realization hits, Jinx's chest clenches in familiar fear. They're waiting for a rollercoaster. A rollercoaster sitting hundreds of feet in the air. If the replica is somewhere on that roller coaster, she just might—no, definitely—will have to sit this one out.

While Jinx panics about their current altitude, Desdemona looks frantically for Felix. Finally, her eyes meet his familiar blond hair and black tennis shoes. She finds him sitting at one of the tables overlooking the packed city.

"I found him!" Desdemona slaps Jinx on the arm to get her attention. Desdemona begins to run towards him, but Jinx stops her just in time.

Jinx surveys the scene where Felix sits. Everything seems too calm. "Hold on, Mona."

Desdemona looks at Jinx with crazy eyes. "What do you mean, 'hold on?' Our brother is in trouble!"

"But look," Jinx points. "He's sitting at the table all by himself. He doesn't appear to be in any trouble at all. In fact, everything here seems a little too perfect..."

"But..." Desdemona shakes her head in continued disbelief. "He came into my head. He said that he was in trouble. I can't wait any longer, J." Mona rips her arm from Jinx's grip and runs over to Felix before her sister can stop her.

With his back turned to Desdemona, Felix doesn't notice her sprinting towards him. When she reaches his table, she doesn't waste any time on formalities. Her earlier anger forgotten, Mona throws her arms around Felix's neck, squeezing him tightly. Felix lets out a loud "huff," with the wind having been knocked from his throat.

"Felix! Oh, I am so happy you are okay!" Desdemona squeals with excitement. A few people sitting at nearby tables turn their heads, but go back to their food as Felix turns around to greet Desdemona.

Just like his sister's greeting, Felix doesn't hesitate. He squeezes Desdemona back tightly, letting her know all is forgiven.

Just to make sure, however, he pulls away from her grasp. "You were right, Mona. I am too trusting." Desdemona shakes her head. An hour ago, she would have loved to hear him say that, but now she doesn't care one bit.

Jinx takes a hesitant step towards them and taps Desdemona

on the shoulder. "Hey, something still doesn't feel right to me."

Of course, Desdemona ignores her entirely. "I was so worried when I couldn't reach you through my thoughts, but then you told me that you needed help and we got here as fast as we could."

Felix's body language hardens and his eyes squint in confusion. "What? I didn't tell you anything."

Desdemona, not even noticing his tension, continues joyfully, "Yes you did! You came into my head and told me that you were in danger and that we needed to hurry here." As soon as the words come out of her mouth, her face morphs into skepticism. "You did... right?"

Felix shakes his head. "No, I was completely avoiding you and I blocked out all of your thoughts. I was too mad to make the first move."

Desdemona shares an uncomfortable look with Jinx. Desdemona knows what she heard. It was Felix's voice inside her head—or was it? "Now that I think about it, I did notice that your voice sounded kind of... weird. It was really quiet, but I just said that it was because you were scared and in trouble." She pauses for a moment and lets this sink into her siblings' heads. Felix and Jinx shift uncomfortably as Desdemona poses the question, "And if it wasn't you in my head... then who was it?"

"It was probably the Council trying to mess with us," Felix reasons.

Jinx's eyes move rapidly, side to side, always on the lookout. "No, they already used our powers against us with the first replica. I don't think they would do the same thing twice."

Desdemona's voice is shaky and hesitant. "But... that only leaves one other person."

"Jane," Jinx finished with a hardened expression. Her voice is emotionless and her hands are clenched into fists by her side.

"Or one of her minions," Felix adds.

"But... how did she get in my head like that?" Desdemona asks.

Felix wonders the same thing, but he can only think of one possible explanation. "It's Jane. She can do whatever she wants."

All three of them have a moment, a moment where they

realize Jane truly is here to stay. Jinx reacts with stone cold, unfeeling detachment. Desdemona, on the opposite side of the spectrum, fights away tears. Felix is angry. So angry his face turns red and his breathing quickens.

"But you know what? We're not going to let her do what she wants!" Felix announces triumphantly. "Because we know she's weak. Desdemona saw it in her vision. She's weak and we're stronger than ever. Right, guys?" Both Desdemona and Jinx nod furiously in agreement." We took her down once; we'll do it again. Jane Anchor is messing with the wrong Asterians."

At his words, Desdemona wipes her eyes and Jinx allows a smile to cross her face. "You're right. She definitely is," Desdemona agrees with him.

"Let's get this replica and remind Jane who she's dealing with!" Jinx celebrates victoriously, turning on her heel to begin their search for the replica. Desdemona follows close, eager to prove herself to be as strong as her sister.

Felix is the only one who stops to think. "Wait... This still isn't right. Jane or one of her followers got into Desdemona's head for a reason. They wanted you two to come here to meet me, which means that we're..."

Before he can finish his sentence, Felix notices the cab driver who took them to the M&M's World their first day, Jinx's stalker, across the platform. Felix's eyes wander the area looking for Jane, but instead, he sees a small glimmer of fake gold. There, in the stalker's hand, is the replica they need to continue in the competition. When Felix once again inspects the stalker's face, he meets Felix's gaze. The corner of the stalker's mouth turns up in a wicked smirk.

"Umm... I think I found the replica," Felix tries to alert his sisters in a quiet, yet forceful whisper yell. Both Desdemona and Jinx follow Felix's line of sight directly to the stalker, now standing across the platform.

"I don't suppose there is any chance this is just part of the competition and the Council set this up?" Desdemona squeaks when she sees the man.

Jinx answers and pushes her short hair behind her ears. She expects she will need a clear line of sight for whatever goose-chase is about to come next. "There's no way in hell."

The stalker, knowing he has their full attention, waves the replica tauntingly in front of them from across the way. For a few tense seconds, nobody moves. Now fed up with waiting, the stalker turns towards the roller coaster hanging off the edge of the Stratosphere. After sharing a few words with the coaster operator, he cuts the line and goes right to the front.

"We have to follow him," Felix announces, leading the pack.

It only takes a second for Jinx to realize "following him" means getting on a roller coaster way, way, way up in the air. Jinx has never been a fan of roller coasters in the first place, much less one higher than any she's ever seen before.

"What's the point of following? He's just going to have to get off and come back anyway!" Jinx argues, making a half-hearted attempt to convince her siblings to abandon their plan.

"Unless he doesn't," Desdemona contradicts.

Felix agrees with Desdemona. "The only way to make sure we don't lose that replica is to follow him."

Jinx stutter steps forward before jumping backward. Desdemona, who follows Felix closely, casts back a few words. "J, we need to stay together. You can do this." After a few moments of weighing the advantages and disadvantages of taking this step, Jinx reluctantly decides to follow. If Jane has another one of her followers set up to try to capture one of them, she could be the next victim. Besides, she will never be able to win this competition by herself.

As they cross the platform, Felix ponders how they will get the roller coaster operator to let them skip the line. If they don't get to the front, there's no way they will be able to keep up with the stalker. The triplets rapidly approach the front of the line and they don't have much time to get the coaster operator on their side. Felix knows he must act quickly. He knows it's wrong to use his powers on humans, but desperate times call for desperate measures.

Felix quickly pushes into the operator's mind. *Let us go to the front of the line,* Felix orders. Then, just to make sure the operator know they mean no harm to him or anybody else on the platform, Felix adds a quick, *please.*

What? The operator looks around with a confused and flustered expression, no doubt wondering who said that.

As the conversation continues, the Anchors reach their destination near the front of the line. Felix, closest to the operator, looks him directly in the eyes. *Let us into the front of the line.*

The operator, obviously disturbed by how Felix just spoke to him without moving his mouth, shakily opens the ropes and allows the Anchors to enter at the front. Now only a few people separate them and their target.

"Maybe I can just grab it," Desdemona whispers to her brother and sister. Though neither thinks it's going to work, they let her try anyway. Desdemona squeezes between the few people separating them and the stalker. She reaches out her hand to grab it, but just when her fingers feel the cool metal of the replica, the stalker pulls it out of her grasp. Instead of charging forward, Desdemona retreats, sprinting back into her place in line. The stalker turns around to give them another nasty smile as if to say "You didn't think it would be that easy, did you?"

All three of the Anchors now have their hands on their concealed weapons, looking around from all angles, at the ready if Jane has more tricks up her sleeve. Meanwhile, the coaster returns to the loading dock. As passengers slowly rise from the coaster cars and return to the platform, Jinx feels her heart race. It is almost their turn. Nearing the gate, Jinx realizes the cars are much larger and hold many more people than she originally thought. In fact, the cars allow the triplets to file into the same car the stalker has just entered.

Perfect. That replica is ours, Desdemona thinks to Felix.

I'm not so sure... Felix's voice trails off inside Desdemona's mind. *This feels like a trap.*

During this mental disagreement, Jinx battles fear. She takes one step onto the coaster, only to realize that it is, in fact, open air.

"Wait..." Jinx mumbles. Her limbs tremble as she sits in the middle of her siblings in the car. "You're telling me that if I can pull up on the lap restraint, I could fall out? From 550 feet? To my death?"

"J, you're not going to fall out," Desdemona tries to comfort her sister as a worker comes around to check their lap restraints. Much to Jinx's relief, when she tugs on her lap bar, it stays firmly locked in place. If she is going to die today, the cause of death will not be flying out of a rollercoaster.

Just a few seats in front of them sits the stalker who now holds the replica high above his head, childishly taunting them. Workers exit the ride area and a loud voice booms over the speaker. "All clear and ready for takeoff. Enjoy your sky-high tour of Las Vegas."

The coaster begins to pick up speed as it revolves around the top of the sky needle. Again, to Jinx's relief, she sees that the coaster doesn't actually go up or down any hills. It makes repeated circles around the top of the sky needle, increasing speed with every rotation.

As the ride picks up speed, the stalker turns around again with that wicked smirk of his. Jinx, hoping to take her mind off the height, finally decides to say something. "What do you want, you freak?"

As the words leave Jinx's mouth, the stalker winks at her. And then, all at once, the stalker is gone. The seat he occupied half a second ago is now empty. The lap bar is pushed up (which doesn't make Jinx feel good about its security) and the seatbelt is unbuckled. The object of their search—the replica—has also vanished. Without a trace, they have disappeared. Just like that.

"Umm..." Jinx begins as the coaster picks up even more speed after another rotation. She has to speak increasingly loud because of the coaster's noisy acceleration. "You guys saw that too, right?"

"Teleporter," Desdemona determines in a yelling voice.

Jinx groans. "What power doesn't Jane have?"

Felix wonders aloud what they will do next. The coaster has them stuck for the next minute and a half or so while that man runs off somewhere with the replica.

"There's no way we can reach him until we get off," Felix says, frustrated.

"You're telling me that I got on this coaster of death for NOTHING?" Jinx yells. She seethes with a mixture of anger and fear.

Felix ignores his sister's comment and decides to enjoy the few more moments he has on the coaster. There's nothing they can do until it ends and, besides, he will probably never see Las Vegas like this again. From the territory of the birds, Felix can see nearly the entire city. They pass by the left side of the building and for the first time, he can see where the Strip ends and the "suburbs" begin. In fact, the end of the city craziness causes him to remember. In just a few short weeks—or days, maybe—they will be going back to the House, returning to their "normal" lives.

Unless Jane messes things up again.

After two more rotations, the ride finally comes to a screeching stop at the loading dock. The triplets turn their attention back to the competition. They frantically search the platform, weaving in and out of patrons, looking for the stalker.

"Why is he playing games with us?" Felix yells as they end up back at the table where their reunion occurred.

Desdemona wonders the same thing. "If he wanted to make us lose the competition, he could have just walked away with the replica."

Felix, confused just as much as his sisters, replays the stalker's instant escape from the roller coaster over and over in his head. He recalls a lesson from their last semester's Powers and Gifts class at The House. Their professor, Dr. Jilt, said some powers can be similar, but no two are alike. He then explained the difference between two powers which seem identical to the naked eye, but fall into two different power categories: teleportation and speed.

It hits him. "This guy isn't Deadpool. He's Flash!"

His sisters look at Felix like he has just grown an extra arm. "Sorry, Felix, but I don't speak nerd," Jinx insults him. This one is so true even Desdemona can't hide her giggle.

Felix ignores her comment and translates. "His power isn't teleportation. He has super speed!" He waits a few seconds for this information to sink in and then continues. "Mr. Jilt said with a teleporter, all of the surroundings are left exactly the same way they were before the person teleports. But with a speed Asterian, things around them can change when they move."

Desdemona jumps in to finish his sentence. "Which is why the seatbelt in that guy's seat unbuckled and the lap bar pulled up!"

Jinx, who obviously doesn't remember this particular lesson, counters. "Okay, he has super speed. What are we supposed to do with this information? It's not like we're going to be able to catch up with him."

Before Felix can answer, a quick movement just inside his field of vision catches his attention. What was an empty space just a second ago is now filled with the stalker. The elevator begins to ding from all the way across the platform, signaling the closing of the doors. Felix now suddenly sees the stalker standing in the closing elevator doors.

For a moment, the triplets don't make a move. "C'mon, what are we waiting for? We're slower than him as it is!" Jinx orders Felix and Desdemona as she makes her way to the elevator through the crowds of people gawking at the city below.

This is a trap, Desdemona thinks to Felix.

Felix listens and nods his head. *But we can't just let Jane continue to gain strength. Maybe if this guy takes us to Jane, we can kick her while she's down.*

What? Desdemona asks. Felix always uses weird sayings like this at the worst times. Like when they are running headfirst into a trap set by the most powerful Asterian woman ever known.

Felix chuckles as they stop, waiting for the elevator. *Maybe we can stop her before she becomes strong again.*

Why didn't you just say that in the first place? Desdemona kids with her brother. Their mental conversation comes to an end as the elevator door opens and they slowly walk in. Desdemona knows there's really no need to hurry. If the stalker wanted to get away from them, he could. He obviously wants them to follow. The stalker will wait an extra minute or two.

A tense silence falls between the triplets as they anxiously wait for the elevator to reach the bottom floor. After a minute it hits the ground with a thud and the doors roll open. The Anchors scan the area, knowing they'll see him lurking somewhere soon enough.

"I'm still not sure this is a good idea, guys," Desdemona's voice is shaky and nervous. Memories of Truchas Peak continue to flood back. "We can just tell the Council Jane is messing up the competition and they'll take care of it."

"Hey, that's not a bad idea, you know," Felix agrees. "The Council will understand and we'll still be able to finish the competition."

Jinx shakes her head furiously. "Oh no, there's no way I'm just going to give in like that. If we do, Jane will know she has us scared again and she'll have all the power."

"But..." Desdemona leans in closer and whispers. "We are scared."

Jinx rolls her eyes. "Speak for yourself!" Before Felix and Desdemona can continue trying to convince her, the stalker makes himself known again. This time he stands directly by the large double doors at the Stratosphere Hotel exit. Suddenly, Jinx breaks out in a sprint after him.

"We can't just let her do this alone," Felix admits to Desdemona as they watch Jinx run. Even though it's not what she wants to hear, he needs to say it. "She could get hurt."

"We could get killed!" Desdemona yells, throwing her arms up. The last thing she wants is to see Jane again.

Felix grabs onto his sister's hand and gives her a light tug. "If we don't go, Jinx WILL be killed. If we go, we might all make it back alive."

After just a second's more of hesitation, Desdemona starts running to the exit to catch up with her sister. Once Felix and Desdemona reach Jinx, they find her standing, confused and frustrated. Jinx swings her head from side to side and looks around furiously.

"Agh! He's got to be around here somewhere!" She yells, tugging at her hair with her hands.

Just before Jinx prepares to take off in the opposite direction, she feels a whoosh of wind hit her hair and the stalker materializes a few feet in front of them. The replica dangles from his outstretched hand. "Are you looking for this?" Jinx reaches her hand out to grab the golden replica, but—of course—she is too slow. The stalker disappears in an instant, leaving them in a gust of swirling air.

Letting out a sigh of anger, Jinx again runs after him. Felix follows, knowing he's following the stalker's silent orders; doing exactly what the stalker wants him to do. And yet, for once, he doesn't care. He's had it up to here with Jane's games and tricks. If following this stalker gives him a chance to end Jane once and for all, it will be worth it.

The triplets run down the Strip, weaving in and out of gawking tourists while trying to follow the stalker. A few people glance their way, but most don't pay any attention. Far crazier things have happened in this city.

As they run, the stalker appears and disappears within seconds. The hot sun beats down on their faces and Desdemona feels sweat beading up on her forehead. Anger starts to build in her stomach. She's just about had enough of this guy's tricks, even if his tricks might help them end Jane. They pass the Coca-Cola Museum and the stalker makes himself known once again.

Desdemona rolls her eyes as she expects the stalker to vanish into thin air again, but this time the man's arms folded over his stomach and he lets out an "oof." Someone, or something, just delivered a blow to his gut. His expression goes blank and he crumbles to the ground, hitting the concrete with a smack. If he hadn't spent the last fifteen minutes taunting them and leading them on a wild goose chase, Desdemona might be worried for his safety. The replica rolls from his outstretched hand onto the pavement.

"What just...." Jinx begins. None of the Anchors know exactly how or why the stalker, who just a minute ago raced around the city at top speeds, now lies incapacitated on the sidewalk. Jinx sprints quickly forward, grabbing the replica to ensure they advance in the competition. But before the Anchors can celebrate, another person materializes out of what appears to be nowhere. Slowly, the person's face comes into view. Desdemona sees blonde hair shagging over his eyes.

"Jason?" Desdemona lets out a surprised gasp. For the first time, she doesn't find herself frustrated with one of his random appearances—which have seemingly occurred in every phase of this competition. Instead, she feels a perfect mix of the gratitude and suspicion.

"What just happened?" Jinx questions. Both Desdemona and Felix think the exact same thing.

Instead of verbally responding, Jason slowly disappears from his spot by the crumpled man. In a few second, he reappears just a few feet from the triplets. "Invisibility. That's my gift."

Desdemona peers at him through squinted eyes and takes a step back, keeping a safe distance from Jason. "Why are you helping us?"

Jason's face goes red and he shifts uncomfortably in his spot. "Um... I thought I made my intentions clear earlier... And besides, you seemed to be having some trouble and I thought I could help."

Felix matches his sister's untrustworthy tone and favors a full interrogation. "But why aren't you out getting your own replicas? Don't you want to win?"

Jason reaches into his backpack and pulls out a replica identical to the one now firmly grasped in Jinx's closed fist. "Mine was at the Stratosphere Hotel too. I was on my way out when I saw you." He pauses. When the Anchors don't say anything, he continues. "Who was that guy anyway? Was he part of the competition?"

Felix readies to tell Jason the truth when Desdemona grabs onto his jacket sleeve, shutting him down before damage can be done. "Oh, yeah, it was. Or we guess it was—we think it was. It definitely was," Desdemona stutters. "Yeah."

Smooth, Felix thinks to Desdemona, hardly able to hide his laugh.

"Well, I think we better be getting back to the hotel now," Jinx tries to free her siblings from the now very awkward situation. "We have some things we have to do before round one ends tonight." They bid Jason goodbye, hesitantly thank him once again, and walk down the sidewalk towards their hotel. Jason, sensing their desire to be alone, pretends to be preoccupied with the Coca-Cola Museum.

Once out of earshot, Jinx launches into giving Desdemona the third degree. "Okay, I haven't seen you stutter like that with anyone before! What's going on between you two."

Desdemona fills Jinx in on what happened in the elevator earlier this morning, but makes sure Jinx knows she does not reciprocate Jason's feelings. "Jason is just... I still don't trust him."

Felix raises his eyebrows at his sister. "Okay, whatever you say, Mona. Or should I say Professor Quirrel!"

"What?" Desdemona asks incredulously. "Felix, nobody understands your references."

"See, it's funny because Professor Quirrel from Harry Potter has a stutter and Desdemona gets all stuttery around Jason!" Felix enthuses as they continue towards the hotel.

Desdemona laughs at him all in good humor. "If you have to explain why things are funny, they aren't funny!"

Felix rolls his eyes at his sisters. One day he will find someone who understands and appreciates his references. But for now, his family will do just fine.

13

"The following list contains all of the families advancing on to the second round of competition!" Council member Eileen Tary's voice booms through the open ceiling of the Ironwell. Anxiety-ridden Asterians pack the lobby area, each cuddling close to their siblings in anticipation. Obviously, those who obtained three replicas, like the Anchors, know they *should* advance, but nothing is ever official until names are announced. If the Council suspects foul play, they have every right to disqualify a family even if they retrieved a third replica.

As Mrs. Tary reads out each name one by one, families let out sighs of relief, screams of excitement, and even tears of joy. All three Anchors hold a different replica, one from each encounter in the competition. Jinx clutches the one from the M&M Museum. Desdemona holds hers, beaming in remembrance of her performance in "O." Felix holds the third replica. Although getting the last replica technically wasn't his doing, he likes to think he led them to the Stratosphere, even if he didn't really mean to.

After Ms. Tary calls nearly twenty names, the triplets become slightly worried. What if the incident at "O" or the run-in with Jane's minion disqualified them? As they wait, Mrs. Tary announces some names they the recognize from the House. The French Family... The Poppers... and the Defrates. Jinx feels her heart twist in agony at the sound of his last name and for a moment she worries she will tear up. But then she remembers her earlier resolution and lifts her head high. She has a competition to win.

"Jason Curb," Mrs. Tary announces next. Normally Mrs. Tary announces only the last name, but with Jason, she said his first name as well.

Hm, is he an only child? Felix asks Desdemona.

Desdemona shrugs. *His sister died, remember?*

Finally, just when the Anchors truly begin to worry their name will not be called, Mrs. Tary says, "And last, the Anchors. Congrats to all our advancing families!" Jinx lets out a heavy breath she hadn't realized she held in. To have Kade advance and not her would have been unacceptable. Other families hang their heads in disappointment and file solemnly out of the lobby area to pack their bags.

Once the losing families depart, leaving less than half of the remaining participants, Mrs. Tary continues. "Now, the moment I know you have all been waiting for anxiously: the announcement of the next stage of the competition." All the young Asterians shush one another in anticipation. Everyone has guessed about what the next stage will be, but now they will truly find out.

Mrs. Tary pauses to build the suspense, then smiles softly from her pedestal in the sky. "As all of you know, the entire purpose of the Asterian race is to protect humans from dangers across the earth. Although I realize most of you are still in training or have just recently finished, I would like to put your skills to work. Tonight you will be given a scenario a real human will be experiencing tomorrow at 10 a.m. It is your job to find this person and help them before it is too late."

Many of the young Asterians turn to their brothers and sisters and whisper to one another. Hushed voices fill the room with a mix of excitement and anxiety.

"I know what you are probably all thinking now. 'What if I don't make it in time and the human gets hurt?' Well, don't worry. We have paired each family up with a Council member or an employee of the Council. If you fail to help the human, your guide will ensure the human's safety."

"Oh good," Desdemona relaxes. "I was worried it was all on us."

"One day, it will be all on us," Jinx points out.

"Yes, but thank goodness that day is not today," Desdemona whispers to her sister.

Mrs. Tary finishes her explanation with only a few more words. And it's a good thing too because the chattering between families makes it obvious their attention has already turned to the next phase of the competition. "The three families who complete their tasks most efficiently according to the Council's opinion will move on to the final round of competition. I will remind you that although it might be slightly harder to hide your powers from humans this round, you must not make a spectacle of yourself. Do not attract more attention than needed. You will find your scenario laid out in your hotel room when you return."

And with that, Mrs. Tary closes the ceiling once again, waving her arms and leaving the Asterians with a mess of emotions. For some, it's excitement about the endless possibilities of their scenario. For others, it's anxiety about the quality of their performance. For the Anchors, who decide to take the stairs down to their room instead of the elevator, it's anticipation. Tomorrow can't come soon enough for the triplets.

"As much as I want to win, I can't wait to get back to the House," Desdemona admits.

"Why?" Jinx asks.

"The longer we wait in this competition, the stronger Jane will get. We need to get out of Las Vegas and back to the safety of the House as soon as possible," Desdemona brainstorms as they enter the dimly lit staircase. Their shoes tap softly against the stone stairs as they descend.

Felix, despite agreeing with Desdemona on almost everything, pushes back. "No, we're at our safest here. Think about it, the eleven most powerful Asterians in the world are here protecting us. Jane won't try anything while they're so close."

Desdemona scoffs. "I wouldn't put it past her."

Desdemona's ominous comment brings the group back to reality as they and the other hundred or so remaining families walk back to their rooms. When Felix opens the door to their temporary home, there is, just as Mrs. Tary promised, a small piece of parchment perfectly placed on the bedside table. For a moment Desdemona wonders why the Council has been so simple with their presentations. They could have done anything they wanted to show them their scenarios, and yet they have chosen old-fashioned hand-written notes.

Desdemona and Felix feel it only appropriate to allow Jinx, the one most excited about the tournament, to have the first glance at their task. The sound of crinkling paper fills the air as Jinx roughly unfolds the letter. Desdemona and Felix lean in close to read over her shoulder.

> Time: 10:00 a.m.
> Location: Siegfried & Roy's Secret Garden
>   and Dolphin Habitat
> Scenario: In the dolphin habitat, a human child
>   finds himself drowning.
> You must save him by using your powers
>   without detection.
> Without your intervention, he will die.

"What?" Jinx gasps, outraged. "How are we supposed to stop a kid from drowning? It's not like we can breathe underwater!"

"And we're not animal tamers either," Desdemona adds.

"We could just watch and try to pull him out, but that wouldn't be using our powers. I expected a scenario somewhat related to our power category..." Felix trails off, not sure exactly what to say.

Desdemona pictures the scenario in her head. A young child, no older than six, drowning and there's nothing they can do to save him. "And the Council is sure someone will be there to save the kid in case we can't, right?"

"Yeah," Jinx affirms. She folds the paper up and tosses it back on the nightstand. "But, we won't need that person because we're going to save the little devil."

"And how are we going to do that? You said it yourself. We don't have any powers to help us with this," Desdemona reminds her sister, disappointed they won't get to show off their powers to the Council.

Jinx shakes her head. "No, we do have powers to help us. Think about it; our powers are basically universal. We can solve any problem. Desdemona, you can see the past side by side with current time, Felix can basically read minds, and I can see anywhere from a few seconds to years in the future."

"We're going to have to be very strategic about how we structure our visions," Felix goes along with what Jinx is saying. She's right; their powers can be limitless—as long as they use them correctly.

"One wrong vision and we're screwed," Jinx says, realistically. In the real world, they won't be able to save people if they misread or take too long with their visions.

Desdemona, excited about the plan, contributes. "We need to take a route of prevention."

"What do you mean?" Felix asks.

Desdemona begins brushing her teeth, speaking through a mouthful of toothpaste. "We can'f breaf underwater and we can'f speak to dolfins. If the boy ne-er getz in the water, then he can'f drown!"

"We just need to make sure he doesn't get near the pool at all," Felix finishes for her. Desdemona nods in excitement and spits out the toothpaste. "We can use our visions to find out which boy it is and then we can try to create some distraction to keep them from getting in the pool."

"I have to hand it to you, sis," Jinx teases. "You might actually be onto something here."

Desdemona folds her hand over her heart and beams sarcastically at Jinx. "Aw, wow! Finally, you admit that I might have some brains inside my head!"

After a few more laughs and a little more brainstorming, they decide to call it a night. Desdemona painfully sets her alarm for 8:00 a.m., too early for any sensible person to get out of bed. They turn the lights off and within a few minutes, Desdemona is fast asleep.

In the middle of the night, a small rustling sound causes Desdemona to stir. Across the room, she sees Jinx's shadow moving. Jinx reaches into the closet, then sits down on the bed to put shoes on her feet. Trying to be as quiet as possible, she flinches a little every time the bed squeaks.

Desdemona blinks her eyes sleepily and glances at the clock. *2:17? What is Jinx doing up at 2:00 a.m.?*

"Hey," Desdemona mumbles. "Where are you going?"

Jinx mutters much like Desdemona, showing she too apparently just woke up. "I'm just going up to get some water. We ran out and I'm thirsty."

With this, Jinx puts her mind to rest. Desdemona begins to doze back off, falling to sleep easily. But, if she had stayed awake just a few more seconds, she would have seen Jinx throw a bag across her back. Desdemona surely would have wondered why someone would need a bag to get water.

14

"Alright guys, this is it," Jinx says as she, Felix, and Desdemona arrive outside the Secret Garden and Dolphin Habitat at 9:00 a.m. the following morning. The sun is low in the sky, shining brightly against the sidewalk, making it twinkle and sparkle like a precious jewel. They have an hour before the boy starts drowning—an hour to get into the Dolphin Habitat area, find the boy, and stop him from getting into the water. On their way to the Mirage Hotel, the Anchors agreed again on the plan. Prevention is the best way to can save this boy. If he doesn't get in the water, he can't possibly drown.

In some ways, The Mirage Hotel looks similar to other hotels in Las Vegas. It's gigantic, at least thirty stories tall, and rectangular. On the other hand, the Mirage has something the other hotels don't—a miniature zoo and dolphin encounter right in its backyard.

As the Anchors enter the hotel, they realize the Mirage differs from other hotels in more ways than just one. Instead of the classic Vegas lobby with golden statues and marble walls, this lobby fills ceiling to floor, left to right, with flowers, trees, and bushes. The Mirage's lobby houses every imaginable flora.

"Wow! I feel like I just walked into the rainforest!" Desdemona oohs and ahhs at the variety of flowering plants, enchanted by their beautiful colors.

Felix, like Desdemona, is also intrigued, but for a very different reason. "Oh! I just read a scientific journal about botany." When his sisters don't respond, he pushes again. "It's a great read. You guys should try it sometime."

Jinx, on the complete opposite side of the spectrum from her brother and sister, has no interest whatsoever in the plants. The total opposite of stopping to smell the roses, Jinx makes a beeline for the front desk. On the wall behind the concierge desk, a rectangular fish tank spreads from one side of the desk to the other. Of course, she ignores that also.

"Excuse me, can you direct me to the Dolphin Habitat?" She asks the concierge. The worker points her towards the left, down a narrow pathway in the vegetation. Jinx hurriedly thanks her and returns to grab Felix and Desdemona.

"I know you all want to geek out about this, but we don't have time," Jinx reminds them. "In case you've forgotten, we have a child to save in fifty-six minutes."

As much as they want to enjoy the scenery, they know Jinx is right. If they want to stay in this competition, they need to keep moving. Felix and Desdemona walk on either side of Jinx as they head down the path, frequently resisting the urge to stop and look. As if it weren't already hard enough, the urge becomes more difficult to fight as they advance from the hotel's garden area to its small zoo.

They exit the lobby area and once again find themselves outside in the already blazing sun. The path guides them past animals of all sorts, with a focus on large cats. Felix sees tigers napping far off to the sides of their enclosures, white lions walking lazily to get a drink from the pond, and mountain lions bouncing from rock to rock as they play.

This hotel sure is something, Felix thinks to Desdemona.

Even though he didn't say it out loud, Desdemona still nods her head in agreement. *If we ever get some free time, this is where we are coming.*

"Guys," Jinx interrupts their conversation. "I think we're getting close to the habitat. Turn your powers up."

Just up ahead, Felix sees sunlight bouncing off sparkling water and he knows Jinx must be correct. He begins listening for the thoughts of a nearby family, one with a relatively young child; old enough to know how to swim, but not old enough to figure out how to save himself. Meanwhile, Desdemona expends a large amount of energy to use her new-found side-by-side view of the past. She too looks for a young family, one which discussed their excitement about going to the dolphin encounter today. Jinx repeatedly skips thirty seconds into the future, trying to zone in on people preparing to enter the dolphin pool.

As they continue to walk, a few voices in Felix's head become louder and louder, letting him know he's closing in on their source. One is the voice of a dolphin trainer. Felix shakes his head and blocks out the voice. That's not the one he needs to hear. A few seconds later he hears the thoughts of a young couple and thinks he might have found the target. However, the more he listens he hears the woman thinking about how their honeymoon has been magical. Nope, not them either. Finally, just as he starts to get frustrated, he zones in on the voice of an overjoyed mother.

Nate is absolutely going to love the dolphins. I can't wait to see the look on his face when he gets to touch one! When he hears this, Felix knows he has found the one.

"Nate. His name is Nate," Felix tells his sisters. Jinx and Desdemona adjust their searches based on his information. After just a few more seconds of walking, Desdemona agrees.

"If you're right, it's a family of three. The mother has blonde hair and the father has brown. The boy can't be older than five. In my vision, I saw them planning this visit with the Mirage concierge yesterday."

Jinx continues to search thirty seconds into the future as if hitting fast-forward on the remote of time.

Jinx sees a young family of three all dressing into wetsuits with the "Siegfried & Roy" logo in bold script. The son, a young boy as Desdemona described, informs his parents of all the facts he learned about dolphins in his science class at school. He raves about how they live under the sea, but still manage to breathe air just like people. The parents, a happy couple probably in their early thirties, beam at their son. It's obvious he's their pride and joy.

Jinx pulls herself quickly back to reality, knowing hardly any time has passed since her vision started. In fact, Felix is still describing what he saw of the present, reassuring Jinx she hasn't missed anything.

"We need to hurry up," Jinx orders Desdemona and Felix. "They're already putting on their wetsuits." Desdemona and Felix quicken their pace to match Jinx. Everyone understands the severity of the task at hand. Even with a designated Asterian to save the boy if the Anchors fail, they remain on edge.

The lush greenery surrounding the animal habitat clears, revealing an opening with beams of light shining in. Excited families prepare for their dolphin encounter, putting on their sunglasses and, of course, donning their cameras. No water vacation endeavor would be complete without slightly blurred, disposable camera family photos.

A gleaming pool of blue sits at the center of the clearing and a movement beneath the crystal water catches Felix's eye. A curved fin rises and a smooth, grey dolphin emerges for just a moment. As a child, Felix never went to the beach and his hometown wasn't anywhere near a big aquarium. For the first time in all his fifteen and 3/4 years, Felix finally sees a dolphin.

You know, they're a lot bigger than I imagined, Felix thinks to Desdemona. As Desdemona agrees, Felix finds himself wishing they could stay for a day to swim with the dolphins like the other tourists. Because they can't, he adds "swim with dolphins" on his mental bucket list before re-focusing on the task at hand.

"Oh!" Desdemona exclaims, pointing to the locker rooms. "There they are." The brunette boy, already decked out in his wetsuit, bounces as he waits impatiently for his parents to catch up. Mona watches the excitement dance in his eyes and feels a pang of guilt. "Guys, we're about to crush this little boy's dream of swimming with the dolphins."

Jinx rolls her eyes at her sister's sympathy and speaks practically. "Mona, if he goes in that pool, he could die. If he's alive, he'll have more opportunities to swim with the dolphins later in life."

"When he's older, maybe he'll get the chance to swim with the dolphins somewhere even better... like the Bahamas!" Desdemona imagines enthusiastically.

The Anchors sneak over to the locker area and peer around the corner at the happy family. "How are we going to stop them from getting in that pool?" Felix asks.

"Why don't we just tell them what we know?" Jinx asks in a loud whisper. "Telling them straight up that their son is going to drown will get our point across."

Desdemona hits Jinx on the shoulder. "We can't be so blunt like that. The Council told us not to reveal ourselves to humans, remember?"

No matter how frustrating, Jinx knows Desdemona is right. If humans find out Asterians exist, they will become reckless, believing they'll be saved no matter what they do. There aren't enough Asterians to save the whole human race from self-destruction.

"Is there a fire alarm around here? If we pull it, everyone will have to evacuate," Desdemona brainstorms as she takes another glance at the family. Felix, initially thinking Desdemona's idea could work, quickly finds its fatal flaw. "We're already outdoors. Fire alarms are for indoor structures."

Soon, Jinx devises a plan which just might work. It's far from foolproof, but better than nothing. "Mona, Felix, we're going to need some wetsuits. And a clipboard. And some candy."

What a weird combination... Desdemona thinks to Felix as they approach the small hut with a sign above that advertises "wet suit rentals." When they reach the hut, it dawns on them. They haven't exactly paid for a dolphin encounter and therefore cannot rent a wetsuit.

"Maybe there is a back door to the stand..." Jinx wonders aloud. She slowly wanders around the side of the hut, finding a heavy metal rack with every inch taken up by wetsuits on plastic hangers.

"Holy Asterian! We've hit the jackpot." Felix exclaims.

Jinx casts a sly glance at Felix, but laughs a little under her breath as she picks out three wetsuits in their sizes. "Give it up. Your catchphrase is not catching on, dude."

Figuring they shouldn't lurk around the back of the wetsuit rental hut, they grab wetsuits from Jinx and return to the locker area. Jinx notices a clipboard on the desk of the wetsuit hut. Jinx makes sure the coast is clear, snatches the clipboard, and tucks it under her arm.

At this point, more and more families arrive, making it easier for the Anchors to blend in. They put their black, slick wetsuits on over the bathing suits they wore under their clothes as the guests chatter in anticipation around them. After zipping the wetsuits up in the back, they are ready.

"I've got some candy in my bag," Desdemona says as she shuffles through her knapsack. Felix hears a small rustling of wrappers before her hand emerges, clutching at least ten mini-packs of M&Ms.

"Where did you get those?" Felix asks.

Desdemona bites her tongue and gives off a guilty expression. "I may or may not have picked them up at the M&M Museum..." When Felix raises his eyebrows at her, she defends herself. "Okay, there was no way I was going to visit the biggest M&M Museum and not take home a souvenir! Besides, they just left them sitting on the counter like they wanted us to take them!"

Jinx shakes her head and tries to steer her siblings back to the task at hand. "It doesn't matter where she got them. It only matters that kids love candy." She pauses and peers around the corner once more at the family. She sees them put their clothes in a locker, which means they have finished changing and will soon walk to the pool. "Alright, it's go time. Hang back and make sure the coast is clear."

"If any of the workers come this way, the code word is Beluga Whale," Desdemona determines. "We will yell Beluga Whale." At first, Jinx opens her mouth to protest, saying the code word is stupid, but then closes her mouth. They don't have time for disagreement right now; it's already 9:45.

Jinx tucks the clipboard under her arm and straightens her back to look as professional and confident as possible. She takes a deep breath before swerving around the corner to greet the small family with a cheery tone.

"Hi! Welcome to Siegfried and Roy's Dolphin Encounter!" She begins with a smile bigger than any she's ever managed before. "Are you three ready to have a great day?"

Behind her, she hears a muffled giggle from Desdemona and Felix. This new side of Jinx presents a sight never seen.

"Of course!" The mother answers, matching Jinx's level of joy. "I am Annie Kelly. This is my husband Jim, and this is our son Nate."

Jinx waves to Nate, who offers a half-toothless grin. She smiles back before turning her attention towards the parents. "Now, there are a few things we have to clear up before we start. First..." Jinx pauses. It just now dawns on her that she doesn't exactly know what she's planning on saying. She commits to do what she does best and wing it.

"Would you like some candy?" Jinx offers Nate, trying to stall as she thinks. He voraciously agrees and Jinx hands him a pack of M&Ms to keep him momentarily distracted. "Alright, let's get down to business. You checked in before you got your wetsuits, correct?" Jinx continues. She struggles to keep up her cheery tone, but manages with maximum effort. The mother and father nod in response. "And you all are signed up for the 10 a.m. dolphin...encounter... correct?"

"Yes," the mother answers. "We were thinking about doing the 11 a.m. session originally, but we decided to do the 10 a.m. so we could have lunch as a family afterward."

Jinx fakes another smile. "Aw, how sweet of you!" Behind her, she hears another laugh-cough mix come from Desdemona. "Lastly... how old is your son?"

The mother grabs onto Nate's arm, holding him in place while she answers. "He's five, actually, but he turns six in three weeks."

Jinx lets her smile fall and sighs heavily through gritted teeth. "Ooo... I'm so sorry, but we have a strict policy that children under age eight cannot swim with the dolphins."

Even though Jinx has no sympathy for children, the look on Nate's face tugs at Jinx's heartstrings. His joyous smile and laugh disappear to reveal a dumbfounded, confused expression.

If this weren't for his own good, she might take back her previous statement.

The mother's sweet disposition shifts as soon as she sees her son's face; her sugary personality morphs into one of anger. "But the lady we spoke to when we booked this tour said the age minimum was FIVE." She enunciates her last word as if this will change Jinx's mind.

Jinx has to think on her feet quickly. "Actually... Um... We just changed the policy a month ago due to a... a dangerous situation."

The woman's rage seems to seep through her pores as she takes a step closer to Jinx. "My son has been talking non-stop about how excited he is to meet the dolphins."

Even though everything in Jinx's nature screams at her to fight back and get in this woman's face, Jinx restrains herself. A real employee of some upscale Las Vegas hotel would *not* get in a customer's face. Instead, she takes a deep breath and manages another smile.

"We can get you a voucher for a free dolphin experience when he turns eight. For now, if it helps..." Jinx tries to think of an alternative to the dolphins. She runs through all the animals they saw when they walked in. "I can get you a close-up with the white tigers and lions!"

As quickly as Nate's face turned to sadness just a minute ago, it again changes to elation and he attempts to imitate a lion with a "ferocious" roar.

Annie's face softens. "He seems even more excited about the lions than he does the dolphins. I guess that's alright." Just when Jinx feels like she has this under control and her plan will work, she hears Desdemona's loud whisper travel through the locker wall separating them.

"Beluga whale!" Desdemona warns. Out of the corner of her eye, Jinx sees a *real* worker—a muscular surfer boy—rapidly approaching them. A little louder this time, in case Jinx didn't hear it the first time, Desdemona says "BELUGA WHALE!"

With a less than confident voice, Jinx politely excuses herself from the family. "One moment, Miss. I am going to go discuss

your voucher and your lion encounter with my... my colleague."
Jinx swerves away from the family and practically throws herself
into the fire by meeting the approaching worker head on.

"The Kelly family has decided to change their dolphin
encounter for a lion encounter," Jinx informs the worker with
the utmost certainty. "I was just going to talk to the front desk
about an exchange."

The worker opens his mouth as if he has something to say,
but then closes it again. For a moment, Jinx knows she's about
to be called out for her ruse, but Surfer Dude nods his head.
"Okay... Are you new here?"

"Yes!" Jinx blurts out. "I actually just transferred here a
week ago from... from a dolphin habitat in the Bahamas."

The surfer boy smiles. "Aw! Those are the best ones! Why
did..."

Before he can finish his question, Jinx cuts him off. "Hey, I
hate to interrupt, but I'm sure the Kelly family doesn't want to
wait any longer. I should probably get back to them."

Surfer Dude puts his hands up in concession and wishes her
luck during her first week. *Phew, I didn't think I would make it
through that one,* Jinx thinks to herself as she struts back to the
family with renewed conviction.

"Now, I will give you all a few minutes to change out of
your wetsuits and by the time you're done, we should have your
lion encounter tickets all set up and ready to go," Jinx informs
them with a smile. Nate, now sprouting off facts about lions and
tigers, beams. Jinx surprises even herself by returning a real
smile. Maybe not all kids are as bad as she thinks.

Soon after, she excuses herself and rushes back around the
corner to Felix and Desdemona.

"Wow, J!" Felix praises, holding his hand up for a high five.
"I don't know how you did that."

Jinx quickly returns the high five before diving into the final
steps of her plan. Lucky for her, Felix and Desdemona changed
out of their wetsuits while she talked to Surfer Dude. "As fast as
you can, I need you to get to the front desk and buy tickets for
the lion encounter. You can put it on this card." Jinx produces

a shiny silver credit card. Before Desdemona and Felix can ask any questions, she fills them in. "Hilga gave it to me before I came to the House. I've just never needed it until now."

Desdemona and Felix run as fast as they can back the way they came. As they run, both think about the way Jinx managed to completely change her attitude and transform into a character of some sort.

"Has Jinx seemed any different to you lately?" Desdemona wonders aloud in between heavy breaths.

Felix thinks for a moment. "You know, I think she has. She seems more... focused, I guess."

"She has only been focused like this since Kade and her... broke up or had their fight? Whatever it was." Desdemona questions. "The competition is all she ever talks about now."

Until this point, Felix hasn't noticed it. But now, he realizes she is right. "It's probably just her coping mechanism. I mean, Kade is really the only person who seems to actually get her. And that seems to be over."

Before Desdemona can respond, they quickly approach the front desk. Desdemona hangs back while Felix goes to the desk and buys the tickets. As she waits, she thinks more about Jinx and her struggles with Kade. She makes a mental note to ask Jinx tonight before bed. Felix returns with three paper tickets clutched in his hand.

They sprint back even faster than they came. This time they have no room to chat between heavy breaths. Once again, Desdemona wishes that she had taken conditioning more seriously while at the House.

When they re-enter the pool area, they hear the clock strike 10:00 a.m., which means they have officially avoided the time when the accident was supposed to happen. However, they aren't off the hook just yet. They find Jinx waiting exactly where they left her. She watches the family like a hawk to make sure they don't wander off.

"We got them," Desdemona informs Jinx in between heavy, weighted breaths. Jinx, without saying a word, gives the family the tickets and points them in the direction of the lobby, where they can receive more information. She beams at them once again and feels a heavy sigh of relief when they leave the pool area once and for all. The minute they turn the corner and are out of sight, Jinx feels a large weight on her back as Desdemona jumps on her in excitement.

"I can't believe we did it!" She shouts, squeezing Jinx's neck from behind. Felix comes up and joins in on the hug just as Jinx begins to protest.

"Hey, you know what you can do to thank me?" Jinx says, grinning, and in a voice slightly muffled by Desdemona's arms around her face. "Get off me."

Laughing, Desdemona dismounts and looks back the way the family just left. "Wow. We actually saved a life today." After saying this, she takes another glance at the large pool holding the swimming mammals. One of the girls standing in the pool supervising the dolphins meets Desdemona's gaze and gives her a wink. At first, the wink confuses Desdemona, but then it dawns on her. This must be the girl the Council placed here to save the boy if they failed. A sense of pride and joy rushes over Desdemona. They did it all on their own!

A few staff members begin to give the triplets some weird looks and Felix nudges his sisters. "Hey, we should probably be getting out of here before people start asking questions."

With both of his sisters in agreement, Felix walks back onto the jungle-like path. When he checks his watch, he realizes that it's only 10:15.

"Guys! We have tons of time before we need to be back. We can spend some of it looking around here!" Felix suggests. Desdemona's face lights up in response and he knows she's in.

On the other hand, Jinx turns her lip up with a bit of a snarl and dismisses his proposal. "You guys can stay. I think I'll go on back to the hotel."

For a moment, Felix and Desdemona both fight with themselves. Is it a good idea to let her go back by herself in a big city? Is it a good idea to let her be alone after she's had such a rough time with Kade?

We're not going to be able to do anything to stop her from going back, Mona, Felix tells Desdemona. As much as she didn't want to admit it, Felix is right. Giving in, Desdemona and Felix caution Jinx to be safe and not to do anything stupid while they're apart.

Jinx rolls her eyes, but agrees. "Have a good time in Nerdland."

Jinx trudges into the elevator to get down to her room, dragging her feet. The only thing she wants to do now is get into bed and take a long, long nap. A nap so long that when she wakes up, Kade will stop infesting her every thought. She slams her hand on the correct button and breathes out. Finally. She's alone.

Until the elevator abruptly stops at a floor that isn't hers.

The door opens to reveal Hazel and... someone Jinx left behind in her memory.

"Maxine?" Jinx asks aloud. Her long red hair and Margret look-alike face are impossible to miss. The earlier vision of Maxine fighting against her sister swims back into her mind, causing Jinx again to wonder what exactly happened between them.

"What are you doing here?" Jinx acts surprised to see Maxine. "You don't have enough training to be in the competition."

"That's the same question I was wondering," Hazel tells Jinx with a hesitant side glance at Maxine. "I found this one wandering in the upper hotel lobby."

Maxine casts her gaze downward to avoid Jinx and Hazel's eyes. "I... I just didn't want to miss out on anything."

Jinx lets out a huff as Hazel asks, "How did you get here anyway?"

Maxine shrugs as the elevator begins to move. "I... um... I snuck out of the House during the night... And caught the first plane here."

Jinx squints at Maxine and tilts her chin upwards. "When did you get here?"

Maxine answers immediately with a determination too quick to be real. "Really late last night."

Liar, Jinx thinks to herself. Maxine must have been in Vegas for at least a few days, and she must have met with Margret in that disgusting, abandoned hotel.

"Hazel, can you give Maxine and me a minute?" Jinx asks Hazel with a wink. Hazel agrees curtly, getting the message and jumping out of the elevator at the next available floor. Jinx jabs the "emergency stop" button on the elevator and it screeches to a halt. She turns to Maxine with a blaze in her eyes.

"Alright Maxine, I need answers. And don't try to lie to me because I know more than you think I do." Jinx orders. Maxine opens her mouth to say something, but then closes her mouth and waits for Jinx to ask her first question. Maxine looks small crouching in the corner of the elevator, tense as a bow.

"When did you *really* get to Las Vegas?" Jinx says first.

Maxine twiddles her thumbs nervously, realizing she has been caught red-handed in her lie. "Four days ago."

Jinx wonders where she has been staying this entire time, but that's not the important question right now. "Where is your sister?"

Maxine clears her throat and runs her hand through her hair. Obviously, her sister is a touchy subject right now. "With... with Jane."

Jinx throws her arms in the air. "As if I didn't already know that! I mean, where is she?"

"Underneath the Treasure Island Pirate Ship..." Maxine answers, shifting her feet uncomfortably.

Jinx recalls passing Treasure Island the other day when they went to the M&M Museum. She recalls the large blue lake outside its front with a life-size, wooden pirate ship floating on top. "It's... underwater?" Jinx clarifies.

Maxine nods. "There's an abandoned space under there. That's where she's been hiding while Jane..." Maxine gulps. "Recovers."

Desdemona's vision was right. Jane was weak, but now she seems to be getting stronger. It's only a matter of time... Jinx tries to shake off the feeling of dread and turns her attention back to Maxine.

"Where's the Asterian Jewel and why does Margret want it?"

This question seems to make Maxine the most uncomfortable of all. She starts biting her lip and rubbing her face. "Margret thinks it has healing powers to help Jane. But I don't know where it is."

"You don't have it, right?" Jinx repeats from her vision. Maxine squints her eyes, obviously wondering how Jinx knows this.

She brushes it off. "No, I don't. And now I don't know what to do..."

Jinx pushes the emergency stop button again and the elevator squeezes into motion. It dings almost immediately on Jinx's floor.

As she gets off, she turns around and gives Maxine her last word. "You don't do anything. Let us handle it."

Jinx whips around and prepares to stalk away, enjoying the feeling of telling Maxine off. But then it dawns on her they need all the help they can get. Hanging her head slightly, Jinx swallows her pride. "Just let me know what else you find out, okay? We could use the help."

With a flustered look, Maxine shakes her head and the elevator doors close, blocking her from Jinx's view. While she returns to her room, Jinx ponders what Maxine told her. If the Asterian Jewel will heal Jane, does that mean she can't survive without the rock? And if her new hideout is underneath the Treasure Island lake, how does she get under there? Is there a secret entrance?

As she ponders all these questions, she realizes that it doesn't matter how she gets in there. Only that she does.

15

"J!" Desdemona screams as she and Felix barge into their hotel room. It is pitch black in the room. The lights are turned completely off. Jinx's soft snore stops as she lets out a groan and rolls over in bed. Just a few minutes after finding out the location of Jane's new headquarters, Jinx decided she needed a nap to process all the information. With her siblings back from their adventurous excursion at Siegfried and Roy's, Jinx knows she can't hide in bed any longer

"J," Desdemona repeats a little softer this time. As she says this, Felix flips the light on, shining a spotlight on the pile of blankets that is Jinx. "It's almost noon and the announcement for the third challenge starts in 10 minutes."

Before they go up to see if their rescue was efficient and discreet enough to get them to the next round, Jinx thinks she should share with her siblings what she learned from Maxine. She throws off the blankets, rubs the sleep out of her eyes, and fills in her brother and sister.

After spilling, Jinx declares "I think we need to drop the competition and go find her right now."

Immediately, Felix and Desdemona shoot down her idea. "That would be like jumping from the frying pan right into the fire," Felix says.

Before Jinx can ask what Felix means, Desdemona clarifies. "What he means is that we're already in enough danger here as it is. Leaving the Council's supervision would be..."

"A death wish," Felix finishes. He knows Jinx is stubborn, but he isn't going to let her be stubborn now. They must stay together on this.

"We have to hang back. There's no question," Desdemona agrees with Felix. At first Jinx wonders if she should argue, but then stops herself. Maybe her siblings are right; maybe she is being impulsive.

"C'mon," Desdemona jumps up off the bed and pulls Jinx up with her. "We're going to be late if we don't leave now."

And just like that, the conversation topic drops. No ifs, ands, or buts about it. The trio heads up to the lobby of their underground Caesar's Palace, talking about anything and everything just to keep their mind off Jane. If they're silent for too long, their thoughts will begin to wander. The last thing that they need is another one of Jane's mind tricks.

Most of the remaining families anxiously mill around the lobby. Some are visibly upset for having been unsuccessful at saving their humans without Council intervention. Others seem nervous as if they saved their human, but maybe not in the most efficient way. The Anchors fall into the latter category.

Across the room, Jinx sees Kade talking with Hazel. His expression is calm, per usual. Jinx begins to wonder if their breakup has affected him at all. She feels a pang in her chest at the thought of him moving on within a matter of days, but suppresses it. She has bigger decisions to make.

While Jinx dissects Kade's behavior, Desdemona closely monitors Jason's movements. With no siblings, he sits alone in silence. His face is collected, but a slight twitch of his thumbs every few seconds gives his nerves away. She is curious about how Jason did today. Did he save his human and if so, how did he do it? She'll just have to ask him later herself.

Before either girl gets too lost in her thoughts, Mrs. Tary descends from the ceiling on her small platform. Other members of the Council descend with her, hovering a few feet above so as not to attract too much attention. Instantly the crowd quiets to the point where she doesn't even have to ask for the talking to cease. Every young Asterian eagerly awaits their fate.

"First," Mrs. Tary begins with a half smile. "I would like to congratulate each of you for making it this far. However, we can only choose three families who will continue to the final round. Twenty-eight families successfully saved their human, which means this last wave of judging has not been easy for us. Remember, even if you are not chosen to continue today, we hope you will collaborate with the Council for many years to come. All of you can make wonderful Council members or liaisons someday."

As Mrs. Tary pauses, the large lobby has become so quiet even the slightest mouse squeak could be heard. No one dares speak.

"Now, I know you are all anxious. I won't make you wait any longer. The family, according to the Council member scores, which performed the best and is currently in first place for round two is... The Defrates!"

Initially, Jinx feels a smile burst onto her face as the crowd of Asterians claps half-heartedly. Her first instinct is to be wildly happy and proud for Hazel and Kade, but then selfishness casts a dark shroud over her joyfulness. What if Kade advances and Jinx doesn't? As she watches Hazel and Kade humbly moving to the front, shame and anxiety fill her.

Mrs. Tary silences the crowd and continues. "The family currently in second place, which will be competing in the final round is... The Anchors!" Whatever nerves Jinx had in the moment wash away as her sister jumps on her in excitement. Hand in hand, Felix, Jinx, and Desdemona skip up to the front, extravagantly proud of their achievement and extremely thankful Jinx's performance got them this far. They line up next to Hazel and Kade, with Jinx and Kade acting as bookends—as far as possible from each other.

"And our third and final family that will be competing in the final round is... Jason Curb!" Mrs. Tary announces. Hundreds of distasteful sighs erupt from the audience, with seemingly no reaction from the boy whose name was called. Jason, with a stone-cold expression, joins the Anchors and the Defrates up front by the fountain. Desdemona casts a sly glance at Jason, but when he meets her gaze, she quickly averts her eyes. She can't have Jason thinking she's suddenly comfortable with him.

Mrs. Tary shushes the disappointed crowd with a wave of her hand. Despite crushing their dreams, she continues to retain immense power over them and their actions. "Please, allow me to explain the final round of the competition. We have chosen three popular Las Vegas hotels and starting at 10:00 a.m. tomorrow morning, the three remaining families will be locked in one of these hotels. It will be their job to escape as fast as possible. The first family to escape will win. Afterward, the Council will choose one member from that family to fill the empty spot."

As Desdemona hears this, she realizes the weight of Mrs. Tary's announcement. If the Anchors are the first to escape and win the competition, one of them—and only one of them—will be chosen to serve and they will have to stay in Las Vegas. They will not return to the House with the other two.

Mrs. Tary interrupts Desdemona's worrying thoughts by continuing with her spiel. "The Defrates will get to choose their hotel first because they came in first place. Kade, Hazel, pick your captor: The Golden Nugget, the Venetian, or Treasure Island?"

After a moment of conference with his sister, Kade steps forward and loudly announces their choice. "The Golden Nugget." Jinx tries to ignore the shivers the sound of his voice sends down her spine.

Mrs. Tary nods and turns to the Anchors to ask them to make their decision. Instead of conferring out loud, Felix pushes into both of his sisters' minds. *Treasure Island, no doubt. It's the perfect way to confront Jane while still being under the protection of the Council.* Both his sisters nod in fervent agreement. The hotel options could not have turned out more perfect.

"Treasure Island," Felix steps forward to exclaim. Because the other hotels have already been chosen, that leaves Jason with the Venetian, the largest and most flamboyant of the three hotels. With their fate decided, Asterians in the crowd impatiently shift on their feet.

In response, Mrs. Tary quickly wraps up her speech. "Everyone except these three families may return to their rooms and pack their bags. Flights will be returning home tomorrow." Respecting her orders, the Asterians shuffle out of the gleaming lobby and return to their rooms. As they walk, the platforms go back into the ceiling, causing all the council members except Mrs. Tary to disappear. Mrs. Tary lifts herself off the platform and floats through mid-air down to the marble floor. Felix tries to snap shut his hanging jaw as the tip of her toes touch the stone to give her the softest possible landing.

"Ooph! Sometimes, it gets tiring standing up there and craning my neck down like that. I just wish I could be down here like y'all!" Mrs. Tary says. Instantly, her colloquial, conversational tone and her slight country twang take the Anchors by surprise. It's like someone flipped a switch on and off within her; the moment she's no longer present in front of a crowd she drops the act. Instantly, Felix feels comforted. The real Mrs. Tary isn't some scary, intimidating councilwoman. In fact, she's a real person with a goofy sense of humor just like the rest of them.

"Alrighty, the competition starts at 10:00, so why don't y'all meet down here in the lobby at 9:00? That should give us plenty of time to get y'all to your separate hotels," she suggests. Desdemona sees Jason nod out of the corner of her eye and mentally hits herself for paying so much attention to him.

Just before she dismisses them for the night, Mrs. Tary adds, "Also, congrats on making it this far! I am sure every single one of you would make amazin' council members!"

The Asterians thank her profusely for this opportunity before bidding her good night and leaving to go back to their rooms for a restful sleep. Desdemona finds herself watching Jason again and she knows that she can't take this anymore. She has to do something about it.

"Go on, guys. I'll be down in a minute," Desdemona tells Felix and Jinx.

"Don't be too long. It's getting late," Felix reminds her, playing the dad as usual. Desdemona waves him off and makes sure they're fully out of sight before turning around to look for Jason. She finds him sitting on the steps by the fountain, turning his thumbs in circles around each other. She marches up to him, prepared to give him a piece of her mind, with her hands on her hips and her lips pursed.

"What is going on here?" Desdemona asks, motioning back and forth between herself and Jason.

Jason looks up at her, meets her eyes, and takes a moment before responding. "I don't know."

Desdemona lets out a huff and moves to sit next to him on the steps, making sure to keep a few feet between them. "Well, that answer isn't good enough. You know something I don't." When Jason looks at her with a confused expression, she continues. "Why are you so interested in me?"

"I've already told you," Jason answers as the last Asterian exits the lobby, leaving them as the only two people in the giant atrium. "I think you're the most beautiful girl I've ever seen." He blushes furiously and averts her gaze.

"No, that's not it..." Desdemona pauses and then asks the question plaguing her ever since she first saw him on the Asterian news that day at the House. "What gave you the strength to leave Jane like you did?"

Jason lets out a long sigh. "You and your brother and sister. When I saw what you did... what the three of you did... I realized that there's more out there than her. There's more to the story than just good vs. evil. It's a constant battle raging between the two inside everyone and the three of you chose well. I realized... I realized I could, too."

Completely touched by his confession, Desdemona scoots closer to Jason on the fountain steps, closing all but a foot between them and allowing him to continue. "When I saw you that morning in Ramsey's restaurant, it was the first time I had seen you since the day you beat Jane on Truchas Peak. I instantly recognized you. A face like yours is hard to forget."

Desdemona feels her heart clench at his words. This is NOT how she was expecting the conversation to go! Sure, guys have called her beautiful a thousand times, but it never quite created a flutter in her chest like Jason just did. She finds herself searching his vulnerable eyes, practically begging him to continue. "Why have you been following me?" Her voice, just a little above a whisper, echoes through the empty lobby to interrupt the sound of the rushing fountain.

"I've wanted to tell you that for a really long time... Ever since the day at Truchas, but I didn't know how. I've wanted to thank you for almost a year now, but I didn't have the nerve...."

"What do you know about Jane?" Desdemona asks. No matter how much she wants to keep hearing him compliment her, she knows the most pertinent information right now revolves around Jane.

Jason shakes his head and his eyes grow sad. Simply discussing Jane seems to make him nervous and depressed. "Not much. I know that she's alive and weak, but I bet you do too."

"Yeah, we do. Do you know anything about the guy who is following us?" Desdemona asks, recalling all the situations in which they have "run into" Jane's minion: the cab, the Paris Hotel, the Stratosphere.

"I knew him when I worked under Jane," Jason tells Desdemona in a heavy voice. "His name is Fargui and ever since Margret failed in her mission to get you three killed, he's been one of Jane's right-hand men."

"Margret?" Desdemona's ears perk up. "Did you know Margret?"

Jason nods furiously. "Oh yeah, I knew Margret. Heck, I thought I was in love with Margret." Desdemona furiously suppresses the jealous feeling when she hears this. "Jane blames Margret for ruining the day on Truchas Peak. I don't know where she is now, but I know she's still with Jane. "

Desdemona processes this information, recalling a vision Jinx had earlier during their time in Las Vegas. Maxine was trying to get the information from Margret, but Margret isn't one of Jane's trusted minions anymore. "Do you remember anything about the day you thought Jane was dead?" Desdemona asks Jason.

"I remember it like it was yesterday..." He pauses, thinking something over. "But why should I explain it to you when you can see it for yourself? I know you can see the past."

Even though they still sit a distance apart, for the first time, Desdemona knows she can trust Jason. He can't lie to her in his past, right?

"Say something. It will trigger my vision," Desdemona says, looking him directly in the eyes for the first time.

"If you can see the past, see mine."

The dry, cool air atop Truchas Peak rushes into Desdemona's nose and blows through her short hair. When Desdemona runs her hand through her hair, she realizes it is a boy-cut. She sees directly through Jason's point of view.

Not too far in the distance, a giant pile of what used to be Jane's lair covers the pale brown, rocky ground. Margret furiously drags an arm from under the rubble and in a few seconds, Desdemona can see the body connected to the arm.

"She's alive!" Margret squeals as she sees a small rise and fall on Jane's chest. Around Desdemona, the remaining Asterians gasp and whisper to each other. Desdemona feels an instant urge to run, to get out as fast as possible. She turns to her left and finds herself face to face with Margret's look-a-like and little sister, Maxine. Maxine looks younger than she does now. Her baby face holds a terrified expression.

Desdemona kneels down next to Maxine and in a voice much deeper than her own says, "It might be too late for me to live a normal life, but it's not too late for you. Nobody has to know you were here if we get out now." Desdemona outstretches her hand to Maxine.

It takes Maxine a moment to process the words as she glances, torn, back and forth between Desdemona and Margret. Eventually, with a look of pure determination and resolve, Maxine takes Desdemona's hand and they run as fast and as far away as possible.

"Maxine?" Desdemona asks incredulously. "She wasn't even fifteen yet. She didn't even have her powers! What was she doing there?"

Jason sighs. "I have no idea. That's why I was trying to get her out of there. I wanted her to have a normal Asterian life without anyone knowing her secret."

Jason's selfless act touches Desdemona. "But... if it's supposed to be a secret, why are you telling me?"

"You need to know. You need all the possible information I can give you if you're going to beat Jane for real this time," Jason says. He takes a deep breath. "Alright, it's my turn for a question. Why did you hate me?"

"I didn't hate you, I just... I just didn't trust you. Listen, when you live a life where Jane and her minions are practically at every turn, you don't know who you can trust. It's easy to be stabbed in the back by someone you thought was your friend... I was just sure you were going to make me regret meeting you."

During a moment of brief silence, Desdemona feels strange and yet completely at peace. She doesn't have to look over her shoulder every time she sees him. She will no longer worry about him being one of Jane's followers. And most importantly, she will no longer worry about the awkwardness between them.

"I wonder how many other people think that about me..." Jason says, running his hand through his hair in mild distress. "I wonder how many other people are afraid of me because I used to be on Jane's side."

"If you're worried about that, why did you do that Asterian News broadcast? You could have just made up some story about why you were gone for so long," Desdemona points out.

"Lying to each other is only going to make Jane stronger. I wanted Asterians to know what it feels like to be under Jane's spell and what they can do to stop it."

As he speaks, Desdemona remembers the Asterian rune Kade and Hazel brought to the Anchors just a few days ago. *Be wary not only of former enemies, but of yourself,* she recalls. She quickly interrupts him. "Asterians need each other to protect themselves from their own evil."

Jason pauses for a moment, confused. "Um... What?"

Desdemona fills Jason in on the rune they transcribed. "Asterians are made to do good, right? Not evil. But there is evil in every one of us. Normally, the good overrides the evil, but when we forget about our families and our purpose, evil can win. I mean, it happened to Jane, didn't it? She turned her back on her brother and sister and focused on greed and power. She turned into a monster."

Jason gulps audibly and his voice cracks in pain. "It... It happened to me."

Desdemona's heart breaks for Jason and she scoots even closer to him, leaning her head on his shoulder as he continues. "I had a sister, you know. Julia. She was just a year older than me. And when I got to Gregoria—our version of the House—we were inseparable. She could make objects invisible and I could make myself invisible. But one day Jane visited me in a dream and I stopped spending time with Julia. I was so drawn in that I forgot what we are here to do... Julia tried to stop me from leaving, but by that point I was way too far gone."

"Where is Julia now...?" Desdemona asks hesitantly.

Jason wipes furiously at a tear that escapes and runs down his cheek. "She's... ah-um... dead."

Instantly, Desdemona feels horrible for having asked that question. She heard on the news broadcast that Julia was dead, and yet she forgot and asked the question anyway. "Jason, I'm so sorry," Desdemona says. It's the only thing she *can* say at this point. A heavy silence follows and Desdemona checks her watch. She is surprised to see an hour has passed. It feels like minutes.

"I should be getting to bed," Even though speaking just above a whisper, her voice travels around the lobby walls. "And you should too. We've both got a long day tomorrow."

Jason nods and stands on the fountain steps. Desdemona begins to walk towards the elevator hallway. However, she only gets a few steps away when Jason calls her name. "Mona?"

She stops and turns around with a heavy heart. "Yes?"

And just then, Jason presents Desdemona with the biggest surprise she's ever received. He closes the gap between the two of them and kisses her. Mona instinctively begins to push him away, but she stops herself. Facing what she cannot admit,

Jason has occupied a space in her heart. And tonight, the night when he let her in, he cemented that spot. Despite the awkward beginning, Desdemona enjoys the kiss. When he pulls finally away, she wishes he hadn't.

Jason begins blushing furiously and stuttering. "Wow- um— I'm really—ah—sorry. That's so... SO unlike me. I just—don't know what came over me."

Desdemona smiles at his shyness and leans in to kiss him sweetly on the cheek. As she pulls away, she whispers, "Don't be sorry." Mona walks away, leaving Jason alone in the vast lobby.

The minute she walks into the hotel room and shuts the door behind her, Felix raises his eyebrow at her. "Care to tell me what happened? You were gone for a long time."

Desdemona, hardly able to contain her smile, raises her hand to cover it up. "Nothing happened. I just had a long talk with Jason and we sorted everything out. As it turns out, he's not working with Jane. He's actually very nice."

Felix laughs. "Okay, but there's something you're not telling us. I can tell your thoughts are running a hundred miles per hour." He pauses and gives Desdemona time to explain, but she remains silent. "Hey, don't make me come in there and find out for myself!"

Desdemona hits Felix across the head and curls up, criss-cross, on the bed next to him. "He kissed me!"

Felix's jaw drops. "Wow. I was expecting you to say a lot of things, but not that. Weren't you the one just telling me I am too trusting? Now you're going around and smooching on the person you thought, just yesterday, was a spy for Jane."

"I already apologized for that," Desdemona reminds him. "And besides, you were right about Jason. He's one of us." For a moment, she debates telling all the things Jason shared with her. But she decides to keep the story between the two of them, a story of their own.

"Hey, where's Jinx?" Desdemona asks. For the first time since she arrived, she realizes her sister is nowhere in sight.

Felix shrugs. "She said she was going for a walk about thirty minutes ago." Desdemona furrows her brow, anxious, prompting Felix to ask, "Should we be worried about her?"

"Vegas is a big city..." Desdemona points out the obvious. "But I think she'll be alright. She won't go far, and if she's in trouble, she can always call for us through her thoughts."

"I'll make sure I'm listening carefully," Felix assures Desdemona. Soon after, they both turn in for the night, fast asleep within minutes. It isn't until almost five hours later that Jinx finally creeps in through the door, undetected, slipping into bed as quietly as possible.

16

An astonishing range of contrasting emotions fly through the air at 9:00 a.m. the following morning. Three families, all of whom know one another, convene together in the upstairs lobby at Caesar's Palace. Desdemona talks excitedly to Hazel and Kade, telling them all about her revelation surrounding the rune last night, while periodically exchanging glances with Jason. Felix shares his nervous anxiety about confronting Jane, while Jinx avoids all possible interactions with Kade. Jason, as usual, waits in silence for Mrs. Tary to arrive, but also shoots Desdemona half-smiles whenever she meets his eye.

"Morning, young'uns!" Mrs. Tary shouts as she approaches the group. The difference between her voice in front of crowds and with small groups once again takes Desdemona aback. This morning Ms. Tary has ditched the usual Council robes for normal clothing, probably to make sure she doesn't stand out. "I hope y'all are ready for a crazy day! A day that will change one of your lives forever."

The Defrates and Jason both smile in anticipation of their upcoming task, but the Anchors lack the same excitement. The Anchors know the task now has nothing to do with the spot on the Council. It's about jumping straight into the fire and ending Jane before she begins again.

"Now remember, y'all are in no real danger here," Mrs. Tary reminds them. "If one of you is seriously hurt or in trouble, we will know and a Council member will step in."

This announcement slightly calms the churning in Felix's stomach. If they are really in trouble with Jane, the Council will be able to help them. And there's no way they can lose with the Asterian Council on their side!

"Oh! I see the taxis outside now. Are you little ones ready?" Mrs. Tary asks again. A chorus of "I guess" and "As ready as I'll ever be" follows. Mrs. Tary wishes them luck before she shoos them outside to the heat. Under the hotel's golden overhang stands three classic, yellow taxis, each with a driver holding a white sign naming a family. Just as the Anchors climb into their designated taxi, Jinx feels a firm tap on her shoulder.

When she turns around, she is inches away from the Kade's familiar eyes. She considers ignoring him altogether and getting back in the cab as quickly as possible, but she stops herself. Kade wouldn't have taken a hit to his pride like this without a specific purpose.

"It's not about the competition anymore, is it?" Kade asks. Jinx feels a lump rising in her throat. She doesn't trust her voice enough to speak. Instead, she simply nods with ice in her veins. Kade's eyes search her face, but Jinx offers no expression.

"If you need help... I'll keep my mind open," Kade offers, suggesting that if the Anchors find themselves in trouble, Felix can call for Kade and he will do as much as he can. His gesture warms her heart and for a moment, Jinx finds herself wanting to forgive him, to throw her arms around him and kiss him in front of all of these people. But she knows she can't.

Instead, she takes a deep breath, clears her throat, and closes the taxi door behind her.

"What was that about?" Desdemona asks as the cab pulls out of the overhang into traffic.

Jinx shakes her head and tries to force the rock out of her throat. "It was nothing," Jinx manages. When Desdemona hears Jinx's voice crack slightly, she begins to feel sorry for her sister. Desdemona knows how close Jinx is—or was—with Kade, and now that all seems to be gone. Jinx refuses even to entertain discussing the topic.

"When we get in there, we head straight for the pirate ship, right?" Felix suggests.

Before either of his sisters can answer, a familiar voice chimes in from the driver's seat. "So that's why you chose Treasure Island? Because of the pirate ship?" The Anchors meet the driver's comment with stunned silence. The driver removes her hat and lets her slightly graying hair fall. It only takes a moment for Felix to recognize Lilianna, and he instantly wonders what she wants with them.

"What's going on here?" Felix asks. He still hasn't mentioned to either of his sisters the daunting message Lilianna left with him the last time he was in her taxi. And frankly, Felix had been hoping that he wouldn't have to revisit that conversation.

Lilianna continues to drive as she explains. "Are you three going to confront Jane?"

"Uhh... Yes?" Felix answers. For a moment, he wonders how exactly Lilianna knows about Jane even though neither her nor her husband are Asterians anymore. Then, he figures this is not the important question to ask. Maybe Lilianna has something to say that will help them.

"I know you are planning on going in there and ending Jane once and for all, but think about it. Would it be so bad if the Council wasn't in charge anymore?" None of the Anchors say anything, mainly because her words shell-shock them into silence. "The Council has so many strict rules for Asterians... They can only use their powers in times of crisis; they can't tell humans about their powers, they can't even marry humans. The list goes on and on. What if these rules weren't there? Then, and only then, could Asterians reach their full potential."

"Why do you care?" Desdemona snaps. "You're not an Asterian and you never were."

Lilianna takes a deep breath as she drives them closer to Treasure Island. "The Council ruined my husband's life. Took everything he knew, everything he loved... Now, it's too late to get my husband's powers back, but it's not too late to prevent others from going through the same thing."

"He chose you," Felix reminds Lilianna. "He had the choice between you and his powers and he CHOSE to give up his powers. It wasn't the Council's fault."

At this point, Lilianna's voice appears to go up an octave in anger. Apparently, she expected the Anchors to give in easily. "But the Council forced him to have to make that decision. Without them, he would have both." She pulls the car into the parking lot in front of Treasure Island. "You are the only ones who can defeat Jane. If you're on her side, she can't be defeated and the Council will be overthrown. And Asterians will be stronger than ever before. Make the right choice before you go in there. Make it while you still can."

The minute the car squeaks to a halt, Felix opens the door and gets out as quickly as possible. His sisters follow with similar urgency, and Desdemona slams the door behind her. The resort rises high into the sky above them, with seemingly endless rows of windows and rooms, each acting as the temporary home of a guest or two. To their right, a large, fenced-in lake extends from the hotel and a ship floats on top, acting as the temporary home of one Jane Anchor.

After a moment of tense silence, the Anchors approach the door to Treasure Island. They pause. Once they enter, the trap will begin and their sole focus will be to find Jane.

"Do you guys think a lot of people think that way? Like Lilianna does? Do other people think that the Council holds Asterians back and Jane would let them reach their full potential?" Desdemona asks her brother and sister.

"Maybe," Felix says.

"She must have gotten the idea from someone," Jinx chimes in sarcastically, continuing with snippy comments since her run-in with Kade.

After a few moments of contemplation, Felix realizes they are now standing outside the hotel for absolutely no reason except to stall. "So... Are you ready to go in?" He asks his sisters. Desdemona nods, but runs her hand over the faint scar still marring her face from their last encounter with Jane. Her eyes hint at fear and Felix knows the last thing she wants is to meet Jane again, less than a year after their epic battle.

You saw it yourself, Mona, Felix pushes into Desdemona's mind to try to comfort her. *Jane is weak. Not even close to the force she used to be.*

And we beat her then, Desdemona responds. *And we can do it again.*

Felix exchanges one more glance with each of his sisters before turning with confidence towards the doors of the hotel. They cross the threshold of the doorway with hardly any hesitation.

"I don't feel any different," Desdemona says. Jinx sees a guest walk out the entrance with ease, but when she turns around to test the walkway, she runs face first into an invisible wall. Despite being able to see through the doorway to the outside as clear as day, Jinx can't walk through it. It's like an invisible forcefield blocks her way.

"Guess I shouldn't have expected it to be that easy," Jinx laughs. When neither of her siblings laughs, Jinx gets back to business. Instead of trying to escape the hotel as they were told to do, they switch their focus to Jane. "Alright, follow me. I know where the pirate ship is." She leads Desdemona and Felix through the hotel, weaving her way in and out of crowds. The hallways are decked out to match the theme of the hotel, with skull and crossbones flags adorning the light fixtures and giant treasure chests posing as ATMs. They pass a casino with pirate ship card tables and gold coin roulette wheels. As usual, Vegas has attended to the smallest of details.

Jinx leads with the utmost assurance, not pausing for even a moment to second-guess herself. "How do you know where you're going?" Desdemona asks with labored breathing. "There was a map back there if we want to check to make sure!"

"No, I promise I know where I'm going," Jinx responds without missing a beat. They enter a dimly lit stairwell with fake torches attached to the wooden walls. Their senses adapt to the low lighting and the sound of their footsteps grows much louder.

"Okay, but *how* do you know where you're going?" Desdemona asks. Even though she's grateful to have someone who knows their way around, she can't help but be curious as to how Jinx acquired this mental map.

For the first time since they entered the hotel, Jinx stops. "Uh... I visited yesterday. When I went for my walk, I came here to, ya know, scope things out."

"Get it?" Felix starts laughing as he points to a telescope hanging from the wall. "*Scope* things out?"

"Wow," Jinx says, not even the slightest bit amused. "That one is a knee-slapper, isn't it?"

Felix shoots Jinx a disapproving look. "Hey, lighten up a little."

Jinx continues walking, but doesn't stop herself from getting in the last word. "Lighten up? In case you've forgotten, we needed Kade's help last time to beat Jane and he's not here this time. I've made up my mind to win, have you made up yours?"

Instantly, the Anchors fall quiet and stop walking. Desdemona gulps as the realization sinks in. In about ten minutes, they will meet true evil for the second time in their lives, this time with no help. This time, the weight falls on their shoulders.

"Are we sure we've thought this through?" Desdemona asks as she nervously rubs the scar on her face. "Maybe this isn't such a good idea after all."

Jinx disagrees and continues leading the way. Her brother and sister follow with slight reluctance. "Mrs. Tary said it herself. There will be an Asterian Council member watching after us, remember? We're going to be fine."

Jinx is right, Mona, Felix comforts Desdemona as they exit the stairwell. *I'm not going to let her hurt you again. I promise.*

Before Desdemona can stop herself, she throws her arms around Felix. Even though he's just a few minutes older than her, sometimes it feels like he's much wiser and experienced. Even though he may not be the strongest man in the world, he does have the strongest heart. Desdemona would put her money on him over anyone else.

When Desdemona pulls away, she finds herself on the outskirts of a large pool area. The pool, in the shape of a pirate's face, has been filled to the brim with sparkling, artificially blue water. Guests of all ages (but mostly children) splash around and battle the heat, enjoying the cool water. A patch of green turf appears on their left. On the top of the turf stands the object of their search: the pirate ship.

Jinx walks with absolute conviction directly towards the ship as Desdemona wonders how Jinx can be so confident. Only Desdemona's vision from a few days ago keeps her moving forward. Jane is weak, and maybe, just maybe, she will be the one outmatched this time.

When they reach the pirate ship, they follow Jinx around to the boat's stern. She touches the wood and puts her face very close to it, feeling and looking carefully for something in particular. Something that will get them in.

"What are you looking for?" Desdemona asks. She crouches down next to Jinx and motions for Felix to follow her. They must be discreet to avoid drawing the attention of other guests.

Instead of speaking, Jinx continues her search. After a few more moments, the tip of her finger meets a bent, rusty nail and she pulls on it gently.

"Ouch!" Jinx lets out a grunt of frustration as the nail breaks the skin of her finger and draws blood. Jinx wipes the blood on her shirt, smearing the blue fabric with an angry red.

"You should wash that off with water, J," Felix cautions his sister. "That nail was rusty and-"

But before he can finish his warning, Jinx gives the nail another tug and the wooden planks of the ship split at the seam, opening and revealing an entryway to a dark passage. Musty stairs lead down into the earth and a horrid stench rises from the walkway.

"Whoa, I am not going in there," Desdemona states as she waves her hand in front of her face.

Jinx grabs her sister's hand and pulls her forward. Desdemona cringes and pulls her tank top up to cover her mouth and nose. "Don't worry. The smell passes," Jinx says.

Desdemona squints at Jinx. "How would you know that the smell passes?"

Jinx laughs uncomfortably. "Oh, I meant that the smell *would* pass... Probably." She clears her throat and avoids their gaze, trying to change the subject. "Now, c'mon, if we don't move fast, someone will see us."

They enter the darkness and stench. Each of them audibly gags and cough, doing everything they can to get the smell out of their nose and throat.

Desdemona thinks to Felix, knowing he is listening. *How does she know all this stuff? Doesn't it seem weird to you?*

Felix nods and thinks to Mona. *Jinx has finally put some work into doing her research and she wants to show off. Besides, she knows what she's doing. Don't bite the hand that feeds.*

Desdemona muffles a laugh after hearing yet another of her brother's silly phrases. Once she breathes in heavily, the smell enters her throat roughly, scratching and tearing at the nerves in her windpipe. She begins coughing uncontrollably.

"I've only smelled something like this once before..." Desdemona manages in between coughs. As she struggles, she recalls the stench that filled her driveway when a raccoon died in their trash can, where it decayed there for nearly a week.

"Death," Jinx finishes Desdemona's sentence. Desdemona nods, and although it cannot be seen in the darkness, Jinx and Felix hear her hair swishing against her back as Desdemona moves her head. Another sound suddenly joins in. Footsteps. Following them from a distance. Jinx pulls out her wallet and taps the photograph three times before feeling her knife belt appear around her waist. Desdemona grabs her hair clip and quickly loads an arrow into her bow. The book in Felix's hand morphs into a sword and he yields it in front of him. The Anchors stand shoulder to shoulder, ready to defend themselves for whatever Jane will throw their way.

"J?" Kade's voice reaches them quickly from above. The footsteps speed up as Desdemona and Felix lower their weapons.

"No," Jinx whispers to Desdemona and Felix. "Keep your weapons ready. It could be an imposter." They follow her command and raise their weapons once more. The footsteps stop and a shadow appears in front of them.

"Jinx? Mona? Felix? That's you, right?" Kade asks in a voice a little above a whisper.

"It's us," Desdemona answers. "But is it really you?"

Kade scoffs. "Of course it is. Who else would it be?"

Jinx speaks up with a shaky, nervous voice and thinks of something only the two of them would know. These are the first words she's said to him since their breakup. "What did I order at the restaurant the night you took me to the Paris Hotel?"

Kade laughs as he remembers. "Just lettuce and ranch dressing." When she hears this answer, Jinx puts her knife back in her belt, but it feels like she's putting the knife straight into her chest. His laugh... the way he fondly remembers... Jinx feels a pang of regret for what she has done and what she's about to do.

"What are you doing here?" Desdemona asks when Jinx stays silent. "Did you get out of your hotel already?"

"I never went in the hotel. The taxi took us there and just as I was about to step through the door... I stopped. There are bigger things than this competition. I knew I needed to be somewhere else."

"We can do this on our own, thanks," Jinx sneers at Kade. She whips around and continues walking down the hallway. A dim light appears in the distance. Jinx picks up her pace, nearly sprinting towards the light. Felix and Desdemona know they must keep up with Jinx. But before they follow, Felix grabs Kade's hand and gives him a pull.

As they follow, Felix does something he hasn't done since his first training session with Kade. He pushes into Kade's mind. The only difference between that time and this time is that now, Kade doesn't push Felix away immediately. *Thank you for coming. We can always use your help, and I'm sorry about Jinx.*

Don't be sorry, Kade says. *I'm here to prove something I said to her earlier.*

Felix knows they have no time for questions. They rapidly approach the light and as they close in, they can see the source: a torch. A torch hung high up on the wall, illuminating the sandstone below. Finally, they reach the torch and realize it stands at the end of the hallway. A fancy script has been etched into the stone, but not in English. Asterian runes, barely visible, covered in dust and eroded stone, have been placed at the end of their path.

"Felix, you were always the best in runes class. What does it say?" Desdemona asks. Felix leans in very close, reaching up to try to clear some of the debris blocking the writing.

"Watch your..." Felix answers before letting out a frustrated grunt. "I don't know what the last word is." As he speaks, Jinx feels a vision coming on and it overtakes her.

Jinx looks from afar as she watches herself, Felix, Desdemona, and Kade study the rune. Just as it was a moment ago, Felix leans in close, trying to translate the rune. Desdemona stands by Felix's side, doing everything she can to help. Jinx and Kade stand as far away from each other as the small passageway allows.

From behind, Jinx hears a slight ticking, almost insect-like, noise. She taps Kade on the shoulder, temporarily forgetting about the awkwardness between them, and points in the direction of the noise. Suddenly, the noise stops and transforms into a distinct hissing noise directly behind Jinx and Kade.

As fast as they left, her senses return and she hears Jane's voice. Jinx's pulse beats faster than ever. Jane's voice behind their backs fades, having been replaced by Jinx's own voice.

"Back," Jinx shouts as she escapes her vision. "The rune says 'watch your back'!" Jinx tears her knife out of her belt and prepares herself to face the coming danger. But when she witnesses her vision coming true, she sees only a splitting image of herself staring back at her.

To Jinx's side, Desdemona screams at the top of her lungs. "Jane, this time we will kill you, once and for all." As she hears this, Jinx wonders why Desdemona is screaming. Jane is nowhere to be seen.

As she does this, Felix groans and shrinks away. "Beetles! Why does it always have to be bugs?"

Kade curses. "Snakes. Of course."

Jinx looks around, flustered, at her siblings and Kade. She sees her double, but she sees no beetles, snakes or other danger. Kade, Desdemona and Felix each appear to be facing something entirely different, equally terrifying and yet invisible to her. To her right, she sees Kade pull out his ax and swing it furiously at the air. To Jinx, he hits nothing, but the satisfied look on Kade's face tells her something good *must* have happened.

Felix follows Kade's lead and reaches for his sword. He begins stabbing it into the mushy, earthy ground. After a few moments, he stops and sheaths his sword.

Desdemona, just as confused as Jinx, figures the only way to make the Jane look-alike go away is to kill it. She reaches around her back and loads an arrow into the bow, pointing it directly at Jane's chest. She takes a deep, steadying breath before launching the arrow. When it pierces Jane's skin, Desdemona alone sees the look-alike disappear with a puff of smoke.

Jinx is the last one left with an enemy. She turns to face herself and raises her hand to her belt to grab a knife. As she does, Jinx's doppelganger does the same thing, as if she stares into a mirror. When she sees a knife appear in the hand of her double, she wonders if it will mimic all of her movements, even when she throws her knife. If she hits her double in the chest with the knife, will she be stabbed as well? She feels her heart beat rapidly and she looks to Kade for.... for something. For guidance. For help. For reassurance.

"It's not real, J," Kade tells her. "Whatever it is, you have to kill it."

Jinx nods slowly, feeling encouraged. If it's not real, she can't be hurt, right? Jinx raises the knife above her head, staring directly at herself, and throws it. She looks away, not wanting to watch until she hears a squish as the knife hits its mark. Jinx's double disappears as fast as it appeared and she lets out a shaky breath. Instantly, the previously sturdy wall behind her opens up to reveal an extension of the dark hallway.

"What just happened?" Desdemona asks. Neither Jinx or Felix can answer her.

Kade, who has more schooling than the Anchors, jumps in. "It's called a dulia. It's a trap, usually set by someone who wants to protect something. It forces someone to face their deepest, greatest fear."

"No, but that doesn't make sense," Jinx counters, knowing Kade must be mistaken. "I saw myself."

A tense air falls over the group and Jinx shifts awkwardly on her feet. "Then your biggest fear is yourself. Trust me, the dulia knows. It knows you better than you."

"Asterians need to protect themselves from their own evil," Desdemona repeats the message of the rune. When she hears this, Jinx feels her pulse accelerate and she quickly avoids everyone's eyes.

"We should keep moving," Jinx says, changing the subject. Keeping her hand on her knife, Jinx leads the group with Kade close at her heels. As they walk they begin to hear faint voices. Whispers, it seems. The whispers grow to speaking as a light again appears in the distance. Before the speaking can turn to shouting, Jinx pauses and convenes with the group.

"What do you think is down there?" Desdemona asks, standing on her tiptoes as if that will help her see in the darkness. "It sounds like a big group."

"But not nearly as big as the group Jane had at Truchas," Felix says in a voice much louder than a whisper. The speaking from down the hallway quiets, leaving Felix's voice as the only noise. Instantly, he shuts up. Jinx shares a strained look with Kade and everyone holds their breath, praying the voices decide to go back to their conversation. After a few moments, the voices pick up again.

Kade sighs, holding his axe up, speaking in a tone so soft Jinx can hardly hear him. "There goes the element of surprise. Looks like this isn't going to be as easy as we thought."

Desdemona rubs the scar on her face. "You know, it's not too late to turn back. We can get help." Just as Desdemona says this, dirt falls from the ceiling and cordons off the passageway from which they entered. They cannot return to the area where they defeated the dulia.

"Apparently, it *is* too late," Kade says. He turns his attention away from the group and towards the rest of the hallway. Their only option at this point is to keep moving forward with confidence. Kade, not able to control his instinct to protect his former apprentices, steps in front of Jinx and leads. All frightened in their own way and for their own reasons, the Anchors are more than happy to let him lead.

Nervously, they walk down the hallway and as they near its end the light grows bigger and the voices grow louder. Eventually, the sound of clanking dishes and glasses becomes clear; it must be meal-time for Jane's minions.

Desdemona grabs Felix's hand and squeezes it tightly as they near the hallway's exit. The last time they went to face Jane like this, Desdemona found solace in her brother and tonight, she finds it once again. They have moved only a few steps towards the bright light and louder noises. They can now hear particular voices. Margret, their stalker, and others with unrecognizable tones. The Anchors bear their weapons, ready to defend themselves if Jane's minions try to attack them upon entry.

Finally, knowing they can't wait any longer, Jinx, Kade, Felix, and Desdemona step into the light.

17

The beauty and wonder of Jane's new lair outshine the enormity of her old headquarters on Truchas Peak. In the past, she needed a giant complex to accommodate her followers. A smaller following and headquarters suits Jane just fine, at least for now.

What the room lacks in size, it makes up for in flair. A gleaming table stretches from end to end of the large foyer. From the soft ceiling hangs three large chandeliers, causing Felix to wonder how in the world soil can support that kind of weight. Red velvet wallpaper sticks to the walls, reflecting the light shining from the chandeliers. Golden silverware and table decorations accent the table perfectly.

This is a room fit for a queen, not a murdering witch! Felix thinks to Desdemona. Felix tears his attention away from the decorations and focuses on Jane's followers. The followers have fallen silent, staring directly at Felix, Desdemona, Jinx and Kade.

"Wow, these people sure know how to treat guests, don't they?" Kade jokes to Jinx in a hushed tone. Jinx doesn't respond. She stares at the throne adorning the furthest wall. In contrast with the brightly lit room, the throne is black. Pitch black, much like the ground of the bewitched canyon the Anchors found themselves stuck on that first day of their journey up Truchas Peak. Spikes rise from the sides of armrests on the throne like unsheathed swords. The throne screams power.

The one thing about the throne that does not scream power is the person sitting in it. Her choppy black hair lets Desdemona know it is—in fact – Jane. At least, it is what's left of the malicious, fear-inducing woman they faced a little under a year ago. Red, scabbed cuts and blue-black bruises cover her skin. Her arms lay limp over the spikes as if she has no strength in them. Her tight shirt reveals a protruding rib cage. Her eyes seem lifeless, careless, lost. Dead.

The moment Jane raises her head to greet her visitors, her eyes reveal what's left of her devilish persona. Jane waves her hand weakly and Margret, as striking as ever, rushes to her side. Apparently, her rightful place as Jane's right-hand man has been restored. Jane leans into her and whispers something inaudible even in the dead silent room. When she finishes, Margaret turns to address the Anchors and Kade.

"Jane would like to welcome you to her new, temporary headquarters and thank you for taking time out of your busy schedule to pay her a visit," Margret recounts to them. Desdemona feels shivers run up and down her spine as she remembers the sweet, yet evil tone of Jane's voice. At least for her sake, Jane isn't doing the speaking this time.

Margret leans down once more and listens. "Jane would also like to thank you for bringing along your friend. She says he will make a great addition."

A great addition to what? Desdemona asks Felix in fear. She isn't sure if Jane means an addition to her army or to her list of people she's killed. At this point, Desdemona isn't even sure which one would be better.

Jinx tenses up as Jane turns her feeble attention towards her. Jane whispers something to Margret and Margret smiles. "Jane wants to know if you are ready."

Desdemona and Felix look at each other, confused. Kade does the same. What does she mean? What are they supposed to be ready for?

Jane says something else to Margret. "Come up here," Margret repeats.

Desdemona and Felix stare at Jinx, absolutely dumbfounded. There's no way she will go up there and stand next to Jane. She'll get herself killed!

But Jinx knows otherwise. With sad, regretful eyes, Jinx turns to her siblings and Kade. A single tear rolls down her cheek. "I'm sorry," she whispers in a barely audible, shaky voice. Before she turns away, she gives Kade one last look. "I love you," she whispers. When Kade says nothing, Jinx approaches Jane, walking around the golden table. Jinx stares at her own feet and avoids the stares of Jane's minions. Once again, dead silence engulfs the lair. Moving up to the throne of spikes, Margret hands Jinx something she hasn't seen since their last day on Truchas Peak. Its gleaming appearance is one that cannot be mistaken. The Asterian Jewel. She offers it to Jinx.

A deafening scream breaks the silence. "WHAT? HOW COULD YOU?" Desdemona spits at Jinx. Mona throws herself forward, but feels Felix's strong hands grabbing her from behind, restraining her. "I CAN'T BELIEVE THIS! YOU WICKED, CONNIVING BITCH!" Desdemona continues to yell. Jinx desperately tries to wipe the tears from her face and wishes Kade would just block out her senses. But no, he doesn't do that for her. She betrayed him. She betrayed everyone.

Desdemona's yells subside and she now fills the silence with something much worse. She speaks in a tone more frail than the day Jane cut her face on Truchas Peak. "You're our sister... Does family mean nothing to you?"

Jane reaches out her hand to take the jewel from Jinx's grasp. When their fingers touch, shivers run through Jinx's body. For the first time, Jinx sees Jane's wounds up close. They vary from small surface cuts to deep, gashes. In Jane's mauled hand, the spiky side of the jewel faces upward, representing darkness and hardship.

Everyone in the room watches in tense stillness as Jane's shaky hand brings the spiky side of the stone up to her face. She presses the sharpest end to the left side of her neck and presses hard. So hard that it draws runny, crimson blood.

In an action so revolting even Jinx has to turn away, Jane drags the stone from the left side of her neck to the right side, cutting it shallowly all the way across. By the time she's done, it appears Jane has slit her own throat. Blood rushes down her neck as she hands the Jewel to Jinx. With a deep, jagged breath, Jinx grips the Jewel in her left hand and glances at the cut the nail on the pirate ship created just a few minutes earlier. She raises the jagged side of the Asterian Jewel to her hand and slashes, making the already seeping wound gush crimson.

In a moment she will never forget, Jinx watches as she holds her hand up and allows the blood to cover her whole right hand. She reaches up and grabs Jane by her injured throat. At first, it appears as if Jinx is going to strangle Jane. But she does not kill her. Quite the opposite.

Slowly but surely the cuts and bruises on Jane's skin fade; the flesh stitches itself back together to heal her wounds. Her choppy hair turns shiny and her skin takes on a healthy, flushed hue. Over the next minute or so, the group stands in stunned silence as the brittle, beaten Jane transforms into the one who haunts their nightmares.

Wounds healed, Jane stands and beams at her audience. Her minions break out into a rambunctious cheer, clapping and shouting. Jane basks in their adoration for a moment before raising her hand, effectively silencing them. When Jane turns to Jinx, Jinx sees her own reflection.

"The blood bond is successful! J, I always knew you would come around," Jane says adoringly at Jinx. When a traitor tear escapes down Jinx's face, Jane reaches up with her blood-soaked hand to brush it away.

"Don't cry, my child. You knew all along that I was leading you towards your destiny. Fargui following you, the rope snapping, Felix's voice in your head when it wasn't really him. It was all my doing. Finally, you've chosen the winning side. Asterians have always been destined for more than serving humans. Just look how the humans have ravaged their own planet! Together, my J, we will usher in a new age. We will lead an Asterian revolution!"

Jane's minions cheer wildly, banging objects on every piece of wood and metal in the lair. Meanwhile, Jinx can hardly bear to look over at her family and Kade. When she finally looks, she wishes she hadn't. Desdemona's tears flow with anger and pure hatred—an expression Jinx has never seen on Desdemona. Felix does a better job of hiding his pain. The expression in his eyes, pain-filled and sorrowful, is the only thing that gives him away.

Kade. Kade is the worst one of all. He stares at Jinx, completely devoid of emotion. Cold eyes, mouth set in a straight line, just like the first day they met at the House. They lack all warmth, all sadness, all... anything.

Jane moves away from Jinx and glances where Felix, Desdemona, and Kade stand. She smiles, seeming to enjoy their agony. "Now, what should we do with the three of you?"

"Let them go," Jinx manages through gritted teeth. "You promised you would."

Jane ponders this for a moment. "Ah, yes, I did. But you should know better than to trust all my promises, sweet J."

"Jane," Jinx puffs out her chest and wipes her tears, staring at Jane. She has already betrayed them. The least she can do for her family at this point is to get them out of here safely.

Jane grins and hesitates for effect, but eventually caves. "You have done much greatness for me, my J. In return, I *will* let them go."

Jinx briefly feels a weight lift off her chest, but it falls back to her when she turns to her family and Kade. It falls back ten times heavier. Desdemona, Kade, and Felix will be leaving, but she won't be going with them. Even if Jane allowed it, they wouldn't want her. Some Asterians are stronger than others at resisting the darkness.

Jinx tries one last time to grab the attention of her siblings and Kade, but they ignore her. Stone-faced and silent, they turn to walk back down the hallway. But just before they move out of view, Desdemona stops.

"Goodbye, Jinx."

Book One in the Ascension Series!

Desdemona, Felix and Jinx live as only children in their ordinary houses with their ordinary parents. But on their fifteenth birthdays, at the stroke of midnight, they come to realize nothing is as it seems. Thrown into a world completely unknown, they learn the identity of their biological mother, Jane Anchor, a member of the mysterious Asterian race and a woman whose goal is terror and destruction.

As the Anchor kids enter The House, a group of Asterians who secretly co-exist with us to help mankind, Jane sets a plot in motion to lure her progeny to a fortress atop Truchas Peak. Seven days is all the Anchor kids have to liberate Asterians from Jane's threatened reign of terror. Can three naïve, yet powerful kids confront evil and preserve a community of guardian angels on earth?

"A magical tale of three siblings who rise to embrace a perilous calling, Lauren knocks it out of the park with her first installment of the Ascension series."

—Award Winning Young Adult Author Barry Kienzle